WAITING FOR GODALMING

ROBERT RANKIN

WAITING FOR GODALMING

Doubleday

LONDON · NEW YORK · TORONTO · SYDNEY · AUCKLAND

TRANSWORLD PUBLISHERS
61–63 Uxbridge Road, London W5 5SA
a division of The Random House Group Ltd

RANDOM HOUSE AUSTRALIA (PTY) LTD
20 Alfred Street, Milsons Point, Sydney, NSW 2061, Australia

RANDOM HOUSE NEW ZEALAND
18 Poland Road, Glenfield, Auckland 10, New Zealand

RANDOM HOUSE SOUTH AFRICA (PTY) LTD
Endulini, 5a Jubilee Road, Parktown 2193, South Africa

Published 2000 by Doubleday
a division of Transworld Publishers

Typeset in 11½/13pt Bembo by Falcon Oast Graphic Art

Printed in Great Britain
by Mackays Chatam plc, Chatham, Kent

1 3 5 7 9 10 8 6 4 2

For my bestest buddy
NICK REEKIE
A great Sherlockian
You work it out!

I really hated the doctor's office.
  It smelled of feet and fish and fear. A fetid fermentation. And I really hated the doctor too. He was a wrong'un, that doctor.

On the outside, to the naked eyeball, he looked fine. He looked just the way that a doctor should look. The way that you would expect a doctor to look. But that's what they do, the wrong'uns. That's how they survive amongst us. They look just right. Just how they're supposed to look. Which is why no-one ever suspects them of being what they really are.

Wrong'uns.

But I know. Because I took the drug. I can see them for what they really are. Foul demonic creatures of Hell. And I can stop them too. I could put paid to their plans for world domination. I could drive them back to the bottomless pit. I could. I really could. If only I could stay awake for a little bit longer. Just a couple of days. That's all I need. Just a couple of days.

'So,' said the doctor, glancing up from his case notes, *my* case notes. 'Do you want to continue with the consultation?'

'Buddy,' I told him. 'All I want is some more of those

wide-awake tablets. So I don't keep falling asleep.'

'The tablets help then, do they?'

'Tablets always help,' I said. 'That's what tablets are for, isn't it?'

'Some of them.' The doctor peered at me over his spectacles. I'd had a pair like them once. Special lenses in mine, though. Invented them myself.

2D spectacles. The opposite of 3D spectacles. When you looked through mine, they made the world go flat. Like you were watching a movie, see? Like you were *in* a movie. Ken Kesey once said, 'Always stay in your own movie,' and that's what I do. That's how *I* survive. I made the frames of my spectacles long and narrow, so that my world was a widescreen movie. But they weren't a success.

I had some really hairy moments on the motorway.

So I don't invent things any more. I just stick to what I do best. And that is being the greatest private eye in the business.

'Do you want to talk about your dreams?' the doctor asked.

'No,' I told him. 'I don't have any time for dreams.'

'Let's talk about you then. Let's talk about you, Mr Woodblock.'

'The name's Wood*bine*,' I said. 'Lazlo Woodbine, private eye.' And I added, 'Some call me Laz.'

The doctor leafed some more through his case notes. 'Mr Woodbine, yes, and you describe yourself as a living legend.'

'I am the man,' I said. 'The one and only. The last of a dying breed.'

'And just what breed would that be, exactly?'

'The nineteen-fifties American genre detective. The man who walks alone along those mean streets where a man must walk alone.'

'Not entirely alone,' said the doctor, flick flick flicking

through those case-note pages. 'There is this Gary character who works with you.'

'It's *Barry*,' I said. 'His name is Barry.'

'Ah yes, Barry. And Barry is a sprout who lives inside your head.'

'He doesn't *live* there. I've told you before.'

'He's a dead sprout?'

'He's a theophany. And before you ask me *again* what that is, it's a manifestation of the deity to man, in a form which, although visible, is not necessarily material. And before you ask me *again* whether I can see Barry, the answer is no. I can only hear him. And only *I* can hear him. He speaks to me from inside my head. He's my Holy Guardian Sprout.'

'As in Holy Guardian Angel?'

'As I have told you many times before. There are more people on Earth than there are angels in Heaven. God improvises. He shares out the produce of His garden. I got a sprout named Barry. Perhaps you have a pumpkin called Peter.'

'Are you suggesting that I have a very big head?'

'If the elephant man's cap fits, wear it.'

'What did you say, Mr Woodbine?'

'I said, you have an elegant man's head. Now please can I have some more tablets before I fall asleep again?'

'All in good time,' said the doctor, doing that thing that doctors do with their pencils. 'Let's talk a bit about this case you say you're on. It involves a handbag, doesn't it?'

'No,' I said. 'My last case involved a handbag. This case involves a briefcase.'

'Is there always luggage involved in your cases?'

'That's what a case is, luggage.'

'I don't think I quite understand.'

9

'Well, we all have our luggage to carry around. That's what makes a man what he is, his luggage.'

'Surely you mean baggage.'

'Luggage, baggage. A man *is* what he carries around. A handbag, a briefcase, a doctor's bag, carpet bag, Gladstone bag, kit bag, duffel bag, saddle bag, portmanteau, suitcase, attaché case, despatch case, guitar case, overnight case, weekend case, vanity case, satchel, knapsack, rucksack, haversack . . .'

'You certainly know your luggage,' said the doctor.

'Buddy,' I told him, 'in my business, knowing your luggage can mean the difference between looking through the eyes of love and staring down the barrel of a P45. If you know what I mean and I'm sure that you do.'

'I don't,' said the doctor.

'Well *I* do,' said I. 'There was one case I was on back in ninety-five and I confused a sabretache with a reticule. That case cost me my two front teeth, my entire collection of Lonnie Donegan records, my reputation as a connoisseur of pine kitchen wall cupboards, my pet duck named Derek and . . .'

'What?' asked the doctor.

'Zzzzzzzzzzzzzzz.'

'Wake up!' shouted the doctor.

And I woke up in a bit of a sweat.

'Listen,' I said. 'All I want is the tablets, so I can stay awake. You want me to stay awake, so I can tell you all about the case. I want to stay awake, so I can close the case. For pity's sake, man, we both want me to stay awake. So why don't you just give me the damn tablets and then I'll stay awake?'

'All right,' said the doctor. 'I'll give you a tablet now and you can have another when you've finished telling me all about your case.'

I could see he was lying. It shows up on their heads when they lie, the wrong'uns. Their quills go blue at the tips. But of course he didn't know that I could see his quills. He didn't know that I was on to him. But I was. I could see his quills and his terrible reptilian eyes and those awful insect mouthparts that kept chewing chewing chewing. I could see it all, because I had taken the drug.

And so I told him all about the case. Just to pass the time. Just so I could stay awake for a couple more days and wipe him and his kind from the face of the Earth. I didn't tell him all of it. Because I didn't know all of it. And even if I had, I wouldn't have told him. I told him my side of the story, when I was called in on the case. I don't know for sure just what happened earlier, because I wasn't there to see it happen. I guess it all really began in that barber's shop. But like I say, I wasn't there, so I couldn't say for sure.

1

Now you don't really see barber's shops any more. They've gone the way of the Pathe News and Raylbrook Poplin, the shirts you don't iron. But once, in a time not too long ago, the barber's shop was a very special place. A shrine to all things male.

Here men of every social order gathered for their bi-weekly trims. The gentry rubbed shoulders with the genetically deficient, princes with paupers, wide boys with window dressers. Here was egalitarianism made flesh. Here was a class-less society. Here all men were equal beneath the barber's brush.

A mile due north of Brentford, as the fair griffin flies, the Ealing Road enters South Ealing and for a space of one hundred yards becomes its high street. And here, in the high street, hard upon the left hand path, betwixt a wool shop, where the wives of wealthy men felt yarn, and a flower shop where they fondled floral fripperies, there stood at the time when our tale is told, a barber's shop that went by the name of Stravino's.

And Stravino's was a barber's shop as a barber's shop should be.

Above the door and rising proud as a porn star's pecker, the red and white striped pole, encased within a cylinder of glass and powered by an unseen engine, spiralled ever towards infinity. The front and only window, bathed on rare occasions by bob-a-jobbing Boy Scouts, displayed in ten-by-eights of gloss-gone monochrome the fashionable haircuts of a bygone day. The face of King Gillette, creator of that famous blade of blue, stared sternly from a box of safety razors. And dead flies, belly up, arrayed themselves in pleasing compositions.

Bliss.

Ah, perfect bliss.

But if 'twere bliss to view it from without, then what of it within?

Ah, well, within.

'Twere poetry within.

For

> Stravino's shop was long and low
> With walls of a nicotine hue.
> The floor was ankle-deep in hair
> And if you dared to stand and stare,
> That hair would soon be round your leg
> And filling up your shoe.
> The Greek himself was a colourful man
> Who rejoiced in the name of Smiling Stan
> And worked his trade with great élan
> And sang some opera too.
>
> There were hot towels in a chromium drum
> And a row of cinema chairs

Where the patrons sat to await their turns
And savour the screams from the hot towel burns
And open the old brown envelope
And dodge the flying hairs.
For the Greek could snip with incredible zest
He'd have at your head like a man possessed
And few could help but be impressed
By his knowledge of cosmic affairs.

And so on and so forth for many verses more. But we have not come here to versify. We have come here with a purpose and that is to meet the hero for our tale.

For the present, he is unaware that he is the hero. Indeed, by the looks of him, he seems hardly cut from that cloth of which heroes are tailored. He is slender, slightly stooped and sits with downcast eyes, patiently awaiting his turn for a trim. He speaks to no-one and no-one speaks to him. He is eighteen years of age and his name is Icarus Smith.

It's a good name for a hero, Icarus Smith. Encompassing, as it does, both the mythic and the mundane. But other than his having a good name for a hero, what can there be said about the man who bears this name?

Well.

If you were to approach young Mr Smith and ask that he recommend himself, he would like as not ignore you. But if the mood to communicate was upon him, as seldom it was without a good cause, for he rarely spoke to anyone other than himself, he would probably say that he considered himself to be an honest God-fearing fellow, who meant harm to no man and called each man his brother.

His brother by birth, however, might well choose to take issue with this particular statement, letting it be known that in

14

his opinion, Icarus was nothing more than a thieving godless ne'er do well.

But then that's brothers for you, isn't it? And Icarus, for his part, considered *his* brother to be barking mad.

So can any man be truly judged by the opinions of others, no matter how close to the man himself those others might be? Surely not. By a man's deeds shall you know him, said the sage, and by his deeds was Icarus known.

To most of the local constabulary.

He did not consider himself to be a thief. Anything but. Icarus considered himself to be a 'relocator'. One who practised the arts and sciences of relocation. And to him this was no euphemism. This was a way of life and a mighty quest to boot.

To Icarus, the concept of 'ownership' was mere illusion. How, he argued, could any man truly 'own' anything except the body that clothed his consciousness?

Certainly you could acquire things and hold on to them for a while and you could call this 'ownership'. But whatever you had, you would ultimately lose. Things break. Things wear out. Things go missing. You die and leave the things that you 'owned' to others, who in turn will 'own' them for a while.

You could try like the very bejasus to 'own' things, but you never really truly would. And if you didn't hang on like the very bejasus to the things that you thought you owned, then like as not you wouldn't 'own' them for very long.

For they would be relocated by Icarus Smith. Or if not re-located by Icarus Smith, then simply stolen by some thieving godless ne'er do well.

Now for the cynics out there, who might still be labouring under the mistaken opinion that relocating is merely thieving by another name, let this be said: Icarus had not become a relocator by choice. He was an intelligent lad and could have

15

turned his hand to almost anything in order to earn himself a living. But Icarus had dreamed a dream, a terrible dream it was, and this dream had changed the life of Icarus Smith.

Icarus had dreamed the Big Picture. The Big Picture of what was wrong with the world and the method by which *he* could put it to rights. And when you dream something like that, it does have a tendency to change your life somewhat.

In the dream of Icarus Smith, he had seen the world laid out before him as the Big Picture. People coming and going and doing their things and it all looked fine from a distance. But the closer Icarus looked, the more wrong everything became. The Big Picture was in fact a jigsaw puzzle with everyone's lives and possessions slotted together. But it was a jigsaw that had been assembled by a madman. A mad God perhaps? The more closely Icarus examined the pieces, the more he became aware that they didn't fit properly. They were all in the wrong places and had been hammered down in order to make them fit.

Icarus realized that if he could take out a piece here and replace it with a piece from over there and move that other bit across there and shift that bit up a bit and so on and so forth and so on and so forth and—

He had awoken in a terrible sweat.

But he had seen the Big Picture.

And he had found his vocation in life. As a relocator.

Icarus realized that the world could be changed for the better by relocating things. By putting the right things into the right people's hands and removing the wrong things from the wrong people's hands.

It was hardly a new idea; Karl Marx had come up with something similar a century before. But sharing out the wealth of the world equally amongst everyone had never been much of an idea. Anyone with any common sense at all realized that a week after the wealth had been distributed, some smart blighter would have wangled much more than his fair share from the less than smart blighters and the world would be back where it started again.

It had to be done differently from that.

But Icarus was working on it. For, after all, *he* had had the dream. *He* had seen the Big Picture. *He* was the chosen one.

He realized from the outset that he would not be able to do it all alone. The task was far too big. It would be necessary to take on recruits. Many many recruits. But that was for the future. Everything had to start in a small way and so for the present he must go it alone.

And it had to be instinctive and *not* for personal gain. He had to eat and clothe himself and attend to his basic needs, but above and beyond that there must be no profit.

Icarus also knew that the 'powers that be' would not take kindly to his plans for changing the world. The powers that be thrived on the concept of ownership. Icarus, in their eyes, would be a dangerous criminal and subversive who could not be allowed to walk the streets.

A few early run-ins with the local constabulary had taught Icarus discretion. And, having read a great deal on the science of detection and seen a great many movies, a *very great many* movies, Icarus had become adept at covering his tracks and leaving no clues behind at the 'crime scene'.

But, as relocating had to be instinctive, rather than pre-meditated, there was always a margin of error. And the possibility of capture and internment was never far away.

On this particular day, being the one on which our epic tale begins, Icarus sat in Stravino's shop in the cinema seat nearest the door. Sunlight, of the early morning spring variety, peeped down at Icarus through the upper window glass and grinned upon his hairy head.

The seat that Icarus occupied was number twenty-three and had once been number twenty-three in the three and ninepenny stalls of the Walpole Cinema in Ealing Broadway.

But the Walpole Cinema had been demolished and, during the course of that demolition, the rows of seats numbered from twenty-three to thirty-two had been relocated.

By Icarus Smith.

In fact there were a great many items to be found amongst the fixtures and fittings of Stravino's shop that owed their presence to the science of relocation. An understanding existed between the barber and the relocator and Icarus Smith was assured of free haircuts for life.

Today he thought he'd have a Tony Curtis.

There were three other clients in the shop of Stravino. One sat in the barber's chair, the other two upon the relocated seats. The one in the chair was Count Otto Black, a legendary figure in the neighbourhood. Count Otto possessed a genuine duelling scar, a Ford Fiesta called Jonathan and a bungalow with roses round the door. Count Otto was having his mustachios curled.

Two seats along from Icarus sat a soldier home on leave. His name was Captain Ian Drayton and he was a hero in his own right, having endured sufficient horrors to qualify for a medal. Between Captain Ian and Icarus Smith sat the third man. He was not Michael Rennie.

The third man's name was Cormerant and Cormerant worked for a mysterious organization known as the Ministry of Serendipity. Cormerant wore the apparel of the city gent, pin-striped suit and pocket watch and bowler hat and all. Cormerant muttered nervously beneath his breath and shuffled his highly polished brogues amongst the carpet of clippings. On his lap was a black leather briefcase, containing, amongst other things, a pair of black leather briefs.

Icarus Smith was aware of this briefcase.

Cormerant was unaware of his awareness.

At the business end of the barber's shop, Stravino went about his business. He teased the tip of a mustachio with a heated curling tong and made mouth music between his rarely polished teeth.

'Living la vida loca in a gagga da vida,' sang the Greek.

'Cha cha cha,' sang Count Otto, in ready response.

It might well be considered fitting at this point to offer the reader some description of Stravino. But let this only be said: Stravino looked *exactly* the way that a Greek barber should look. *Exactly*. Even down to that complicated cookery thing they always wear above their left eyebrow and the shaded area on the right cheek that looks a bit like a map of Indo-China.

So a description here is hardly necessary.

'Hey ho hoopla,' said the Greek, breaking song in midflow to examine his handiwork. 'Now does that not curl like a maiden's muff and spring like the darling buds of May?'

'It does too,' agreed the count. 'You are za man, Stan. You are za man.'

'I am, I truly am.' Stravino plucked a soft brush from the breast pocket of his barbering coat and dusted snippings from the gingham cloth that cloaked the count's broad shoulders. The professional name for such a cloth is a Velocette, named after its inventor Cyrano Velocette, the original barber of Seville.

Stravino whisked away the Velocette with a conjurer's flourish and fan-dancer's fandango. 'All done,' said he.

19

'Your servant, sir.' The count rose to an improbable height and clicked his heels together. 'It is, as ever, za pleasure doing business with you.'

'One and threepence,' said the Greek. 'We call it one and six, the tip included.'

'Scandalous,' said the Bohemian count. But he said it with a smile and settled his account.

'Captain,' said the Greek, bidding the count a fond farewell and addressing his next client. 'Captain, please to be stepping up to the chair and parking the bum thereupon.' Captain Ian rose from his seat and made his way slowly to the barber's chair. It had to be said that the captain did not look a well man. His face was deathly pale. His eyes had a haunted hunted look and his mouth was a bitter thin red line.

Stravino tucked the Velocette about the captain's collar.

'What is it for you today?' he asked.

'For me today?' The captain gazed at his ghostly reflection in the tarnished mirror. The mirror was draped about with Spanish souvenir windmill necklaces and votive offerings placed there to honour St Christopher, the patron saint of barbers. On the glass shelf beneath were jars of brilliantine, shaving mugs and porcelain figures, statuettes of Priapus, carved soapstone marmosets and Stravino's spare truss.*

'Do what thou wilt,' said the blanched soldier, who had studied the works of Crowley.

'Then today I think I will give you a Ramón Navarro.'

Outside a number sixty-five bus passed by.

The driver's name was Ramón.

Stravino took up his electric clippers, held them close by his ear, thumbed the power and savoured the purr.

---

* All Greek barbers wear a truss. It's a tradition, or an old charter, or something.

Icarus snaked his hand around behind his seat and sought out the brown envelope. There are many traditions and old charters and somethings attached to the barbering trade. The brown envelope is one of these, but one which few men know.

In the days before the Internet and the invention of the video, the days in fact in which this tale is set, there was little to be found in the way of real pornography. There was *Tit Bits* and *Parade* and the first incarnation of *Playboy* magazine, which was far too expensive to buy and always kept on the top shelf of the newsagent's. But there was only one place where you could view real pornography. Real genuine down-to-business smut. And that was in the barber's shop.

And that was in the brown envelope.

Today things are different, of course. Today the discerning buyer can purchase a specialist magazine dedicated to his (or her) particular whimsy in almost any supermarket.

But way back when, in the then which is the now of our telling (so to speak), there was only the brown envelope.

Icarus peeled back the flap and emptied the contents of the brown envelope onto his lap. There were four new photographs this week. The first was of two Egyptian women and a Shetland pony. The second was of two blokes from Tottenham (who can tie a knot'n'em). The third showed a midget with a tattooed dong and the fourth a loving couple 'taking tea with the parson'.

A musician by the name of Cox would one day write a song about the first three. He would sadly die in a freak accident whilst trying to engage in the fourth.

Icarus perused the photographs, but found little in them to interest him. Cormerant glimpsed the photographs and turned his face away. Icarus became aware of Cormerant's most distinctive watch fob.

21

'Babies,' said Stravino, his clippers purring towards the crown of the captain's head. 'What do you think about babies, then?'

'I don't,' said the captain. 'Why should I?'

'You can't trust them,' said Stravino. 'They pee in your eye when you're changing their nappies. And do you know why that is?'

'I don't,' the captain said.

'Ancestral voices,' said Stravino. 'All that gurgling they do. That's not gurgling. That's an ancestral tongue. You have to keep babies apart, you can't let them chat, there's no telling what they might plot amongst themselves.'

'Twins plot,' said the captain.

'Exactly,' said Stravino. 'Because they were together as babies. Twins are all weirdies, deny that if you can.'

'I can't,' said the captain. 'I have a twin sister.'

'And she's a weirdie?'

'No, she's a unisex hair stylist.'

'I spit on those, whatever they are,' said Stravino. 'And also I spit upon architects. They will be the death of us all.'

'Because they design blocks of flats? Ouch!'

'Sorry,' said Stravino. 'I just took a little off your ear then. But not enough to affect the hearing. But blocks of flats, did you say? Well, that's right, but it's not for why you think.'

'How do you know what I think?' the captain asked.

'I interpret,' said the Greek. 'But answer me this. Why do you think the world has all gone potty mad today? Why are people all stony bonker and devil take their hindparts? Answer this.'

'A lack of discipline,' the soldier in the captain said. 'Or a lack of hope,' the man inside the soldier added.

'No no no.' Stravino hung his electric clippers on their

hook, took up a cut-throat and gave it a strop. 'It's the houses,' said he. 'And I am a Greek, so I know what I say. The Greeks were famous throughout the old world for their classical architecture. Am I right or am I barking up a gum tree?'

'The Greeks were famous for many things,' said the captain, peering ruefully at the reflection of his ruined right ear.

'I put the styptic pencil on that,' said the Greek. 'But many things, you're right as tenpence there.'

'Notable shirtlifters,' said the captain. 'Their armies had platoons of them. No offence meant, of course.'

'And none taken, I assure you. But when they weren't lifting each other's shirts, they were building great temples and amphitheatres and harbours and hippodromes.'

'Hippodromes?' said the captain. 'The Greeks built music halls?'

'Race courses,' said Stravino, now taking up a shaving brush and lathering the captain's head. '*Hippos* means horse in Greek. *Dromos* means race. Did they teach you nothing at Sandringham?'

'Sandhurst,' said the captain. 'But where is all this leading?'

'Architecture, like I say. It is all in the proportions of the buildings. The size and shape of the rooms. You go in some houses, you feel good. Others and you feel bad. Why is that? Don't tell me why, because *I* tell *you*. The proportions of the rooms. The rooms are wrong, the people in them go wrong. People need the right sized spaces around them where they live.'

'There might be something in what you say,' said the captain.

'More than you know,' said Stravino, now applying his cut-throat. 'And babies are little, so to them all rooms are big. Deny that if you please.'

23

Cormerant opened his mouth and spoke. 'I have an urgent appointment,' said he. 'Will I be kept much longer?'

'Do you eat out?' the barber enquired.

Cormerant made the face that says, 'Eh?'

'Do you insult the chef before your soup is served? The chef he spit in your soup, I'll wager. I not care to dine with you.'

'Eh?' said Cormerant. 'What?'

'Look at this poor soul,' said Stravino, pointing to the captain in the chair. 'This man is my friend, but by the caprice of fate, he has all but lost an ear. Think what might befall the man who hurries up his barber.'

'I think perhaps I'll come back another day.'

'No no,' said the Greek. 'I'm all done now.' And he wiped away the shaving foam and dusted down the Velocette and hummed a tune and smacked his lips and then said, 'What do you think?'

Captain Drayton stared at his reflection. His stare became a gawp and his gawp became a slack-jawed horror-struck stare. Of his hair little remained but for an unruly topknot.

'But,' went the captain, 'but . . .'

'But?' asked Stravino.

'But,' the captain went once more, 'you said a Ramón Navarro. Ramón Navarro doesn't have his hair cut like that.'

'He does if he comes in here,' said Stravino. 'Two and six-pence please.'

Cormerant declined the offer to become the next in the barber's chair. He left the establishment in a fluster and a hurry. He dropped his bowler hat and he tripped upon the out-stretched feet of Icarus Smith and fell down on the floor amongst the clippings and the fluff. Icarus helped him up and dusted him off and opened the door and all. Cormerant hailed a passing cab and Cormerant was gone.

Icarus Smith did not have a Tony Curtis that day. He left Stravino's only moments after the departure of Cormerant. Some might say, when the coast was clear. But then some might say anything.

Some might for instance say that it was yet another caprice of fate that Mr Cormerant tripped. And some might say that his watch and his wallet fell into the hands of Icarus Smith by accident. And some might say that Icarus took up the black briefcase that Mr Cormerant had inadvertently left behind in the confusion in order to run after him and return it. Along with the wallet and the watch of course. And the most distinctive watch fob.

Some might say any or all of these things.

But then some might say anything.

2

Icarus Smith took an early lunch at the Station Hotel. It is popularly agreed that there is no such thing as a free lunch. But Icarus did not pay for his. The barman, who now wore a most distinctive watch fob, gave Icarus a double helping of mashed potatoes and told him that everything was 'on the house'.

An understanding existed between Icarus and the barman. The bar and grill of the Station Hotel was a study in scarlet. The rooms were high-ceilinged and broadly proportioned and would have found favour with Stravino. Long, net-curtained windows looked to the station, where the great steam engines came and went, the mighty King's Class locomotives with their burnished bits and bobs. Icarus sat down at a window table, recently vacated by a stockbroker's clerk, and stared wistfully out through the net curtaining to view a passing train.

There were few men alive who were not stirred by steam and Icarus had long harboured a secret ambition to relocate an engine. Exactly to where, and for why, he did not as yet know.

And though the thought of it thrilled him, it terrorized him too. His grandfather had been an engineer on the Great Northern Railway and had lost a thumb beneath the wheels of *The City of Truro*. Icarus prized his digits, but a man must dream his dreams. And if this man be the chosen one, these dreams are no small matter.

Having concluded his early repast and washed it down with a pint of Large and a brandy on the house, Icarus placed the black briefcase upon the table before him and applied his thumbs to the locks. The locks were locked.

Having assured himself that he was unobserved, Icarus removed from his pocket a small roll of tools and from this the appropriate item. It was but the work of a moment or two. Which is one moment more than one less.

The locks snapped open and Icarus returned the item to the roll, and the roll to his pocket.

He was just on the point of opening the briefcase when a hand slammed down upon it.

'I wouldn't do that, if I were you,' said the owner of the hand.

Icarus looked up and made the face that horror brings.

'Chief Inspector Charlie Milverton,' said he, in a wavery quavery voice. 'My old Nemesis.'

'I have you bang to rights this time, laddo.'

Icarus held up his hands in surrender. 'It's a fair cop, guv'nor,' he said. 'Slap the bracelets on and bung me in the Black Maria.'

'One day it will come to that, you know.' The chief inspector grinned and winked and sat himself down at the table next to Icarus. For he was in truth no policeman at all, but the bestest friend Icarus had.

Friend Bob.

Friend Bob was a tall and angular fellow, all cheekbones and pointy knees and elbows. In fact, he looked exactly the way a bestest friend should look. Even down to that curious thing that fits through the lobe of the left ear and that business with the teeth. So no further description is necessary here.

'Watchamate, Icky-boy,' said Friend Bob.

'All right, Bob-m'-son,' said Icarus Smith.

'You're losing your touch, you know. Opening up a stolen briefcase in a bar.'

'The briefcase is mine,' said Icarus Smith.

'With the corner up,* it is.'

'Temporarily mine, then.'

'That's a bit more like it.'

Icarus smiled upon Friend Bob, and Friend Bob smiled back at him, doing that business with the teeth. Although they had known each other since their schooldays at the Abbey Grange and were as close as best friends could be, it had to be said that Friend Bob did not wholly approve of Icarus Smith. He knew well enough that Icarus did not consider himself to be a thief. But he also knew that Icarus was alone in this particular consideration and that it was only a matter of time before the law's long arm reached out and took him in its horny hand. Friend Bob hoped that by subtle means he might one day persuade Icarus as to the error of his ways.

Icarus Smith, in his turn, hoped that one day he might convert Friend Bob to the holy crusade of relocation. And,

---

*The phrase, 'with the corner up', meaning 'you are a lying git' or 'in your dreams', was first coined by the great boxing cornerman Richard Reekie, dubbed in the sporting press as the Cockney in Clay's corner. Before the now legendary fight between Cassius Clay and 'Our 'enry' Cooper, Reekie was told that Cooper felt he could beat Clay. 'The only way Cooper will win', said Reekie, 'is with the corner [man] up holding Clay's arms behind his back.' These things matter.

after all, if you wish to relocate a steam engine, it takes two. One to drive the blighter and the other to shovel the coal. And Friend Bob, felt Icarus, was a natural shoveller.

'What are you doing here?' asked Icarus Smith.

'Working,' said Friend Bob. 'I am the new washroom attendant.'

'Well, you are a natural shoveller.'

'It's an *honest* living.'

'And the pay?'

'There's room for some improvement there.' Friend Bob fingered his left earlobe.

'You could always work with me.'

'I think not.' Friend Bob smiled. 'So how are things with you?' he asked. 'How's the family? How's your brother?'

'Still barking mad. He thinks he's a detective.'

'You'd better watch out that he doesn't arrest you, then.'

Icarus drummed his fingers on the briefcase. 'Tell me, Friend Bob,' said he. 'If you could be anything you wanted to be in this world, what would that thing be?'

'You know perfectly well what it would be. I would become a successful artist. Famous throughout the land.'

Icarus nodded. 'But you don't feel that your total lack of artistic skill might prove a handicap in this?'

'A considerable handicap,' agreed Friend Bob. 'But a man must dream his dreams.'

'Indeed.' There was a moment of intimate silence, each man alone with his thoughts and his dreams.

'So,' said Friend Bob, when he had done with silence. 'What do you have in *your* briefcase?'

'Let's have a look, shall we?' Icarus lifted the lid of the case.

'Urgh,' went Friend Bob, peering in. 'Leather underpants, you pervert.'

29

'You are, as ever, the wag. Have you eaten your lunch yet? There are some sandwiches in here.'

'I have no wish to munch upon sandwiches that have been hobnobbing with a pervert's knickers, thank you very much.'

'Hello, what's this?'

'What's what?'

'This.' Icarus lifted from the briefcase a small dark electronic doo-dad. 'Transistor radio, I think.'

'It's a Dictaphone,' said Friend Bob, who had a love for all things electrical. 'You can record your voice on that. Here, I'll show you how.'

Friend Bob took the Dictaphone, held it up to his mouth and pressed a little button.

'Aaaaaaaaaaaaagh!' went the Dictaphone.

'Aaaaaaaaagh!' went Friend Bob, flinging it back into the briefcase.

'Surely that's the wrong way round,' said Icarus. 'I thought *you* were supposed to record on to *it*.'

'I pressed the playback button by mistake, you twat.'

Icarus now took up the Dictaphone, tinkered with the volume control and then pressed the playback button.

'No,' screamed a voice of a lesser volume. 'No more pain. I'll tell you everything you want to know.'

'Oh shirt!' said Friend Bob, whose mother had told him not to swear. 'It's someone being tortured.'

'Leather pants in the case,' said Icarus. 'Probably just some recreational activity. Shall we hear a bit more?'

'I'd rather not, if you don't mind.'

'Come on now, what harm can it do?'

Icarus fingered the button once more. A new voice said, 'Tell me all about the drug.'

30

'It's drugs.' Friend Bob flapped his elongated hands about. 'It's gangsters. I'm off.'

'It's probably just a TV programme, or a radio play, or something.'

'Or something. Whatever it is, I've heard enough. I don't want to get involved. Return the case to its owner, Icarus, please.'

'Don't be absurd.'

'It will end in tears.'

'Let's hear a little more.'

'Fug that.' Friend Bob lifted his angular frame from the seat next to Icarus Smith. 'I have tiles to polish. I will bid you farewell.'

'Are you coming to the Three Gables tonight? Johnny G's playing.'

'I'll be there. But listen, just dump the briefcase, eh? Leather pants and tortured souls are not a healthy combination.'

Friend Bob turned upon his heel and had it away on his toes.

Icarus sat and considered the Dictaphone. He turned the volume down a bit more and held the thing to his ear.

'What drug?' came the voice of the tortured soul.

'Red Head,' said the other voice.

'Red Head?' whispered Icarus Smith. 'What kind of drug is that?'

There came a crackling sound from the Dictaphone, followed by another 'Aaaaaagh!' and a 'Stop, please stop, I'll tell you everything.'

And Icarus listened while the tortured soul told everything. And as Icarus listened, his face became pale and his hands began to tremble.

For what Icarus heard was this and it bothered him more than a little.

'Tell me all about Red Head,' said the other voice. 'How did you come up with the formula?'

'From the flowers. It was the flowers that showed me the way.'

'Are you trying to be funny?' said the other voice.

'No. I'm telling you all the truth. And I have to tell someone. I'll go mad if I don't.'

'Just tell it all from the beginning then.'

'All right. As you know I worked for the Ministry of Serendipity. On the A.I. project. Artificial intelligence. The thinking computer. Rubbish, all of it. But we didn't know it then.'

'Why is it rubbish?'

'Just listen to what I'm telling you. From the beginning, OK?'

'OK.'

'I worked on the project with Professor John Garrideb. He was one of three brothers, all of them something in mathematics. John was always convinced that we'd make the big breakthrough. But when we did, when *I* did, it wasn't the way we expected and it's my fault, what happened to him, which is why I'm telling you this.

'We worked on the project for twenty-two months, but like I say we were getting nowhere and we kept getting all these directives from above, saying that our work was in the National Interest and we should hurry ourselves up and that other governments were ahead of ours and all the rest of it. And we were working really long hours and I took to drinking a bit in the evenings. And then a bit more and then a bit too much.

'And one night I left the Ministry and went home on the special train from Mornington Crescent and got off at the wrong stop. And I found myself in Brentford and I fell down on the floral clock in the Memorial Park and that was when it came to me.

'I had a sort of revelation. It was all to do with the flowers on the floral clock. It was well after midnight and as I lay there I noticed that all the flowers were still awake. They had their petals open. And I thought that's a bit odd and then I saw the floodlights. They're on all night, you see, to illuminate the clock and because they're on all night the flowers stay open. The flowers never sleep. The flowers cannot dream.'

There was a pause and Icarus heard sobbing.

'Stop blubbing there,' said the other voice. 'What are you crying about?'

'Because I understood it then. I understood why we could never build a computer with artificial intelligence. Because a computer cannot dream. It's a man's dreams that give him his ideas. A man is what he dreams.'

'Sounds like rubbish,' said the other voice. 'But go on.'

'When we sleep,' said the tortured soul, 'it's only our bodies that sleep. Our brains don't sleep. Our brains go on thinking. If we have problems, our brains go on thinking about them, trying to sort them out, trying to solve them. But the solutions our brains come up with are in the form of dreams that our waking minds cannot understand. People have tried to interpret dreams, but they can't, dreams are too subtle for that. But the way we behave and the solutions we eventually arrive at are guided by our dreams, even though we're not aware of it.

'I suddenly understood all this, you see. Probably because it was ultimately the solution to the problem I had. The problem with artificial intelligence. The answer was right there. In our heads, you see. The brain is the ultimate computer, you just have to know how to use it properly.'

'Which is why you came up with Red Head?'

33

'To enhance the intellect. To speed up the thinking processes. To create the human computer. Why bother to build machines, if the answers to the problems you would set them to solve were all inside your head anyway? Just needing a little chemical help to bring them out. But *I* didn't come up with Red Head.'

'I don't understand,' said the other voice. 'Explain yourself.'

'I was lying there amongst the flowers,' said the tortured soul. 'And it all became clear, like I say. And I realized that if such a drug could be formulated, it could change everything, solve all human problems. A group of human computers dedicating themselves to the good of humanity. Just think what might be achieved. I saw the big picture. The overview. But then I thought, how could I ever formulate this drug? It might take years and years. The rest of my life. What I really needed was a drug to speed up my own thinking processes, in order that I could create a drug that could speed up thinking processes. Bit of a Catch 22 situation there. But the crooked man showed me how to read the flowers and that's how I came by the formula.'

'Crooked man?' asked the other voice. 'Who is the crooked man?'

'He found me lying there on the floral clock. He helped me up and he showed me how to read the flowers. He told me that the flowers would help me, if I helped them. All they wanted was to sleep. It seemed a pretty fair deal to me.'

'You'll have to explain this,' said the other voice.

'The crooked man helped me up. He said he'd been listening to what I'd been saying. I thought I'd only been thinking but apparently I'd been talking out loud. Or according to him I had. He said the answer was staring me right in the face, all I had to do was look at the flowers. Well, I looked at the flowers, but all I could see was the flowers. Lots of different coloured flowers in the shape of a floral clock. But he said, look at the colours. Think of the rainbow. Well, I remembered the poem we'd been taught at school, about how you remember the order of the colours in the rainbow. It's a poem about fairies. It goes, *Some came in violet, some in indigo, In blue, green, yellow, orange, red, They made a pretty row.*'

'I remember that,' said the other voice.

'Yeah, well I remembered it and looked at the flowers. First the violet ones, then the indigo ones and so on. And they spelled out letters. Letters and numbers. They spelled out a chemical formula. The chemical formula for Red Head.'

'With the corner up,' said the other voice.

'It's true. Well, the formula is true at least. The drug works. I wish to God now that it didn't. But it does. When I'd written the formula down, I thanked the flowers and then I smashed the floodlights so that they could sleep and dream and then I walked all the way home and went to bed.'

'Incredible,' said the other voice. 'Insane.'

'Oh yes,' the tortured soul agreed. 'It's quite insane. All of it. I went into the Ministry the next day. Gained access to the laboratory and mixed up a batch of the drug. It was remarkably simple and straightforward. And then of course I had to test it. See if it really worked. So I tested it upon myself.'

'And it worked?'

'It worked all right. But not in the way that I'd been expecting. I thought it would speed up my thinking. But the human brain is not a calculating machine. It functions by entirely different processes. Organically. Thinking is organic, that's what it's all about. The drug enhanced my thinking processes. It opened my eyes and allowed me to see clearly. To understand everything. To see things as they really are. And people as they really

35

are. The ones who actually *are* people. And the ones who aren't. The wrong'uns.'

'Careful,' said the other voice.

'Or what? You'll kill me? You're going to kill me anyway, aren't you? You have to keep your secret. If humanity knew about you and your kind and what you're up to and how to see you—'

'Careful.'

'Be damned,' said the tortured soul. 'Be damned the lot of you. I know you for what you are. And I know what you want.'

'Only the formula.'

'But you won't get it.'

'You'll tell us what we want to know eventually.'

'Not I,' said the tortured soul. 'I've only told you this much because I wanted to spend the last few moments of my life free from pain.'

'What?'

'The poison I've taken will kick in at any moment. You'll never find the drug. But someone will and that someone will learn the truth and they'll put paid to you and your kind. That someone will change the world for ever. That someone will make things right.'

'Perhaps you've told us enough anyway,' said the other voice. 'We know where to find the formula. On the Memorial clock.'

'Oh yeah. Right.' A laugh came from the tortured soul. 'The flowers. I got very angry over the flowers. Because of what they'd done to me. Because they'd given me the power to see something so awful that it would ultimately lead to my own destruction. As it has. So I went back there, to punish the flowers. To stamp them to oblivion. But then I thought no, it wasn't their fault. They were quite mad, you see, the flowers. That's what happens when you're deprived of sleep. When you cannot dream. You go mad. The flowers couldn't dream and so the flowers went mad.

'But I did go back. I made a kind of pilgrimage. I wanted to see whether the floodlights had been repaired. And if they had, then I would break them again. So I returned to the Memorial Park, and do you know what I found when I got there?'

'What?'

'Nothing,' said the tortured soul. 'Nothing whatsoever. You see, there was no floral clock in that park. There never had been.'

'What are you saying? Speak to me.'

Another silent moment, then another voice spoke.

'Save your breath on him,' it said. 'He's dead.'

3

Now this is where I came into this tale, so listen up people and listen up good.

With me you get what you pay for, when you pay for the best private eye in the business. I don't come cheap, but I'm thorough and I get the job done. I know my genre and I stick to it. When I'm on the case, you can expect a lot of gratuitous sex and violence, a corpse-strewn alley and a final rooftop showdown.

And along the way you'll get all the stuff that you get when you pay for the best. You'll get a generous helping of trench-coat humour, a lot of old toot being talked in a bar, running gags about the mispronunciation of my name and my trusty Smith and Wesson, a dame that does me wrong and a deep dark whirling pit of oblivion that I tumble down into, when she bops me on the head at the very beginning of every new case.

That's the way that I do business, always has been, always will be. Because, like I say, I stick to my genre. And because, like I say, I'm the best.

If you're looking to get all fancy and post-modern, then

don't come a-knocking at my partition door. Because if what you want is a lot of psychological fol-de-rol and a tormented detective with a drink problem and a broken marriage, who's coming to terms with a tragedy that happened in his youth and is reaching out to his feminine side, then buddy you've come to the wrong address.

But if your taste is for a hard-nosed, lantern-jawed, snap-brimmed-fedora'd, belt-knotted-trenchcoated, bourbon-swigging, Camel-smoking, lone-walking, smart-talking, pistol-packing, broad-smacking, mean-fighting, hot-pastrami-biting, tricky-case-solving son-of-a-goddamn-prince-among-men, then knock at the door and walk right in and ask for me by name.

And the name to ask for is Woodbine. As if you hadn't guessed.

Lazlo Woodbine, Private Eye.

Some call me Laz.

You see me, I keep it classic and I keep it simple.

I work just the four locations. An office where my clients come. A bar where I talk a load of old toot and where the dame that does me wrong bops me on the head at the beginning of the case. An alleyway, where I get into tricky situations, and a rooftop where I have my final confrontation with the villain.

No spin-offs, no loose ends and all strictly in the first person. No great genre detective ever needed more than that and no detective ever came greater than me.

So, with that said, and pretty goddamn well said too, let's get us down to the business in hand and begin it the way that it always begins.

And it always begins like this.

It was another long hot Manhattan night and I was sitting in Fangio's, chewing the fat with the fat boy. The fat boy's name was Fangio, but the fat we chewed went nameless.

It had been a real lean year for me and I hadn't had a case to solve with style since the big one of '98. Times were getting tough.

It's all well and good being hailed as 'the detective's detective', and having your craggy silhouette on the cover of *Newsweek* magazine and your office featured in *Hello!*, but fame won't buy you a ticket to ride if you don't have the fare for the ferryman.

At the present, I was down.

My bank account was redder than a masochist's butt and the trench had washed out of my trenchcoat. The trusty Smith and Wesney Snipes was gathering rust in Papa Legba's pawnshop and my now legendary snap-brim seemed to suit my landlord who had taken it in lieu of last month's rent.

I was down.

Down. Down.

Deeper and down.

I was deeper and down than a pit lad's purse in a pocket of Pleistocene pumice. More at sea than a Lascar's lunch on a leaking Liberian lugger. Further south than a tired Tasmanian's toe-jam tucker-bag take-away.

But hey, when you're deeper and down as that, my friends, the only way is up. You can't just sit there on your sorry ass, waiting for the wind of fortune to blow in your direction.

You have to lift yourself high above adversity.

You have to make your own wind.

'Holy humdinger,' flustered Fangio, fanning his face with his fat. 'If you make wind in my bar one more time, Laz, I'll kick your sorry ass out.'

Oh how we laughed.

40

'I'm not kidding,' the fat boy flustered further. 'I put up with a lot from you, Laz. The running gags about your trenchcoat and your trusty Smith and West Bromwich Albion. The dame that does you wrong always bopping you on the head in my bar. *And* you calling me the fat boy all the time. But I do draw the line at you making wind. I'm running a business here.'

'But you *are* a *very* fat boy,' says I, faster than a ferret in a felcher's footbath.

'*And* those dumb surrealistic metaphor jobbies you insist on using all the time because you think it gives you your own style. The ones that gradually get more and more obscene and obscure and are neither funny nor clever.'

'Ease up, Porkie,' says I. 'I may be down, but I'm far from out.'

'Do you want to settle your tab?'

'I'm out,' says I. 'You have me there.'

Oh how we laughed again.

'By the by, Laz,' says Fangio to me, when the laughter has died down once more in the bar that bares his name. 'I've been thinking of taking up a hobby. Is there anything you'd recommend to me?'

'How about slimming?' I offered in ribald recommendation.

'Would that involve eating less?' asked Fangio. 'Because as you know I gorge like a pig, for it's my only pleasure.'

'Rubber bondage?'

'Well, *almost* my only pleasure. I was thinking of something cerebral that required next to no exercise, cost but a penny or two and could win me a first prize at the annual bartenders' orchid-breeding competition.'

'How about orchid-breeding, then?'

'What, with my back? Come off it.'

'Hang-gliding?'

'Too high.'

41

'Bass-playing?'

'Far too low.'

'Asking after the good health of folk?'

'Fair to middling. Mustn't grumble.'

'How about a card game?' says I.

'Not with you, you cheating Arab.'

'No, not with me, Fange. How about taking up a card game as a hobby?'

'Well,' the fat boy stroked at his chins and a bird blew by in Brooklyn. 'I used to play cards a lot when I was a grunt in 'Nam.'

'You're still a grunt in my book, Fange.'

'Thanks very much, my friend.'

'So,' says I. 'Card games it is. What kind of card game do you fancy?'

The Fange gave his chins another stroke for luck and asked, 'What games do you know?'

I made the face of thought, and pretty damn well too. 'There's Cribbage, Blackjack, Patience, Parliament, Chase the Ace, Rummy, Chemmy, Piquet, Strip Poker, Stud Poker, Seven Card Stud Poker, Bridge, Whist, Old Maid, Happy Families, Three Card Brag, Smiling Faces, Pontoon, Batter My Old Brown Dog in a Basket, Snap, and Snip Snap Snorum.'

'What about six card walkabout?'

'Yes, there's six card walkabout. Strip Jack naked. Boil my brains in a barrelful of bran, Cock the snoot at the Cockney cowboy, Bury my heart at Wounded Knee and Kick butt west of the Pennines.'

'You're just making these up now, aren't you?'

'Have been for quite some time, actually.'

'So how do you play Kick butt west of the Pennines?'

'With aces wild and one-eyed Jacks worth double if you put one on top of a black ten or nine.'

'Very much the same as Batter my old brown dog in a basket, then?'

'Same rules apply,' says I. 'Do you want me to continue?'

'Have you any more real card games on offer? Or are you just going to carry on making up ones with foolish names?'

'Just carry on, I suppose.'

'Continue then.'

'There's Hamper the Scotsman. Whoosh goes a wimple. Cover the rabbit. Body Chemistry 4 . . .'

'Body Chemistry 4?' says Fangio. 'Surely that's a 1994 movie starring former *Playboy* playmate Shannon Tweed. The one where she has it away with a character called Simon on top of a pool table.'

'Well, you can play cards on top of a pool table, can't you?'

'Not if someone's having it away.'

'No, you're right. Forget about Body Chemistry 4. There's Round my hat with a pigeon on a string, Beat the bad boy Berty, Jump around Shorty and Set 'em up Joe . . .'

'You sure know your card games, buddy.'

'Listen, Fange,' says I, 'in my business, knowing your card games can mean the difference between getting it up on a cold winter's night, or getting them down in a Dormobile. If you know what I mean, and I'm sure that you do.'

'I know where you're coming from there,' says Fange, and who was I to doubt him?

We paused for a moment and chewed some more fat.

'That was good,' said Fange.

'What, the fat?'

'No, the toot. That was a good bit of toot we just talked there. A first class piece of toot.'

'Glad that you enjoyed it. Do you want me to make up a few more card games?'

'No,' said Fangio, shaking his jowls. 'The secret lies in knowing when to stop. But, by the by, Laz. There was a guy in here earlier asking after you.'

'How could he be asking *after* me, if he was in here *earlier* than me?'

'Search me,' said Fangio. 'We live in troubled times.'

'So what did this guy look like?'

'Well.' The fat boy pecked upon a peanut. 'Looked a lot like Mike Mazurki to me.'

I nodded thoughtfully.

'A hint of Brian Donleavy over the eyes.'

I scratched at my gonads with equal thought.

'Spoke a little like the now legendary Charles Laughton.'

I whistled through my teeth with less thought than it takes to pluck a turkey. 'The now legendary Charles?' whistled I.

'Yeah, and he had a Rondo hat on.'*

Oh how we laughed once more.

'But seriously,' said Fangio. 'He left his card for you.'

'Is it a one-eyed Jack?' I asked. 'Because they're worth double if you lay them on a black ten or nine.'

'No, it was his business card. We've done with the card game toot.'

'I've a few foolish names left in me.'

'I'm all too sure you have.' Fangio produced the card from a place where the sun never shines and pushed it over the counter to the place where I sat bathed all in glory.

I read aloud, to myself, from the card. 'Mr Cormerant,' I read. 'The Ministry of Serendipity.'

'Speak up a bit,' said Fangio.

---

* Rondo Hatton, legendary Hollywood star of *The Creeper*. It's a joke, see, Rondo Hat on. Well, please yourself!

'Cormerant,' said I.

'Cormerant?' said Fangio. 'Isn't that an aquatic bird of the family *Phalacrocoracidae* that inhabits coastal and inland waters, having dark plumage and a slender hooked beak?'

'No, I think you'll find that's a cormorant.'

'Ah, thanks for putting me straight.'

'So did this guy say what he wanted with me?'

'No,' says Fangio. 'But if you want my opinion, I'd say that he was looking to engage your services as a private investigator in order that you might track down a briefcase of his that has gone missing and contains certain items which if they fell into the wrong hands, or even the right ones, might spell doom to this world of ours in any one of a dozen different languages, including Esperanto.'

'Well, if I want your opinion, I'll ask for it,' says I. 'Did he say that he might call back?'

'He might have,' said Fange. 'But I wasn't listening. Care for a bit more chewing fat?'

I shook my head in a negative way that mirrored my negative thoughts. There was something about this card that didn't smell right to me. Something foully depraved and loath-some to the extreme. Something . . .

'Turn it in, Laz,' said Fangio. 'You always do that when I give you a card and it frankly gets right up my jumper.'

'There's something about this business card that I don't like one bit.'

'Probably the shape,' said Fangio. 'You can tell a great deal about a man's character by the shape of his business card.'

'But surely they're all the same basic shape.'

'Mine aren't,' said Fangio. 'Some of mine are such horrible shapes that it makes me feel sick to my stomach just to look at them. I figure that any man who owns business

45

cards the shape of mine must be some kind of psycho.'

'And did you choose the shapes yourself?'

'Certainly not. How dare you!'

'I'll sleep easy in my bed tonight then, Fange.'

'Gobbo the gnome who lives in my nose told me the shapes to cut them.'

'I'll lock my bedroom door before I go to sleep.'

A guy along the bar was making waves and rattling his empty glass upon the counter. 'Is there any chance of getting served here?' he was heard to ask. 'Or are you two going to talk toot all night, while the rest of us die of thirst?'

'I'd better go and serve him,' said Fangio. 'He's been standing there with an empty glass in his hand since before we started chewing the fat, let alone talking the toot.'

'You go and serve him then,' says I, 'while I ponder over this card and try to get a handle on the guy who left it here. By using certain psychic powers that I don't like to talk about, I can conjure up a mental visualization of the card's owner, by tuning myself to the cosmic vibrations emanating from the card. I'm already getting an image of Mike Mazurki, with a hint of Brian Donleavy over the eyes and a voice like the legendary Charles L—'

'I'll leave you to it then,' says Fangio. 'I'll go serve the customer. Sorry to keep you waiting there, Mr Cormerant.'

'What?'

I bid the guy the big hello and made my presence felt. The hand that held his liquor was shaking more than a go-go-dancing vibrator demonstrator with a bad case of St Vitus. Or possibly just a little less. Who am I to say?

I looked the fella up and down and then from side to side. He had a definite hint of Brian Donleavy over the eyes. And

46

there was more than a trace of the legendary Charles in the voice he used to speak with. But the thing that struck me most about him had to be his hat.

'Is that a Rondo?' says I, admiring the cut of his jib.

'No,' says he. 'It's a bowler.'

We established ourselves at the table near the rear. The one to the left of the gents. It's a bit of a favourite with me. Secluded. Out of the way. That hint of exclusivity that offers the client confidence. Muted lighting that catches my noble profile just so in the tinted wall mirror and a lot of firm support in the seat, which can be handy if your piles are playing up.

'So,' says I, when we've comfied ourselves, 'what's the deal here, fella?'

'My name is—'

'Cormerant,' says I.

'Cormerant,' says he. 'And I work for—'

'The Ministry of Serendipity,' says I.

'The Ministry of Serendipity,' says he. 'And I . . .'

I paused.

'What?'

'What?'

'What are you pausing for?' says he.

'I wasn't pausing,' says I. 'I was waiting for you to continue. You paused first.'

'Well, you kept interrupting.'

'I wasn't interrupting. I was anticipating.'

'That's the same as interrupting, if you butt in. That's interrupting.'

I leaned across the table and beckoned the guy towards me. As he leaned forward, I butted him right in the face.

He fell back gasping and clawing at his bloodied nose.

'What did you do that for?' he mumbled, pulling out an

oversized red gingham handkerchief to dab at all the gore.

'I just wanted to clear up a matter of semantics,' says I. '*That* was *butting*. I was *anticipating*.'

Naturally he thanked me.

He got us in another brace of beers and then explained his situation. Clearly, without pause. Apparently he wanted to engage my services as a private investigator in order that I might track down a briefcase of his that had gone missing and contained certain items which, if they fell into the wrong hands, or even the right ones, might spell doom to this world of ours in any one of at least eleven different languages.

'There's something you're not telling me,' says I.

He counted on his fingers. 'Yes, you're right,' says he. '*Twelve* different languages, including Esperanto.'

'Just as I thought.'

'And so I came to you,' says the guy. 'Because I've heard you're the best.'

'You heard right,' says I. 'So, do you want to tell me *exactly* what's really in this briefcase of yours?'

The guy gave his head the shake that meant, 'No.'

'Well how's about telling me the last place you saw it?'

'Do you know Stravino's barber's shop?'

I pointed to my crowning glory. 'What does this tell you?' I asked.

'It tells me that you asked for a Ramón Navarro.'

'Precisely, and what did I get?'

'You got a Tony Curtis.'

The guy and I chewed fat for a while and then he took his leave. I returned to the bar to find Fangio shuffling cards.

'Pick a card, any card,' says he.

'Three of spades,' says I.

'Correct,' says he. 'But how did you know?'

'Let's call it intuition.'

'Fair enough,' said Fangio. 'I was going to call it Rush the Flush, but Intuition is better. So how did you get on with Mr Cormerant? Are you going to take the case?'

I nodded in the infirmary. Wherever the hell that was. 'He gave me a thousand big ones up front.'

Fangio seemed lost for words. 'I'm lost for words,' he said.

'The guy left his briefcase in Stravino's, where it was apparently lifted by some petty criminal. It shouldn't be too hard to track it down.'

'Stravino's the barber's shop?' said Fangio.

'You know the place?' says I.

Fangio pointed to his head. 'What does this say to you?' says he.

'It says to me that you have a big fat head,' says I.

'Precisely,' said Fangio. 'Precisely.'

Now I know what you're thinking, my friends. You're thinking, how come this Lazlo Woodbine, a man clearly possessed of a mind like a steel trapper's snap-trap, hasn't seen the glaring continuity error here? Surely he's in a bar in Manhattan and Stravino's shop is in South Ealing High Street many miles far to the east.

Well, hey, come on now.

You're dealing with a professional here. A master of the genre. And though I might have said it was another long hot Manhattan night, that didn't necessarily mean that it *was* night or that it was *actually* in Manhattan. Like I told you, I work only the four locations, but if all my four locations were permanently in Manhattan, that would seriously limit my scope of operations, and as you only ever see the interior of Fangio's bar,

49

it could be anywhere. Like, say, at the end of South Ealing High Street, near to the Station Hotel.

'Remember the time it was in Casablanca?' says Fangio. 'Some laughs we had then, eh, Laz?'

'Shut your face, fat boy,' says I.

'Will you be settling your tab now? What with you having a thousand big ones up front?'

I gave my head the kind of shake you couldn't buy for a dollar. And I took a look at the big bar clock that hung up on the wall. And then I gazed along the bar to where the little brown men with hats on sat, a-strumming at their ukes. And then I peered up at the ceiling where the bumblies hung and the ghost of Christmas past had once appeared to Fangio. And then I glanced down at the floor and then I peeped out of the window.

'Something on your mind?' asked Fangio.

'I'm just wondering where she is.'

'Who's *she*?'

'The dame that does me wrong. The one who always bops me over the head at this point, so that I tumble down into a deep dark whirling pit of oblivion. She should have shown up by now.'

'Oh, I forgot to tell you,' said Fange. 'She phoned earlier. Said she wouldn't be in this lunchtime.* Sent her apologies.'

'What?'

'She said that she has to go and bop some other detective over the head today. Some tormented detective with a drink problem and a broken marriage, who's coming to terms with a tragedy that happened in his youth, and reaching out to his feminine side.'

* See that, it's lunchtime, not night at all.

'*What?*'

'She said that the nineteen-fifties American genre detective is now an anachronism and an anathema. The stuff of cheap pulp fiction. She's moved right upmarket now. Gone all fancy and post-modern.'

'WHAT?'

'So it looks like you're out on your own this time, Laz. Or should that be *in* on your own? Because unless you can get someone else to bop you on the head, I can't see how you'll be able to stick with your genre and do things the way that things should be done. After all, the bopping over the head business is a big number with you genre detective lads, isn't it?'

'*WHAT?*'

'Laz, will you let up on the WHATing already? You're giving me a migraine.'

'But what am I going to do?' I asked. 'She can't do this to me. I'm Lazlo Woodbine! Lazlo Woodbine! Some call me Laz. She can't just abandon me. Leave me stuck in a bar. This could be the greatest case of my whole career. The Big One. You gotta help me, Fange. What am I gonna do?'

'Well.' The fat boy scratched at his gut. 'We might come to some arrangement.'

'What?' I kept my what small this time.

'We're old pals; I might be prepared to do you a favour.'

'Go on then,' says I.

'Well,' the fat boy scratched at his gut again, 'I don't think you'll find that it has to be a dame that does you wrong who bops you on the head. It could be anyone.'

'Anyone?'

'It could even be me.'

'You? *You* would bop me over the head? But why would *you* want to bop me over the head?'

51

'Like I say, we might come to some arrangement. Lend us your ear and I'll whisper.'

I lent Fangio my ear and he whispered. 'That's outrageous,' I exasperated, once his whispering was done.

'That's my offer. Take it or leave it.'

I sighed deeply. 'I'll take it,' says I.

'Look out behind you,' cried Fangio.

I turned and then something hit me from behind.

And I was falling.

Tumbling down.

Down. Down.

Deeper and down.

Into a deep dark whirling pit of oblivion.

Yes siree.

By golly.

4

If Icarus Smith had been sitting on the other side of the Station Hotel's scarlet bar and diner, the side that faced to the lower end of the high street, he would have seen Mr Cormerant leaving Fangio's bar, after his meeting with Lazlo Woodbine.

He would have seen Mr Cormerant muttering to himself and dabbing at his nose with an oversized red gingham handkerchief. He would have seen Mr Cormerant stumbling across the street, narrowly avoiding death beneath the wheels of a speeding Ford Fiesta.

And finally he would have seen Mr Cormerant struggling into the back of one of those sinister long dark automobiles with the blacked out windows, which are positively *de rigueur* with the upmarket criminal fraternity, to be ferried back to the Ministry of Serendipity.

But as Icarus was sitting on the other side of the bar, he saw none of those things.

Had he seen them, and indeed had he been able to follow Mr Cormerant back to the Ministry and stick his ear close to the door of a top secret chamber, he would have heard Mr Cormerant get another sound telling off for losing the briefcase, before being complimented for his good sense in employing the world's greatest private eye to search for it. He would then have heard Mr Cormerant being informed that *certain agencies* had already been despatched, to seek out the petty criminal who had apparently lifted the case from Stravino's and see to it that he came to a most unpleasant but suitably spectacular end.

But Icarus did not hear any of these things. Which may, or may not, have been for the best.

With a trembly hand, Icarus Smith removed the cassette tape from the Dictaphone. Having managed, with some difficulty, to slide it into the top pocket of his jacket, he snatched up the Dictaphone, flung it back into the briefcase, closed and locked the lid. And then sat at his table, quivering somewhat and staring into space.

Now Icarus knew the scenario, every moviegoer did. It had been used again and again on the big screen in crime thrillers and science fiction thrillers and even science fantasy thrillers, in fact in pretty much every kind of thriller that there ever was. It was simple and succinct, and this is how it went.

Petty criminal steals something really important without realizing that it is. Case of drugs, or money belonging to gang-lord, advanced military microchip, mega-dangerous virus, Ford Fiesta with alien corpse in the boot. Tick where applicable.

Then, early on in the plot, the petty criminal comes to a most unpleasant but suitably spectacular end, before the hero, in the shape of the detective, arrives on the scene in search of the stolen something.

It was hardly an original scenario, but it had been tried and tested and found to work very well indeed.

Icarus recalled the movie version of *Death Wears a Blue Sombrero*,* in which small time crook Andy Challis, played by Tom Hanks, steals a patent leather clutch bag from a prostitute played by Meg Ryan. The bag contains a doorway to another dimension and poor old Tom gets sucked through it into oblivion, several scenes before the hero, in the shape of Laz, played on this occasion most unconvincingly by Leonardo di Caprio,† arrives to solve the case.

The small time crook *always* came to a hideous end. It was a great Hollywood tradition. Hollywood knew its own business best and who was Icarus to argue?

'I'm in serious trouble here,' mumbled Icarus Smith. 'Although . . .'

Although?

'Although.' Icarus began to smile.

To smile?

'Just let me think about this.'

Icarus gave the matter some thought. Some deep and serious thought. Surely, he thought, in a deep and serious manner, this can be no accident. Surely, this tape did not fall into my hand through mere chance alone. The nature of my game is in-stinctiveness. To become aware of something and then to relocate it. If I have acquired this cassette tape, then there must be some reason why. And think about it, just think about what's on this tape. A man is being tortured and he dies because of something he has discovered. A drug, created from a formula given to him by a pattern of flowers. A drug designed to create the human computer, which instead opened the man's eyes and

---

* A Lazlo Woodbine Thriller.
† Opinions are divided regarding which actor gave the best portrayal of Laz in a Hollywood movie. Robert Mitchum, Brian Donleavy and Rondo Hatton are up there in the top three.

allowed him to see something incredible. Something terrifying.

'To see things as they really are. And people as they really are. The ones who actually *are* people. And the ones who aren't.'

This was big. This was *very* big. This had to be a part of the Big Picture.

And what else had the dying man said to his tormentor?

'You'll never find the drug. But someone will and that some-one will learn the truth and they'll put paid to you and your kind. That someone will change the world for ever. That someone will make things right.'

'That someone is me,' whispered Icarus Smith. 'I must find this drug and I must take it and then I will be the one to change the world.'

It had to be so. Well, to Icarus it did. To Icarus this could not be one of Stravino's 'caprices of fate'. To Icarus, it was a case of 'I am the Chosen One'. And, as history has proved most con-clusively, it can be a difficult matter arguing with a man who believes that he is the Chosen One.

'There can be no doubt,' whispered Icarus Smith. 'The tape was meant to fall into my possession. It is my destiny to change the world for ever.'

And so with all this thought and said, Icarus set to reopening the briefcase. His hands shook only slightly now, and this from excitement rather than fear. Icarus rubbed these hands together and then began to rifle through the contents of the case.

Disregarding the leather briefs, the packed lunch and the Dictaphone, he addressed his attention to a wad of papers and a notebook bound in a curious hide.

Firstly the papers. Icarus leafed through these. They bore the letter heading of the Ministry of Serendipity, and appeared to

56

be interdepartmental memos, concerning the staff canteen and the poor selection of food on offer.

'Hence the packed lunch,' said Icarus Smith.

The notebook, however, was of considerable interest. There were two stains on its front cover. The first appeared to be marmalade but the second looked like blood. Icarus opened the book and then went ah.

'Addresses,' said Icarus Smith.

On the flyleaf of the book were printed the words:

> *This book is the property of*
> Prof. Bruce Partington
> Wisteria Lodge
> Shoscombe Old Place
> Brentford.

'Aha,' said Icarus. 'No doubt the tortured soul himself. But let's just check.' He dug into a jacket pocket and brought to light the relocated wallet. Flipping this open, he observed a Ministry of Serendipity security card made out to one Arkus Cormerant. The photo displayed the face of the chap in Stravino's. The erstwhile 'owner' of the briefcase.

'Yes,' said Icarus. 'And I recognized your voice on the cassette tape. It was you who spoke at the end and said, "Save your breath on him, he's dead."'

Icarus returned the wallet to his pocket.

'Right,' said he. 'Let's have a little action.'

But before Icarus has a little action, indeed a very great deal of action, let us speak a little regarding the living hero of Icarus Smith. This is best done now, rather than later, because later it would only interfere with the action. And also because it will

demonstrate just how the particular endeavours of this particular hero influence the forthcoming actions of Icarus Smith.

The hero of Icarus Smith is a master criminal, wanted in
several countries.

His name was, and is, a secret known to only a few, but as
his best-known pseudonym is the Reverend Jim de Licious, we
shall know him by this name alone.

Jim originally worked at Fudgepacker's Emporium, a prophouse in Brentford which supplied theatrical properties to the
film and TV industries, and it was there that he got the original
idea for his crimes. Fudgepacker's hired out all kinds of stuff,
mostly Victoriana, but had certain items in stock that other
prophouses didn't, and amongst these was a full-sized fibreglass
replica of a post box.

This used to get hired out again and again for street scenes in
movies, and the thing about it was that it looked so convincing
that when filming finished it inevitably got left behind on the
street corner where it had been placed while the scene was
being shot and the prop man would have to go back the next
day and pick it up to return it to Fudgepacker's.

And nearly every time this happened, the prop man would
find that the post box was half full of letters. You see, people
thought it was a real post box and it never occurred to them
that it hadn't been there the week before, so they posted their
letters into it.

This gave the Reverend Jim an idea. It was a dishonest idea,
but it was a good'un. The Reverend Jim took to hiring the post
box himself. He told Mr Fudgepacker that he did amateur
dramatics and Mr Fudgepacker let him hire the post box at a
discount. The Rev would leave the post box on a likely street
corner for a few days, then pick it up in a van in the early hours
of the morning and help himself to the contents.

You'd be surprised just how many postal orders and indeed how much paper money people post.

But it was a pretty heartless crime, because a lot of these postal orders and paper money were being posted off to kids as birthday presents and Jim didn't feel too good about nicking stuff from children.

But he did see the potential.

The prop telephone box that Fudgepacker had in stock was another goody. It looked just like the real thing. It even had the phone and the coin box and everything. And nicking cash from a phonebox is hardly an evil crime, is it?

So the Rev took to hiring the telephone box and setting it up beside a row of other telephone boxes and collecting it after a few days and helping himself to the money in the cash box, which people had put in before realizing that the phone didn't work and using one of the others. Well, he couldn't keep hiring this week after week without rousing suspicion.

But he did see the potential.

There are other prophouses, you see. Prophouses that specialize in other items required by the film industry. There are those that hire out weapons. Those that hire out costumes. And those that hire out vehicles.

The one that hires out vehicles has an AA pickup truck in stock. It's not a real AA pickup truck; it's just been painted up to look like one. It does look very convincing, though.

The Reverend Jim was making quite a lot of money from the telephone box and he'd taken the lease on a lock-up garage, where he used to take the box and empty it. It occurred to him that he might branch out into car theft. And that if he was going to do so, he might as well start at the top end of the market and rip off a Rolls-Royce.

It's remarkable really. If you tried to break into a Rolls-Royce and drive it away, people would look. People would see you. People would call the police. But if you arrive with an AA pickup truck and simply tow the Roller away, people don't even seem to notice.

Those who do, usually laugh. Well, there's nothing more pleasing than a broken down Rolls-Royce, is there? It's nice to see that even rich blighters come unstuck once in a while.

The Reverend Jim would rip off a Roller a week with the hired out AA pickup truck and he probably would have been content with that. He'd made an underworld connection, which was hardly too difficult a thing to do, if you were brought up in the kind of neighbourhood where Jim was brought up. The Hell's Kitchen neighbourhood of Brentford. And this partner in crime was selling the Rollers on to Arabs and the money was pretty good. But one day, when he was returning the AA pickup truck to the prophouse that hired out the vehicles, he spied a new vehicle that they had in stock.

The prophouse had mocked it up for a crime thriller movie about a bullion robbery. The vehicle in question was a Securicor van.

The Reverend Jim was not slow to realize the potential of this particular vehicle. And of course there were those other prophouses. The ones that hired out costumes. So the uniforms wouldn't be too much of a problem.

The Reverend Jim took a week off work. He followed a real Securicor van around. Mapping its routes and logging the times at its various ports of call.

The following week he hired the van and the costumes and he and his partner in crime did the rounds, arriving ten minutes earlier than the real van.

It was a masterstroke.

And once they'd emptied the contents of the bogus van into

60

the lock-up, they returned it and the costumes to the respective prophouses and then drove back to the lock-up in another hired van to pick up the loot and carry it far far away.

And were promptly arrested by the police.

Well, almost.

It was *that* close.

They were returning to the lock-up when they saw the police cars. The police had the lock-up surrounded: pretty quick work, thought Jim. Far too quick, in fact. It occurred to him that the police had probably been tipped off about all the Rollers that had been going in and out and that they'd get quite a surprise when they opened the lock-up and discovered all the newly stolen bullion.

This was just an unfortunate coincidence. A caprice of fate. Jim was pretty rattled seeing all those police cars there, but also felt somewhat proud that he had had the foresight to hire the sort of van he had hired, with which to carry his loot so far far away.

This particular van was a mock police van.

Jim had hired the police uniforms and everything.

Well, let's face it. The police, once alerted to the robbery, would be looking for a bogus Securicor van, not a police van.

Jim got a real kick out of having real policemen help him and his partner load up the van with all the stolen booty.

He told a friend about this over the phone.

Jim was living in Spain at the time.

The Reverend Jim's present whereabouts are unknown. But at least two further crimes committed in this country have his unique stamp on them.

The first one was the great art robbery.

Jim had always had a love for original art. His taste was for certain living artists who produced the kind of abstract stuff that most people wouldn't give you a thank you for, but Jim adored it and wanted to own a collection.

So what Jim did was to take a short lease on a shop premises in Mayfair and open it up as a very prestigious art gallery. He then contacted the various artists for whose work he had his taste and asked them whether they'd care to exhibit. Unlike other art galleries, he would waive the 40 per cent commission on this occasion and allow the artists to keep all the money their paintings sold for. It would be good for the reputation of his gallery, he told them. A one-off event.

Well, you'd be surprised what greedy blighters some artists can be. The ones who said yes to Jim put a really high value on the pieces they exhibited.

Jim insured the lot.

Not that he expected the insurance company to actually pay up. But he felt that it was nice to have the documentation of the art works' values, in case he ever chose to sell the pieces on in the future.

The night before the exhibition – which had been widely advertised in the arts media – was to open, Jim went round to the gallery with another hired van, opened it up with his keys, took down all the canvases and removed them to a place that was far far away.

Spain probably.

You might well know of Jim's final great crime, although it is doubtful that you will have known it for the thing it really is until now. It was a logical progression, though. A matter of seeing potential.

Having graduated from bogus post box to bogus telephone box to bogus AA pickup truck to bogus Securicor van to bogus police van to bogus art gallery, it was natural that Jim would progress to a bogus organization into which millions and millions of pounds might readily pour, week in week out, without anyone ever seeing it for the thing it really was.

So he did.

You probably do know of it.

It's called the National Lottery.

Allegedly.

But let us return now to Icarus Smith, who is about to have a little action. A great deal of action, as it happens.

But no.

Wait.

Let us not return to Icarus just yet. Let us return instead to Lazlo Woodbine, which is to say, the world's greatest private eye. Because Laz is about to meet up with an old companion, a very important companion, and that companion is about to impart certain information to Laz which is of major importance to our tale. Information which will change the direction of Lazlo Woodbine's investigations, and indeed the world, for ever.

We left Laz falling into that deep dark whirling pit of oblivion that all great genre detectives always fall into after they've been bopped on the head by the dame who does them wrong, or, as in this case, the fat boy barman. So let us join Laz as he regains consciousness.

Over to you, Mr Woodbine, sir.

5

I awoke from a dream about a doctor's office and clutched at a dented skull.

'Tongues of the jumping head,' I said. 'That hurts more than a broke-dick dog on the rocky road to ruin.'

I didn't trouble myself with the old 'What happened?' or the even older 'Where am I?' That stuff's strictly for the cheap seats; you're in the dress circle here.

I blinked my baby blues, choked away a manly tear, cast aside all thoughts of pain and even those of taking up a hobby (such as playing Kick butt west of the Pennines, without the aces wild), and copped a glance at my present surroundings.

I lay, sprawled handsomely, though a tad dishevelled, upon a carpet. But it was a carpet of such an unspeakable nature that no words could naturally speak of it. This carpet was spread on the floor of a room which was long and low and loathsome. There was a ghastly hatstand, rising like a gallows tree. A watercooler of evil aspect, dripping poison from its crusted chromium spout. A filing cabinet, coffin black, which surely rotten corpses held. A desk, dark foreboding, and a chair of surly misdemeanour. Above me turned a ceiling fan, its blades slowly cleaving the rank air. Its motion conjured dire thoughts of the pendulum in the tale by Edgar Allan Poe and chilled my soul and placed an icy hand upon my heart.

'What foul and evil den is this?' I cried. 'What fetid wretched chamber of despair? Oh, what has it come to, that I should find myself in such a dismal place? What vile crimes have I committed, that I should be cast into this dungeon of hopelessness? This sordid, filthy—'

'Get a grip, chief. You're back in your office.'

'Aaagh!' cried I. 'The evil one himself speaks inside my head. The father of lies. The spawn of the pit. I am possessed. *I am possessed.*'

'Turn it in, you twat, it's me, Barry.'

'Barry?'

'Barry, chief. Your Holy Guardian Sprout. The cute little green guy who sits in your head and keeps you on the straight and narrow. The little voice that speaks to you and only you can hear. Your bestest friend, who helps you solve your cases. Your little gift from God's garden.'

'Ah,' said I. '*That* Barry.'

'That would be the kiddy, chief.'

'Yeah. Well, I knew it was you all the time. *And* I knew it was my office. I just thought I'd add a bit of atmosphere and excitement. And demonstrate my skills with the old Gothic prose.'

'Best stick to what you do best, eh, chief?'

'Being the best private eye in the business?'

'That would be the kiddy, chief. You wish.'

'I didn't catch that last bit, Barry.'

'I said that would be the kiddy, chief, you're bliss.'

'Thanks, Barry.'

I lifted myself into the vertical plane with more dignity than a belted earl at a defecophiliacs' disco. Made my way across my office with more style and suavity than a dandy in the underground and sat myself down on my chair with more polished aplomb than a plump pink plumber from Plympton.* And with a certain amount of care in comfying up the cushion, as my piles were playing me havoc at the time.

Before me, on my desk, I spied my snap-brimmed fedora and my trusty Smith and Wes Craven.

'My hat, my gun,' said I with some degree of amazement.

'Say "Thank you Barry",' said Barry.

'Eh?'

'Say "Thank you Barry for putting thoughts in a couple of heads and getting my hat and gun back so I can set out once more on a case without looking like a hatless, gunless, gormless git."'

'There's no bullets in this gun,' said I, examining same with my eagle eye. 'I had at least two bullets left, I'm sure. I remember shooting that black guy in the alley who asked if I wanted to buy the *Big Issue*. And I put two in the head of that fat woman, because she was taking up too much space in Fangio's and I've never seen the point of fat people. And one in the kid with the lollipop, because I can't be having with dogs and children either. And . . .'

' "Thank you, Barry" not a happening thing at the moment, then, chief?'

'Yeah, sure, Barry, thank you. But like I was saying, I'm certain I should have had at least two bullets left. And bullets don't grow on trees, Barry. Bullets cost bucks.'

---

* Lobsang Rampa.

'You ungrateful schmuck.'

'What did you say, Barry?'

'I said you're a wonderful buck, chief.'

'Yeah, I guess that I am.' And guessed that I was. That's one of the things that I liked about Barry. He recognized greatness. 'So, little green buddy,' I said. 'What have you been up to? You weren't with me in Fangio's when I got bopped on the head.'

'I always like to miss that part, chief. Rattles me all about inside this empty skull.'

'So where have you been?'

'Been up in Heaven, chief. We Holy Guardians have to check in every week. Put in our expense chitties. Write out our reports. Get a bit of fertilizer rubbed into our leaves by a bra-less Charlie Dimmock lookalike with five-star bottom cleavage. But it's mostly paperwork. You know how it is.'

'I do,' said I and I did. 'So how are things, topside, amongst the choirs celestial? God keeping well, is He?'

'Well, that's the thing, chief. Actually things aren't exactly hunky-dory in Heaven at the moment. God's gone missing again and His wife's getting pretty upset.'

'God's *wife*? I didn't know that God had a wife.' And I didn't. I knew that every dog had its day and that a trouble shared was a trouble halved and I even knew that if you take two mobile phones, call one of them with the other, then place the two of them ten inches apart on a table with a raw egg between them, the egg will be cooked in less than twenty minutes.* But I never knew that God had a wife.

---

* This is true. You can try it yourself if you don't believe me. It's a very expensive way to cook an egg, but it's one of the reasons why I don't own a mobile phone.

'Does He?' I asked Barry.

'Does He what? Own a mobile phone?'

'No. Does God really have a wife?'

'Of course He does, chief. A wife and three kids.'

'*Three* kids?'

'Only one by marriage. The other two, well, you know the story.'

'I don't,' said I, because in truth, I didn't.

'Wake up, chief, you do know the story. Little baby, born in a manger, three wise camel jockeys coming over the desert, nice Christmas presents but a really rotten Easter.'

'OK, yeah.' I dug into my desk drawer and brought out a bottle of Old Bedwetter Bluegrass Bourbon. The taste of the South that makes any day a Mardi Gras. I always like to take a slug of Old Bedwetter at times like these. It adds that certain something that you just don't get from other sippin' liquors. No siree. By golly.

'Don't start *that!*' said Barry.

'Start what?' said I.

'Endorsing products.'

'Sssh,' said I. 'I never was.'

'You lying git.'

'Barry,' I whispered. 'There's a fortune to be made by endorsing products. It's a market that's never been exploited by private eyes. I'm sitting on a gold mine here.'

'I thought you were sitting on your piles. So where was I?'

'You were telling me about God's wife and His *three* kids.'

'Oh yeah. Well, you know about Jesus. He's pretty famous. But what you didn't know was that he had a twin sister called Christene. But she got edited out of the New Testament because God gave Jesus overall artistic control and the full

68

translation rights. Favourite son and all that, you know how it goes.'

'Yeah, OK, Barry, I get the picture.'

'But not the Big Picture, chief. Everyone knows that Mary was the mother of Jesus. Although they don't know about Christene. But there's not many who know that God already had a wife and just how peeved she was when she discovered that God was having a bit on the side and had got His girlfriend up the duff.'

'Hoots a crimbo!' I clapped my hands right over my lug-holes. 'Put a sock in it, Barry, that's big time blasphemy.'

'It's no secret in Heaven, chief. But God eventually managed to smooth things over with His missus. He can be a real charmer when He wants to be. And one thing led to another and the other thing led to the bedroom and Colin was born.'

'Colin?'

'The third child of God. Born within wedlock this time. But he's a bad lot, that Colin, chief. I hate to speak ill of the governor's son, but that Colin. Phtah!'

'Phtah?'

'That was the sound of me spitting, chief.'

'What? Inside my head? You . . .'

'Don't get yourself in a lather. It's only a bit of vegetable phlegm. But anyhow, God's gone missing and His wife is in a right state. She reckons He's down on Earth again, getting up to hanky-panky. He has this thing about Jewish virgins, you see, and—'

'Enough!' I gave my head a clout.

'Ouch!' went Barry.

And 'Ouch!' I went too. 'But turn it in, will ya? You'll bring down the wrath of God on the both of us.'

'I didn't have you down as being pious, chief. I thought you always said you were an atheist.'

'What? With *you* in my head?'

'I thought your psychiatrist told you that I was a delusion and that you were suffering from multiple-personality disorder and that the voice you heard in your head had been caused by some tragedy that had happened in your youth, which, allied to your drink problem and your broken marriage and your need to reach out to your feminine side and—'

'All right! All right! All right! I *do* believe in you. OK, I've said it now. Are you satisfied?'

'Always a pleasure, ever a joy.'

I took another slug of Old Bedwetter and lit up a Camel. I always smoke a Camel on occasions like this. The rich mellow taste of the fine Virginia tobacco gives me that special satisfaction which you just don't find with other smokes.

'I can hardly wait till you put on your pile ointment, chief.'

'Yeah, right. But I can't chitchat with you all day, Barry. I have a thousand big ones up front and a case that needs solving.'

'Forget that, chief. This is *really* big. God's gone missing. Don't you hear what I'm saying?'

'Sure I do, Barry. But if God's got the hots for some piece of kosher tail, that's hardly my business. God knows His own business best.'

'No, chief, you're missing the point. If God doesn't get back on the job, there's no telling what might happen to the world.'

'But I thought you were implying that God *was* on the job, which is why His wife's so upset. Haw haw haw.'

'Chief, pay attention. If God isn't up in Heaven, managing

70

things down here, then things down here are going to get hairier than a prize-winning pooch in a hirsute hound competition.'

'Ease up there. But I don't get you, Barry. What do you mean about God managing things down here? Everybody knows that God doesn't exactly have a hands-on approach to running the planet. God gave man free will. He doesn't intervene. He doesn't take sides. God's neutral. Like Switzerland.'

'That's what God would have you believe. But it isn't so. God has always taken an active part throughout the course of human history.'

'You mean by inspiring people? Like poets and painters? Like prophets and priests?'

'No, chief. They're all just nutcases. God never actually speaks to anybody, but He has shaped human history. And would you like to know how?'

'I would,' I said, and I would and I did.

'The weather, chief. God controls the weather.'

'Oh,' said I, and 'does He?'

'Yes He does. Think about it. The entire colonization of the world depended on which way the wind blew and there are heaps of battles that were won or lost according to the weather. The Spanish Armada blasted away in a storm. Hitler expecting a mild winter in Russia. Rain stopping play each time England get near to winning back the Ashes. Everything in human history has ultimately been governed by the weather.'

'Well, I never knew that.'

'Of course you didn't. But think about this. The only things you can't insure against are acts of God. And that's floods, lightning and earthquakes and all that palaver. And that's God sticking His oar in.'

'You live and learn,' said I.

'Well, some of us do.'

'What's that, Barry?'

'Nothing, chief. But what I'm saying is that God manages the weather and the weather manages human affairs and human history.'

'So what exactly *does* God have against the Ethiopians?'

'I think they nicked the Ark of the Covenant. God does have a very long memory. You never heard of a Jewish saint, did you?'

'No,' said I, 'I did not. But what has all this got to do with me?'

'Wakey-wakey, chief. God's gone missing. His wife wants Him found.'

'Are you saying what I think you're saying?'

'That very much depends on what it is you think I'm saying.'

'*Me?*' I said. 'You want *me* to find God?'

'God's wife wants you to find God. Someone told her that you were the best in the business.'

'*Someone?* Are you saying what I think you're saying?'

'If you think I'm saying that it was me—'

'Barry, I love you.'

'—then you're wrong, chief.'

'What was that?'

'Nothing, chief. Not a thing.'

'Me!' I upped right out of my chair, skipped the light fandango and turned cartwheels 'cross the floor.

'Whoa! Don't do that, chief! Agh! Eeek! Ooh!'

'Sorry, Barry.' I fell into a perfect splits position before backflipping over my desk to land once more upon my chair. There to turn a whiter shade of pale.

'The piles, chief?'

'Urgh!'

I sat upon an ice pack and pondered my position. I was being called in to *find* God. This *was* the Big One. This was *The Case*. Every great detective dreams of *The Case*. And this had to be it.

'Barry,' said I, with more seriousness than a Sudanese sooth-sayer, 'this is the Big One, but I have a problem here.'

'You could strap the ice pack into your underpants.'

'Not that kind of problem. I'm already engaged on a case. I've taken the thousand big ones up front. And although these are now only small ones, compared to the Big One, I can't just quit the case.'

'Chief. A word to the wise here. God's wife is not the kind of creature that you want to keep waiting. If you think that God's been a little harsh with the Ethiopians, believe me, piss God's wife off and you're in a world of hurt.'

I glanced down at my wristlet watch. 'Listen, Barry,' I said. 'It's just turned four. I can have this other case tied up today, easy. Then I could go out this evening, have a few beers, talk some toot, get an early night and find God first thing in the morning. How does that sound?'

'About as likely as Blue Peter sponsoring a Gary Glitter comeback concert, chief.'

'That likely, eh?'

'That, or just a bit less.'

I pondered my position once more. I felt the need to cogitate. To conceptualize. To lucubrate. To cerebrate. To ruminate. To . . .'

'Gimme a break, chief. Dump your case and let's go looking for God.'

73

'Well . . .'

'Chief, would you like me to tell you a little story about God's wife?'

'Does it have a happy ending?'

'No, chief, it doesn't. But I'm going to tell it to you anyway. It's all about how the world really began and it's not the version you've read in the Old Testament. I'll tell it as it happened and I'll do all the voices and everything. I'll even throw in a title for good luck.'

'Go on then.'

'OK.'

GENESIS

At Last the Truth

God's wife wasn't impressed.

'And what is *that* supposed to be?' she asked.

'It's a present,' said God. 'I made it for you.'

'A present.' God's wife did that thing with her mouth. That thing that God didn't like.

'It's for your birthday,' said God. 'You see I didn't forget.'

'I see,' said the wife of God.

'And I've named it after you. It's called the Earth.'

God's wife did that thing once again. 'My name is *not Earth*!' she said. 'It's Earth*a*. You know I don't like you calling me Earth. It sounds dirty, somehow.'

'You used to like it when I called you Earth.' God made a sad and sorry face.

'Well that was *then* and this is *now* and what is that supposed to be?'

'Which *that* is *that*?'

'That little *that* down there on the Earth.'

74

'Ah,' said God, with pride in His voice. 'That little that is Man.'

'Man?' asked Eartha, wife of God.

'Man,' said God. 'I created him in my own image.'

'Ha ha ha,' went the wife of God. 'You never looked as good as that.'

'It's what you call an idealized representation.'

'Yeah, right, sure it is.'

'Look,' God sighed. 'Do you want it or not? It took me days to make.'

'How many days?'

God sighed again. 'What does it matter, how many days? Look at the detail. Look at all the pretty colours.'

God's wife looked. 'And what are those?' she asked.

'Those are trees,' said God. 'And those are flowers. And those are rabbits. And those are birdies. And that's a Ford Fiesta.'

'I don't like *that*,' said Eartha.

'Why don't you like it? What's wrong with it?'

'The design of the inner sill on the wheel arches. You'll get rust there.'

'Ah,' said God.

'And why is Man grinning like that?'

'Because he's happy.' God shook His old head. 'So do you want it, or not?'

God's wife shrugged. 'Suppose so,' she said. 'But what's it for? Can I wear it?'

'No!' God threw up His hands in despair. 'It's not for wearing. It's not even for touching. It's just for looking at. You look at it and it makes you happy.'

God's wife looked. 'Oh no it doesn't,' she said. 'But if you made me another one, I could wear the pair as earrings.'

'I give up,' said God. 'I give up.' And God put on His over-robe. 'I give up and I'm going fishing.'

'Fishing?'

'Never mind!'

God left, slamming the door behind Him. God's wife looked down on the Earth. 'Well,' she said, 'I suppose it's an improvement on that stupid black hole thing He made for me last year. But it needs a bit of tidying up. It needs a woman's touch. The Ford Fiesta can go for a start. And as for you . . .'

God's wife peered down at the grinning Man.

'What you need is a wife.'

The grinning Man ceased grinning. 'I'd rather keep the Ford,' he said.

'And you probably know the rest, chief. Adam gets a wife. The wife gets tempted. Original sin. Adam gets kicked out of paradise and it's another ten thousand years before the Ford Fiesta is invented. And they never sort out the problem with the inner sill on the wheel arches.'

I whistled two bars of 'Mean Woman Blues'.

'You get the picture now, chief?'

'I do. So I'll tell you what I think. I think I'll put the other case on hold for now!'

'I think you've made the right decision there, chief. And it's really nice that you made it of your own free will, without me having to mention the threats and everything.'

'Threats? What threats?'

'Oh, just the threats that God's wife made, regarding what she'd do if you didn't find her husband within twenty-four hours. The most unpleasant but suitably spectacular death, followed by the eternity of hellfire and damnation. But as you've made the decision of your own free will, I won't have to mention them at all.'

'Thank goodness for that.'

'You haven't got a hope, you feeble-minded sod.'

'What was that, Barry?'

'I said put on your hat and coat and let's go and find God.'

'OK, Barry, let's have a little action.'

6

Icarus Smith returned the cassette tape and address book to the relocated briefcase and departed from the Station Hotel. Following Hollywood's example, he then placed the briefcase in a left luggage locker at the station. Put the key into an envelope, addressed this to himself, stuck a stamp upon it and popped it into the post box on the corner.

Having, of course, first assured himself that it was a *real* post box. Well, you never know.

'Right,' said Icarus, when all these things had been done. 'First stop, Wisteria Lodge, home of Professor Partington. If I am to find this Red Head drug, or at least some clue as to its hidden location, the most logical place to begin my search would be there.'

And who could argue with that?

Wisteria Lodge was a grand old Georgian pile. It stood tall and proud with its heels dug into Brentford's history and its head held high towards the changing of the times.

Because, as is often the case, certain additions had been

made to the building over the years.

To the original Georgian pile had been added a Victorian bubo, an Edwardian boil and a nineteen-thirties cyst.

At the rear, work was currently in progress to construct a monstrous carbuncle.

Icarus stepped up to the front door and gave the knocker a knock. He waited a while and then knocked again, but answer came there none. Icarus became aware of the many keyholes in the front door and proceeded to the rear of the building.

The scaffolding was up, but the builders were absent. It was, after all, the afternoon now and builders rarely return from their lunches. Icarus tried the back door and found it to be unlocked.

To some this would be encouraging, but not to Icarus, who reasoned that an unlocked door is a likely sign of occupancy.

'Hello,' called Icarus. 'Anyone at home?'

There didn't seem to be.

Icarus entered the empty house and closed the door behind him.

He stood now in a hallway that could have done with a lick of paint, or a big French kiss of paper. Plaster had been ripped away from the walls and holes driven through the laths. Icarus stepped carefully over the rubble-strewn floor and made his way towards the front rooms.

These he found to be elegant and well proportioned. But utterly utterly trashed. Antique furniture smashed and broken, doors wrenched from hinges, marble fireplaces levered from the walls. Holes driven into the ceilings, floorboards torn from the floors.

Icarus surveyed the terrible destruction.

'It would seem', said he, 'that the men from the Ministry of Serendipity have done some pretty thorough searching here.'

Icarus now stood in what had once been a beautiful dining room. He righted an upturned Regency chair that still retained all of its legs and sat down hard upon it.

'But did they find what they were looking for?' he asked himself.

'Not if their language was anything to go by.'

Icarus turned at the sound of the voice and all but fell off the chair. In the doorless doorway stood a tiny man. He wasn't just small, he was tiny. He had more the appearance of an animated doll than a human being. In fact, it was almost as if a ventriloquist's dummy had been conjured into life.

Clearly this effect was one that the wee man sought to cultivate. For he had slicked back his hair and powdered his cheeks and pencilled lines from the corners of his mouth that met beneath his chin. He wore a dress suit, starched shirt with black dicky bow and patent leather shoes. And he leaned upon a slim malacca cane and eyed Icarus with suspicion.

'So what's your game?' asked the miniature man. 'What are you doing here?'

'Are you Professor Partington?' asked Icarus, rising to his feet.

'Of course I'm not. You know I'm not. I'm Johnny Boy, I am.'

'Pleased to meet you, Johnny Boy. My name is Icarus Smith.'

Johnny Boy cocked his head on one side. 'Icarus Smith?' said he. 'So what are you, Icarus Smith? You're not a wrong'un, like those monsters from the Ministry.'

'Wrong'un?' said Icarus, recalling the expression from the cassette recording. 'Just what exactly is a wrong'un?'

'You wouldn't want to know and you'd better get out of that room real quick if you know what's good for you.'

'Are you threatening me?' Icarus Smith approached the tiny man.

'No, I'm just giving you some sound advice. If you want to hang on to your sanity, I'd advise you to get out of the room before the four o'clock furore starts.'

'The four o'clock furore?' Icarus glanced down at his watch; it was almost four o'clock.

'Starts at the front door there. Goes up the stairs. Then all of that room goes all over the place.'

'What are you talking about?' Icarus peered over the small man's head along the hallway towards the front door and then looked back into the ruined dining room. 'What do you mean, it goes all over the place?'

'Trust me, you wouldn't want to know. Just go out the way you came in and we'll say no more about it.'

'I have some questions to ask,' said Icarus.

'And I have no answers to give.'

'Were you a friend of the professor?'

'Oh,' said Johnny Boy. 'That's how it is, then, is it?'

'What do you mean?'

Johnny Boy looked up at Icarus. Tiny tears were forming in the small man's eyes. 'You said *were*. The professor's dead, isn't he?'

'I'm afraid so,' said Icarus. 'The men from the Ministry tortured him and he—'

'I don't want to know.' Johnny Boy pinched at the tears in his eyes. 'Just go away, will you? You'll find nothing here.'

Icarus placed a gentle hand upon the small man's shoulder. 'I'm sorry,' he said. 'I'm truly sorry.'

Johnny Boy shrugged away the hand of Icarus Smith. 'Go, before it's too late for you.'

'What do you mean? I . . .' Icarus paused. 'There's a

81

child,' said he. 'Standing behind you, beside the front door.'

'It's staring. Close your eyes.'

'I don't understand.'

'Just do what I tell you. Close your eyes.'

'No, I won't. I . . .' Icarus stared. The child was moving towards them now. A little girl with a sweet and smiling face. She had a head of golden ringlets and wore an old-fashioned yellow taffeta dress and a pair of pink ballet shoes.

She skipped along the hallway, seeming oblivious of the rubble and the mess.

'Hello,' said Icarus. 'And what's your name, little girl?'

'You can't talk to them.' Johnny Boy had his eyes tight shut, but he shook his cane about. 'Go out of the back door, quickly.'

Icarus dodged the shaking cane. 'Don't be silly,' he said. 'It's just a little girl. Oh, she's gone. Where did she go?'

A flicker of movement caught his eye and Icarus looked once more into the devastated dining room. A tall man paced up and down before the vandalized fireplace. His face was slim and gaunt with a long hooked nose and a twisted lip and he wore upon his head a periwig. His costume was that of a Regency dandy, all frocked coat and lacy trims. He too appeared oblivious of the rubble and the rubbish, and just paced up and down.

'Who is *he*?' whispered Icarus. 'How did he get past us?'

'Close your eyes, you stupid fool. Do what I tell you now.'

The woman came as a bit of a shock. She seemed suddenly to be there, sitting in a fireside chair. She wore a lavender dress and appeared to be knitting something of an indeterminate shape.

'There's a woman now,' whispered Icarus. 'Where did she come from?'

Icarus sensed, rather than saw, the next arrival. He became

82

aware of a hulking presence, of something oversized, passing him and entering the dining room. It was a giant of a man, with long wild hair, back from the hunt, by the cut of his clothes.

He stormed about the room, ignoring its other occupants and viciously cleaving the air with his riding crop.

The gaunt man continued to pace. The lavender woman, to knit.

Two schoolboys were suddenly playing with an old-fashioned clockwork train set. A crazy-eyed woman, naked but for a speckled band about her neck, danced a lunatic jig. A one-legged soldier with a yellow face hobbled in on a crutch. And then there were more and more and more. And the more and more moved into and through one another. Merging and reforming and blurring and coming and going. And . . .

It was all too much for Icarus, who suddenly found himself falling into that deep dark whirling pit of oblivion normally reserved for genre detectives who are beginning their cases.

He awoke in horror and confusion to find himself in a garden shed. Lacking Woodbine's professionalism, the best Icarus could manage was 'Where am I?' followed by quite a loud 'Aaaaaagh!'

'Calm yourself, lad, calm yourself.' Johnny Boy looked down upon Icarus Smith. 'You fainted, lad. I dragged you out here.'

Images swam before the eyes of Icarus. 'Aaaagh!' he went once more. 'It was ghosts. I saw ghosts.'

'One hundred and six ghosts altogether. I told you not to look.'

Icarus struggled to his knees and glanced fearfully about.

'There's no ghosts here,' said Johnny Boy, doing his best to help the lad up, but not faring altogether well. 'You're quite safe here in my shed.'

'Your shed?'

'Well, the professor's shed. But he lets me live here. *Let* me live here, that is.'

Icarus climbed shakily to his feet. The shed at least looked normal enough. It had the usual broken tools, the usual wealth of old flowerpots, the usual sheddy smell and the traditional half a bag of solid cement that all sheds seem to have.

Upon one wall, however, there was a world map, which looked slightly out of place, but other than that it was all safe shed.

'Bottom of the professor's garden,' said Johnny Boy. 'Beyond the hedge; you have to crawl through. I dragged you through. You're all safe here.'

'But the ghosts.' Icarus sat down upon the half bag of solid cement. 'They were real ghosts. I really saw them. I never believed in ghosts. But they were true. I *did* see them.'

'True as true, all hundred and six of the beggars.'

Icarus took calming breaths. 'Too much,' he said. 'That has to be the most badly haunted house in all the world.'

Johnny Boy shrugged. 'Probably the same as any other. You just can't see them, is all.'

Icarus shook a befuddled head. 'I'm in a right state here,' he said.

'I told you not to look. But did you listen to old Johnny Boy?'

'No I didn't,' said Icarus.

'No you didn't. You've got a white face on you. White as Lady Gloria Scott. You saw her dancing nude, didn't you?'

'You know their names?' said Icarus.

'Researched every one of them for the professor. They were all his fault, after all.'

'I don't understand a bit of this.'

'No, of course you don't. But I'll tell you what. I can see that you're not a wrong'un, so why don't we do a deal? You tell me everything you know and I'll tell you all about the ghosts. Oh, and by the by, I took the liberty of going through your pockets, so I saw the wallet you nicked.'

'I relocated it,' said Icarus.

'So did I,' said Johnny Boy. 'But you can have it back later.'

Icarus sighed and shook his head. 'All right,' he said. 'I'll tell you what I know.' And so he did. He told Johnny Boy everything. About relocating the briefcase and listening to the tape and about what was on the tape and about how he, Icarus Smith, sought to find the Red Head drug and take it and change the world.

Johnny Boy now sighed and shook *his* head. 'Those filthy monsters,' he said. 'I knew they'd do for the professor. They came here two days ago and carted him away. Then they came back and smashed the place up, looking for his formula. I hid in here. They didn't find me.'

'So they never searched this shed?'

'Don't get your hopes up, sonny, there's nothing hidden in here.'

'And you don't know where he hid the formula?'

'I don't need to know,' said Johnny Boy.

'I'll find it,' said Icarus. 'If it can be found, I'll find it.'

'I just bet you will. Would you like to know about the ghosts now?'

Icarus nodded.

'Well,' said Johnny Boy. 'It happened like this. The professor was walking home one night from the station and you know that little passage you go down that leads to Abbadon Street?'

'I do,' said Icarus.

85

'He saw a ghost there. He didn't know it was a ghost at first. He thought it was just a little old lady walking in front of him. It was night and there's two street lamps about twenty yards apart. She passed into the light of one, then into the darkness beyond. And he walked on, but she didn't appear in the light of the next street lamp, so he hurried forward, thinking she'd fallen over, or something. But she hadn't, she'd vanished. And there's high walls on either side, so he knew that she hadn't climbed over.

'Then it occurred to the professor that there was something odd about the old woman. Apart from her just vanishing, of course. Something odd about her clothes. They were wrong, see? Old-fashioned. She wore a plaid shawl and a waxy Victorian bonnet. And then he realized that she was a Victorian old woman. She was a ghost.'

'So he somehow got her here?'

'Don't be stupid, lad. The professor was a scientist. He had a scientific outlook. He reasoned that if he had seen a ghost there had to be a natural, rather than supernatural, explanation and one that science could suss out. So he applied his not in-considerable store of wits to solving the mystery of ghosts.'

'And he solved it?'

'Shut your face, lad, and listen. People have all kinds of theories about ghosts. Lost souls. Shades doomed to wander this Earth in search of justice. Spirits being punished for crimes they had committed as men. Arbiters of doom. Et cetera and et cetera. But what the professor had seen seemed to him so mundane. It was just an old woman walking along. Probably as she had done in that passage hundreds of times. And that was the clue he needed to solve the mystery. Repetition, see. When people see ghosts, those ghosts are always seen doing a particular thing. Just walking along, mainly. So the professor reasoned that what people were actually seeing was a playback of the event.'

'Like a holographic image,' said Icarus.

'What the holy hellfire is that?'

'Something I read in a science fiction book.'

'Yeah, well it ain't that. It's a playback. The professor studied the location of the sighting. He tried to work it all out. Was it something about the location itself? Was it to do with atmospherics? He worked away like one possessed. He was always like that. And finally he worked it out. This world we live on is a bit like a great big capacitor. It stores up energy. You can call it psychic energy if you want, but that's just a word. Everything that's ever happened on this Earth leaves behind a residue. Everything. Like you leave behind a scent that a bloodhound can track. Your ghost is just a recording of an event, which can be played back if the conditions are absolutely right. Are you following this?'

'I think so,' said Icarus.

'So the professor set to work to invent a machine capable of creating the right conditions. An electrical machine, because all people really are, when you get right down to it, all everything is, when you get right down to it, is energy. Electrical energy, atoms vibrating, that sort of stuff. The professor figured that all you had to do was tune into the right wavelength, create the right frequency, beam it at a particular place, create the correct conditions for the playback of a particular event to become visible to the human eye.

'He tested it out in the house. Because he was also no fool, the professor, and he could see the enormous commercial potential for such an invention. Better than theme parks. Imagine if you could go to the Tower of London and actually see all those famous kings and queens of England, played

87

back before your eyes, getting up to all sorts of business.'

'I can imagine,' said Icarus.

'He got all his apparatus set up and we gave it a test run and Winifred appeared. That was the little girl you saw first. The professor was delighted. I was scared witless, but he knew what he was doing. Kind of.'

'Kind of?'

'He tuned the machine back and forwards, up and down the scale, and they began to appear, one after another. You could tune it to Victorian times and see Winifred or Regency times and see Black Peter, the big huntsman, and so on and so forth. And even more creepy, you could tune it back to just minutes before and see yourself doing whatever you were doing then. I'd been having a root through one of his drawers and he wasn't too keen about that.

'But the machine certainly worked and eventually we'd tuned it to every one of the people who had ever been in that front room. One hundred and six of them. Not that many really, considering how old the house is.

'We played them back one at a time and he had me research them from old paintings and photographs and we worked out pretty much who they all were. Apart from a few of them who didn't seem to tie up anywhere. Wrong'uns they were, but we didn't know it then.

'The professor was over the moon. He was all for patenting his machine and becoming very very wealthy. But things didn't work out that way. Winifred kept appearing, even when the machine was switched off. And then, one by one, so did all the others, until you have the four o'clock furore that you saw today. And you can come back and see it all tomorrow if you want.'

'I don't,' said Icarus.

88

'No, I'll bet you don't. This house will be a real stinker to sell, won't it?'

'So you're saying that once the ghosts had been made to appear by the use of the machine, they couldn't be switched off.'

'Seems so. So you can just imagine what would have happened if the machine had been produced commercially. You wouldn't be able to move for ghosts.'

'Does the machine still exist?'

Johnny Boy tapped at his nose. 'Wouldn't you like to know.'

'I would,' said Icarus. 'Because if it did, we could play back the professor and see where he hid the formula, couldn't we?'

'We *could*,' said Johnny Boy, stroking away at his little pointy chin. 'If the machine did still exist. If the professor hadn't smashed it to smithereens.'

'Well, it was a thought.'

'Yes it was, and a good one too.'

'Well,' said Icarus. 'It's an incredible story and an incredible invention, but it doesn't help much with my search. Are you absolutely sure that you don't know where the professor might have hidden the formula?'

Johnny Boy gave his head a shake. 'I wish I did,' he said. 'Because if I did, I'd manufacture the drug by the tanker load and dump it into the water supply. Then we'd see some fireworks.'

Icarus eyed the tiny man. 'You know what the drug does, don't you?'

Johnny Boy nodded.

Icarus sighed again. He got to his feet and stretched out his arms. 'I *will* find it,' he said. 'And when I find it, I'll take it and I'll know too.'

Johnny Boy grinned. 'I hope I'm around to see that,' he said. 'Perhaps you will change the world, eh?'

'Change the world.' Icarus glanced over at the map. 'Why do you have that in here?' he asked.

'It's pretty. It was a present. It arrived in the post yesterday, addressed to me. I don't know who sent it.'

'What?'

'I don't know. The envelope was typed. Free sample probably.'

'I think not.' Icarus stepped over to the map and gave it a bit of close-up perusal. 'There are lines drawn on this map in biro,' he said. 'Did you draw them?'

'I didn't notice any lines.' Johnny Boy pushed in front of Icarus. 'Where are these lines?'

'There and there. All over the place. They're faint but you *can* see them.'

'Well, I didn't draw them.'

Icarus ripped the map from the wall.

'What are you doing that for?'

'Have you a pair of scissors?'

'You're not going to cut up my map?'

'Oh yes I am,' said Icarus Smith. 'I'm going to change the world.'

7

Now I'm not into autoerotic podophilia, so I don't shake in my shoes at the first sign of trouble. Nor am I some taurophiliac, so you won't find me going off like a bull at a gate. I reason things out and *then* I leap into action.

I put my feet up onto my desk and lit up another Camel.

'This would be the reasoning it out bit, then, would it, chief?'

'No, Barry, this would be the me with my feet up on the desk while you get your little green bottom in gear bit, actually!'

'Don't quite follow you there, chief.'

I blew a smoke ring out of my nose and smiled a winning smile. 'Tell me, Barry,' said I. 'How exactly would you describe yourself?'

'Chirpy, chief. Chirpy and chipper and cute as a cuddler's cuddly.'

'I meant, *what* are you?'

'I'm your Holy Guardian, chief.'

'Exactly, and as a Holy Guardian, I'll just bet you have lots of other Holy Guardian buddies, don'tcha?'

'Millions, chief. We're all one big happy family.'

'So why don't you put the word out on the old celestial telephone? Because if God's down here on Earth, one of your big happy family is bound to have seen Him.'

'Smart thinking, chief, but no can do.'

'Come again, please, if you will.'

'Against the rules, chief. We're not allowed to speak to one another.'

'But I clearly recall you saying you'd put ideas into a couple of heads to get me my hat and my gun back. Weren't you talking to the Holy Guardians then?'

'No, chief, just the human schmucks.'

'Damn and blast,' said I. 'Then I'll just have to do this myself. So what *do* we have, Barry? Do we at least have a photo of God, so I have something to go on?'

There was the kind of silence that I for one wouldn't pay you five cents for.

'That would be a no, then, would it, Barry?'

'That would be a *big* no, chief.'

'OK. Fair enough, we'll just have to do it the hard way. If you had a thing about Jewish virgins, where would you go to meet some?'

'Israel, chief?'

'Would you care to narrow that down a little?'

'Isl?'

'Most amusing.' I gave my head a violent shake. 'Ooh' and 'Eeek' went Barry.

'I would go to the Crimson Teacup,' I said.

'The Crimson Teacup, chief? *Not* the Crimson Teacup! Don't tell me you want us to go to the Crimson Teacup?'

'You know the place, Barry?'

'Never heard of it, chief.'

The Crimson Teacup was a gin and ginseng joint on Brentford's lower east side. The Jewish quarter. It was not the kind of venue that I'd want to take my granny to. But hey, I wouldn't want to take my granny anywhere. The old bag's been dead for three years.

The Crimson Teacup was one of those leather bars, where guys and gals who like to dress as luggage get together and sweat it out beneath the pulsing strobes. Fuelled on a diet of amphetamines and amyl nitrate, they strut their funky stuff to the tribal rhythms of the techno beat and discuss the latest trends in nail varnish while the DJ's having his tea break.

I loaded up the trusty Smith and Kick butt west of the Pennines and rammed it into my shoulder holster. Cocked my fedora onto my brow at the angle known as rakish. And, with more savoir-faire than a pox doctor's clown, was off and on my way to glory.

The Crimson Teacup was having one of its specialist evenings. It was a theme night and the theme was 'Come as your favourite food'. Now I thought that I'd seen every kind of cuisine that could possibly be splattered over the human form in my time as a private eye. Because, let's face it, in my business you get to meet some pretty messy eaters. But when I walked into the Crimson Teacup that evening, I was ill prepared for the startling sight that met my peering peepers.

'The joint's empty,' I said.

'It's early yet,' said Fangio. 'Care for a piece of chewing fat?'

I swanked over to the bar and settled my bottom parts carefully onto a stool. 'I didn't know you worked here, Fange,' I said.

'I bought the place. Thought I'd branch out. And a house without love is like a garden overgrown with weeds, I always say.'

'Well, set 'em up, fat boy,' says I.

'Ah. Excuse me, sir,' said Fangio, a-preening at his lapels.

I looked the fat boy up and down, then up and down some more. 'Is this a mirage?' said I. 'Or am I seeing things?'

The fat boy was no longer fat!

In fact he was freer of fat than a scarecrow in a sauna bath. He was willowy as a whipping post and pinched as a postman's pencil. I'd seen more flesh on a supermodel's shadow. This guy was wasted. He was scrawny. He was gangly, wire-drawn, waif-like, spindle-shanked, spidery, shrivelled . . .

'Turn it in, Laz,' said Fangio. 'I'm not *that* thin. I'm svelte.'

'Svelte?' said I. '*Svelte?*'

'Svelte,' said the sylph-like barkeep.

'Now just you turn that in,' I said. 'You're Fangio the fat boy. Always have been, always will be.'

Fange shook his jowl-free bonce. 'Remember our deal?' said he. 'Remember back in my bar at lunchtime, when you didn't have the-dame-that-does-you-wrong to bop you on the head and I whispered to you that I'd do it, if we came to an agreement?'

'Sorry,' I said. 'I must have amnesia. I got this bop on the head.'

'You lying git. I agreed to bop you on the head, as long as I didn't have to be the fat boy any more. As long as you would refer to me in future as the handsome snake-hipped barkeep with the killer cheekbones and the pert backside, and you said—'

'That's outrageous!'

'That's exactly what you said. But you had to agree, so you

could stick to your genre and do things the way they should be done. Am I right, or am I right?'

'Huh!' I made the kind of grunting sound that goes down big in a piggery, but tends to turn a head or two at the last night of the Proms. 'I didn't think you meant *that* thin. I thought you just meant a couple of stone off your big fat bum.'

The handsome snake-hipped barkeep with the killer cheek-bones and the pert backside poured me a gin and ginseng.

I sipped at it and cast a steely eye about the place. It hadn't changed much since the last time I had been in. There was the same old junked-up jukebox, the same old spaced-out salad bar, the same old trippy tables and the same old stoned-again stools. The bar counter looked as if it had been on a five-day freebasing fallabout in Frisco and the ashtrays had chased more dragons than a St George impersonator at an Anne McCaffrey convention.

'Oi!' said the svelte boy. 'Turn that in. There's no drugs allowed in this bar.'

'Since when?' says I.

'Since last week,' says Fangio. 'I recently had a bad experi-ence with drugs. I snorted some curry powder, thinking it was cocaine.'

'Oh yeah?' I said. 'What happened?'

'I fell into a Korma.'

Oh how we laughed.

'But I'm not here to talk toot tonight,' said I. 'I'm here on a case.'

'The briefcase case?'

'No, this case is bigger than that.'

'A suitcase case?'

'No, bigger than that.'

'You don't know how big a suitcase I was thinking of,' said

the wasp-waisted wonderboy. 'This one's really huge. I used to get inside it when I was a kid and go through this doorway into a snow-covered land where I met a lion and a witch.'

'Surely that was a wardrobe?'

'No. It was definitely a witch.'

I whistled a verse of 'You're a twat, Fangio' and sipped on my gin and ginseng.

'So tell me about this case of yours, Laz,' says Fangio.

'Well,' says I. 'I'm looking for this old guy. He might be a regular here. Has a thing about Jewish virgins. Ring any bells with you?'

Fangio stroked at his chiselled chin. 'Well,' says he, also. 'We do get a *lot* of Jewish virgins coming in here. *A lot*. But as to this old guy, what exactly does he look like?'

'Well,' says I, once more. 'Can you imagine what God must look like?'

'Richard E. Grant,' said Fangio.

'Richard E. Grant?'

'Richard E. Grant. Tall and slim and dark with devilish good looks and a twinkle in his eye. Not unlike myself, in fact.'

'With the corner up,' said I.

'He's spot on,' said Barry.

'He's *what*?'

'Who's what?' said Fangio, for none can hear Barry but me.

'I wasn't talking to you.'

'Oh, sorry,' said Fangio. 'Were you talking to Gobbo the magic gnome? Because he's moved out of my nose. He's taken up residence in my pert bottom cleavage now. Hold on a minute while I get my trousers down.'

'Don't you do any such thing.' I took off my hat and holding it carefully in front of my face I feigned an interest in its interior. 'What are you saying, Barry?' I whispered. 'Are you telling me that God looks like Richard E. Grant?'

'Well, wouldn't you, if you wanted to pull Jewish virgins, chief? Or any virgins at all, for that matter.'

I lifted my hat from in front of my face and stuck it back on my head. 'Aaagh!' I went. 'Pull your bloody pants up, Fange!'

The fatless boy buttoned his fly.

'So,' said I. 'A Richard E. Grant lookalike.'

'That's me,' said Fangio.

I shook my head. 'Does a guy who looks like Richard E. Grant ever come in here?' I asked.

'All the time,' said Fangio. 'That would be Mr Godalming.'

'Mr *Goda*lming!' I made the face of the man who broke the bank at Monte Carlo. 'And do you think Mr Godalming might come in here tonight?'

Fangio shrugged. 'He might do. You could wait for him,' and Fangio began to giggle.

'What are you giggling at?' I asked.

'You could *wait* for Mr Godalming. Get it? *Waiting for Godalming*, as in *Waiting for Godot*. That's a good 'un, eh? Haw haw haw.'

'Lost on me,' I said. 'But I'll wait.'

And so I waited.

The Crimson Teacup began to fill up. But not with crimson tea. These dudes and dudesses had taken pretty seriously to the idea of coming as their favourite food.

'Excuse me.' A dame stood before me. And some dame she was. Five feet two and every inch a woman. She had hair the colour of cheese soufflé. Her lips looked more at home around a champagne flute than a chipped enamel mug and her eyes were the windows of her Dover sole. She was wearing nothing but two fried eggs and a doner kebab.

'Interesting hat,' I said. 'How did you sew on the fried eggs?'

'Mr Woodpile?' says she.

'Wood*bine*,' says I. 'The name's Lazlo Woodbine. Some call me Laz.'

'I'm Phil,' says the dame.

'Well, you shouldn't eat so much,' says I. Always happy to inject a little humour into any situation.

'Phil*omena*,' says the dame in a manner which led me to believe that she didn't quite grasp the subtle nuances of my outstanding witticism. 'Philomena Christina Maria O'Connor.'

'That sounds like a line from an Irish jig.'

'You're a real funny guy, Mr Woodpile. It's a pity you'll meet such a tragic end.'

'Tragic end?' says I. 'What's this?'

'I overheard you asking after Mr Godalming.'

'But you weren't in the bar at the time.'

'Walls have ears, as well as sausages,' says she. And who was I to argue with that?

'So what's the deal?' says I.

'The deal is, stay away from Mr Godalming.'

'No can do,' I told her. 'I'm working for his wife. She wants the guy back for his tea tomorrow.'

'His *wife*?' The dame went 'haw haw haw' in a manner I found most upsetting. 'Mr Godalming *won't* be coming home for his tea tomorrow,' she said, and then went 'haw haw haw' again.

'Enough of the hawing, already,' I told her. 'You'll get us picked up by the vice squad.'

The dame raised two fingers, then turned round and left me.

'What was *that* all about?' I asked myself.

'She's a real bad lot,' said Barry.

'I was asking *myself*,' said I. 'Not you.'

'Any luck then, Laz?' The thin boy tapped my shoulder with a delicate digit.

'None,' said I, a-shaking of my head. 'There's no shortage of Grant lookalikes in the place, though. I've seen three Russells, two Hughs, a General, and a council grant for getting your loft insulated. But ne'er a sniff of a Dick, if you catch my drift and I'm pretty sure that you do.'

'Pervert,' said the thin boy, but he said it with a smile.

I cast a professional eye around and about the place. The joint was truly jumpin' now and the DJ was layin' down the good stuff. Above the wild gyrating crowd, the bar's logo revolved, an oversized teacup and saucer crafted from red vinyl and black lace and fashioned to resemble a corseted female torso.

And then I saw him.

'Him, chief, Him. Where? Where?'

'By the gents. I'm going over.'

'Just take care, chief. Take care.'

I elbowed my way through the dancers. Making my presence felt, but taking care that nobody rubbed up against me. I mean these folk were covered in food and this was my best trenchcoat. And although the fabric is waterproofed – in fact I'd had mine double-coated with that special stuff they treat office carpets with – you can still get greasy stains that are the very devil to wash out. Red wine's always a killer, but almost anything from an Indian restaurant can be the kiss of death.

The way I see it is this: the way a man treats his trenchcoat tells you everything you need to know about him. Some say it's shoes, and they may have a point, but in my business, keeping a spotless trenchcoat can mean the difference between cutting a dash at a debutante's do or cutting the cheese in a chop shop.

If you know what I mean and I'm sure that you do.

'Out of the way there,' I went, and, 'Don't you get cream on my trenchcoat, buddy, or I'll punch your lights out.'

I made my way to the gents with sartorial elegance intact, leaving only two men dead on the dance floor. Oh, and one woman too, but that had been an accident.

The Richard E. Grant lookalike had his back to me now and as I didn't really know the correct form when addressing God in person, I thought it best to ask Barry.

'Just be polite,' said the little green guy. 'And call Him sir. He always likes that.'

'Fair do's.'

The dude hadn't come as his favourite food, but I guessed God had more class than that. He wore the kind of suit that doesn't come off the peg, or out of the Next catalogue. I'd only ever seen a suit like that once before and that was on the body of a businessman, who'd spilt soup on me at a Masonic maggot roast in Barking, back in '93.

Mr Godalming was chewing the fat with a dame done up as a Danish. She looked to be about sixteen years of age, had long black hair and a tiny moustache and answered to the name of Sarah.

'So Sarah,' I heard Him say. 'What's a nice girl like you doing in a place like this?' A real class act.

'Er, excuse me, sir,' I said, in a manner calculated to give no offence, 'but are you Mr Godalming?'

He turned slowly to face me and high above the DJ's din I heard the angels sing. He fixed me with a stare from His clear blue eyes and my piles began to shrink. He opened his mouth to speak to me and I knew at that very moment that I, Lazlo Woodbine, private eye, stood in the presence of God.

And I damn near soiled my underlinen.

100

Well, it was *that* close.

'Excuse me, sir,' said I, and I backed at some speed to the gents.

'Very stylish, chief,' said Barry, somewhat later as I washed my hands in the sink.

'The guy's God, for God's sake. I've never been face to face with God before.'

'No, I guess not, chief. I should have warned you. He can have that effect on people.'

'But it *is* Him, Barry. It's definitely Him. I solved the mystery of His disappearance, in less than a couple of hours. Mind you, it hasn't had the usual gratuitous sex and violence, nor the alley full of corpses leading to the final rooftop show-down, but hey, I've solved the Big One.'

'You haven't persuaded Him to go back to His wife yet, chief.'

'Mere detail, Barry. I've found God and that's a pretty big number.'

'So Cliff Richard says.'

'Right.' I dried my hands on a paper towel and readjusted the tilt of my fedora. 'Let's get this done,' said I.

I swung the gents door open and returned to the bar of the Crimson Teacup.

'Damn and damn and double blast,' said I. 'The holy bird has flown.'

I thrust my way into the chaos of culinary cavorters. Pushed past a guy dressed up like a dog's dinner and a dame dressed down in duck à l'orange. Glided by a geezer in gammon gateaux and two in taramasalata. Squeezed between a sassy sal in a sexy seafood salad and a white-faced wimp in a whitebait waistcoat, waving a waffle iron. I was carefully manoeuvring myself around a red-necked raver in a rabbit-fish ragout, when I spotted the sweetmeat known as Sarah standing soberly by the sound system, swigging Sauternes and savouring a sauerkraut sandwich.

I unholstered the trusty Smith and Wessex-Arms-Wednesday-night-chef's-special.

'Where is Mr Godalming?' I shouted in Sarah's shell-like. 'Spill the beans or eat some lead, it's all the same to me.'

She shot me a glance like she was gobbling Gumbo, or chewing on cheap chitterlings. 'You've just missed him. He went out the back door with two guys.'

I beat my way back through the crowd. Battering the bean-feast barn-dancers and shovelling sitophiliacs to the right and left of me. Certainly I would have liked to have indulged in a bit more alliterative whimsy, all that fellow in falafel and a flap-jack fez kind of caper, but I was in a hurry here and when time is tight you don't count sheep or lard the lambs, or even munch the mutton.

Now normally I open doors with caution. I mean, you never know what lies beyond them and like I've said before, I work only the four locations. My office, the bar, the alleyway and the rooftop. So I can't go off kicking open every door that lies before me, no matter how big the temptation. But the way I see it is this, a bar's back door *always* leads to an alleyway. So I put my boot to this one and kicked down the son of a—

BANG BANG BANG and BANG again.

The sound of gunshots came to me and they weren't music to my play-my-ears. I pride myself that I can identify almost any handgun in the western world, simply by hearing it fire. And so I knew right off that the sounds of firing were coming from a pair of P37 Narkals, Greek army issue revolvers, pearl-handled probably, with the blue metal finish.

I took a peek round the doorpost to gauge the situation and then ducked back to regain my wits and then burst forth with my gun held at the ready.

BANG BANG BANG then BANG again.

There were two guys at the alley's end, pumping bullets, thus and so, into a third on the ground. I didn't ask any questions and I didn't offer any deals. I let off just two straight shots and the two guys joined the third.

'Nice shooting, chief,' said Barry.

'Thank you, Barry,' said I.

I made it down the alley, checked out the gunmen to make sure they were dead and then turned over the victim who was lying face down in the mud and red stuff.

And then I leapt up all in a lather and damn near soiled my underlinen for a second time off.

'Oh God!' I cried. 'It's God! I felt His power and now He's dead. Oh God! Oh God! *Oh God!*'

'Hold on to yourself, chief, easy now.'

'But God's dead, Barry, He's dead.' I began to do the wee-wee dance.

'Then he can't have been God, can he, chief? God wouldn't go getting Himself shot dead in an alleyway. That's not how God does business. This must be some other Richard E. Grant lookalike.'

'Yeah, but if God was being a man. So He could pull the Jewish chicks and everything. He'd be vulnerable. He could be killed.'

'Well, chief, I suppose He could. But it's not very likely, is it? God getting Himself shot in an alleyway.'

'So you reckon it's the wrong guy? Do ya, Barry? Do ya?'

'Has to be, chief, has to be.'

I breathed a mighty sigh of relief. 'That had me going for a minute,' I said. 'I mean imagine if it really *had* been God. I'd be in really big trouble with His wife, wouldn't I?'

'Big, chief. Bigger than big. The biggest that ever there was.'

'And what about the weather, Barry? What with God controlling the weather, the way He does. Imagine what might happen to the weather with Him no longer in charge of it.'

'It doesn't bear thinking about, chief.'

'Well, phew,' said I. 'All I can say is phew.'

'I'll join you in that one, chief, phew.'

I straightened my hat and turned up my collar. 'Let's go back inside,' I said. 'It's getting chilly out here.'

'You're right, chief, downright bitter.'

'And it looks like rain.'

'Snow, chief, looks like snow.'

'Not at this time of year, surely?'

Something hit me right upon the snap-brim. 'Hail,' I said. 'It's hail. No, it *is* snow. No, it's rain, no, it's, oh, the sun's come out again. No it's not . . .'

'Chief,' said Barry.

'Barry?' said I.

And then the hurricane hit us.

8

Two hours prior to the terrible death of God and the rather unseasonable change in the weather, Icarus Smith and Johnny Boy knelt on the floor of the late Professor Partington's shed, worrying at a map of the world, which now had been cut into many tiny pieces.

'Try putting that bit there,' said Johnny Boy.

'Please leave it to me,' said Icarus Smith. 'I am the relocator and this is the stuff of my dream.'

'I've got a piece of Afghanistan here.'

'Then kindly give it to me.'

Johnny Boy handed Icarus the piece of Afghanistan, then clambered to his feet and stood with his hands on his hips, peering quizzically over the lad's stooped shoulders.

'The secret', said Icarus, 'is for me *not* to think about it. Just let it happen naturally. Just let the right pieces fall into the right places. That's what the science of relocation is all about.'

'Things don't just fall into place by themselves,' said Johnny Boy, stretching his tiny arms and clicking his tiny neck. 'Things require a catalyst. And the "relocation" theory of yours requires you to be its catalyst. But you're making a right pig's earhole of the map.'

'It will all fall into place,' said Icarus. 'Trust me.'

'Oh, I *do* trust you. Don't get me wrong. I'm just suggesting that you need a little help with this one. I'll pop up to the house and get us a cup of tea. A cup of tea always helps.'

'No,' said Icarus, turning, 'don't open the shed door.'

But it was too late. Johnny Boy had opened the shed door and a breeze from the garden came curling in, lifting the pieces of map from the floor and whirling them into a fine little papery snow storm.

'Oooh,' went Icarus, snatching here and there and everywhere.

'Ooh,' went Johnny Boy, joining him in this.

'Just shut the door. Shut the door.'

Johnny Boy hastened to shut the door.

Bits of map came fluttering down to land here, there and everywhere.

'Sorry,' said Johnny Boy.

'Just hold on,' said Icarus Smith.

'You've got it?'

'Yes, I think I have. Look at the way the pieces have fallen. Look at all the different colours. The colours of the rainbow. Like the flowers on the floral clock. Help me gather them up.'

Johnny Boy helped in the gathering up and in the sorting out.

Icarus Smith did the putting into order and then the laying down. '*Some came in violet, some in indigo, In blue, green, yellow, orange, red, They made a pretty row.*'

'Rainbow,' said Johnny Boy. 'That's pretty.'

'Yes it is. And now the biro lines join up and spell something.'

'What do they spell? What do they spell?'

'Words,' said Icarus. 'They spell, TOP OF THE BILL. What does that mean, TOP OF THE BILL?'

'I know what it means,' said Johnny Boy.

'Then tell me, please.'

'Me and the professor,' said Johnny Boy, and he bowed grandly to Icarus. 'Me and the professor were once top of the bill.'

'Go on.'

'Back in the nineteen fifties. Long before you were even born. The professor was a stage magician, Vince Zodiac, he called himself, or the Vince of Darkness, I liked that one. But he was a pretty crap magician and he was usually near the bottom of the bill. Until he met me. I've always been right down at the bottom. Life's like that, when you're a midget. But anyhow, I met the professor one night in a bar. He stepped on me, people often do. He was rather drunk. Drank far too much, the professor. Mind you, if he hadn't been drunk, he wouldn't have seen the flowers on the floral clock. Even if the floral clock doesn't exist.

'But I digress, he was drunk and I was sore because he'd stepped on me and he bought me a drink and we got to talking and that's how the stage act came to be. Professor Zodiac and Johnny Boy. He dressed up as a headmaster and I was dressed as a schoolboy and made up to look like a ventriloquist's dummy. I had a special box with air holes that he used to carry me in and out of the theatres in. No-one twigged that I was a person and not a dummy. We made it to top of the bill.'

'So where is the formula hidden?' asked Icarus.

'I'm coming to that. Top of the bill we were. But just for the one night. The professor drank too much champagne at the backstage party and knocked me out of my box. I didn't

107

half howl. And the game was up. That was the professor out of showbiz. But he felt a duty to me, because he was a good man and he was never cut out for showbiz anyway, he was a scientist. He stuck with me and I stuck by him. We were good friends.'

Tears came once more to the eyes of the tiny man.

'I'm so sorry,' said Icarus. 'But *do* you know where the formula is hidden?'

'Of course I do. We were only ever top of the bill at the one place and that was the Chiswick Empire. That's where the formula will be hidden.'

'Then let's go,' said Icarus Smith.

'They pulled it down,' said Johnny Boy. 'Years ago.'

'So what's there now?'

'On the site? A multi-storey car park.'

Icarus gnawed upon a knuckle. 'Did the professor own a car?' he asked.

'He did, but he didn't drive it much. He'd drive it drunk and in the mornings he wouldn't be able to remember where he parked it.'

'So where is this car now?'

Johnny Boy shrugged. 'I haven't seen it for weeks. It could be anywhere.'

'Like for instance, parked in a multi-storey car park?'

'Ah,' said Johnny. 'That might just be.'

'Then I will go and search for it. What kind of car did the professor drive?'

'A red Ford Fiesta. But there's millions of them. I'll know the one when I see it.'

'Ah,' said Icarus. 'I was thinking of going alone. There might well be danger. There always is, in the movies.'

'I'm coming too,' said Johnny Boy, stamping his tiny feet.

'I've trusted you from the word off. Why did you think I trusted you?'

'I don't know.' Icarus shook his head. 'I've been wondering about that.'

'Because I can *see*.' Johnny Boy pointed to his little dolly eyes. 'I can see the truth. I can see who's who.'

'What are you saying?'

'Wake up, sonny. I can see because *I* took the drug. I was the only one the professor could trust. And if you're going to take it too, you're going to need me there. You won't like what you see, when you see it.'

Icarus Smith left the house of the late Professor Partington, struggling under the weight of a case. It was not a briefcase this time, although he certainly hadn't struggled under the weight of that, it was a special case. A case with air holes in it.

The conductor of the Chiswick-bound bus wouldn't let Icarus get on with his big case. Icarus was forced to hail a taxi.

The taxi driver tossed the case into the boot and slammed it shut. Icarus winced and climbed into the passenger seat. 'Chiswick High Street and fast,' said he. 'I'll tell you when to stop.'

The taxi took off at a leisurely pace.

Icarus chewed upon his bottom lip.

Had Icarus been looking into the driver's mirror, he might well have noticed the long dark automobile with the blacked out windows that was following the taxi. It was the same long dark automobile that had been parked in a side road opposite Wisteria Lodge when Icarus had entered the house, two hours earlier. And it had driven quite slowly up the road behind him, when he left the house.

But Icarus apparently hadn't noticed the car upon his arrival, nor when he left, and, as he wasn't looking into the driver's mirror, he didn't notice it now.

Icarus sat and gnawed upon his knuckle. He was fully aware that he was in considerable danger. The men from the Ministry of Serendipity would probably stop at nothing to get their hands on the professor's formula. And also Mr Cormerant's briefcase and its contents. Bringing Johnny Boy along for the ride had not been the best of ideas. Although, if Johnny Boy *had* taken the drug and he was right about Icarus needing him to be there when Icarus took it . . .

Icarus gnawed some more. He'd actually considered leaving the boxed-up Johnny Boy on the bus. Someone would have let him out sooner or later. It would have been cruel, but it might have been kinder in the long run. But Icarus certainly didn't think that leaving him in the boot of a taxi was any solution to anything.

'Can't you go any faster?' asked Icarus Smith.

'Of course I *can* go faster,' said the cabbie, in the voice that cabbies use. 'But I won't.'

Icarus glanced across at the cabbie. He was your typical cabbie. He talked exactly as your typical cabbie always talks and looked exactly the way that your typical cabbie always looks. Even down to that curious thing they do to their hair on the left hand side and that odd business with the tongue when they pronounce the word 'plinth'.*

So there was no need to bother here with a description.

'I've done the knowledge, you know,' said the cabbie, doing

---

* Plinth is a really wonderful word. It was Simon Kimberlin, the rubber fetish wear designer, who first drew my attention to it. 'Get a woman to slowly pronounce the world plinth,' said he, 'and watch her mouth, it's one of the sexiest things you'll ever see.' And it is. Try it yourself if you don't believe me.

110

that other thing that cabbies always do. That thing with the eyes. 'And I know the name of every street in Greater and Inner London off by heart. You can test me if you want.'

'I don't want,' said Icarus.

'It might make me drive faster.'

'All right,' Icarus sighed. 'Name a street beginning with W.'

'No, that's not what I mean. *You* name a street in London and *I'll* tell you how to get to it.'

'Chiswick High Street,' said Icarus.

'No, not Chiswick High Street. We're almost in Chiswick High Street. A street that's nowhere near here. One that's on the other side of London.'

'Mornington Crescent,' said Icarus, recalling the address of the Ministry of Serendipity.

The cabbie scratched at his hair on the left hand side. 'There's no such street,' he said. 'You're pulling my blue carbuncle.'

'Your *what*?'

'It's what my wife calls my willy. She's an architect.'

'Could you drive a little faster?'

'Give us another street then.'

Icarus sighed yet again. 'Sesame Street,' he said.

'Sesame Street?' said the cabbie.

'Sesame Street,' said Icarus.

'Right then,' said the cabbie.

'What, you turn right here?'

'No, not here. You turn left.'

'But you said right.'

'No, I said right *then*. I was just plotting my course. It's straight ahead for a quarter of a mile, then turn left into Albert Square. Around the square, right into Coronation Street, third left into Brookside, past Peyton Place, into Tin Pan Alley.

111

Then it's goodbye Yellow Brick Road, past the House of the Rising Sun, into Blackberry Way, down Dead End Street, taking in a Waterloo Sunset, up Penny Lane, then we're on the road to nowhere, a Road to Hell and a long and winding road, then we're—'

'Here,' said Icarus. 'Stop the taxi, please.'

'But I haven't done Route 66, Highway 61, Devil Gate Drive and Desolation Row, and you have to watch out for Cross Town Traffic there.'

'On the corner here will be fine,' said Icarus.

'Turn right at Camberwick Green and you're in Sesame Street.'

'I think you'll find it's left at Camberwick Green then right up Trumpton High Street.'

'Smart arse,' said the cabbie. 'You knew all the time. That will be five guineas please.'

'Guineas?' said Icarus.

'Guineas,' said the cabbie. 'I'm sure a noble bachelor such as yourself is used to paying in guineas. And that includes the fare for your mate in the box. I wasn't born yesterday, sunshine.'

Icarus bid the cabbie farewell and humped the case into the multi-storey car park. Here he released Johnny Boy.

The midget climbed out, coughing and spluttering.

'Are you all right?' said Icarus.

'That really is a very stupid question.' Johnny Boy dusted himself down and straightened his dicky bow. 'Hide the case behind that wheelie bin over there and let's go and look for the car.'

Icarus hid the case behind the wheelie bin and he and Johnny Boy went off a-looking.

Behind them a long dark automobile pulled up beside the

ticket barrier, a darkly tinted window slid down and a hand reached out to press the button.

'There's an awful lot of Ford Fiestas,' said Icarus.

'Most popular car in the world,' said Johnny Boy. 'Even with that design fault on the inner sill of the wheel arches.'

They were up on the second level now.

'Do you know the number plate?' asked Icarus.

'No, but it has a sticker in the back window that reads ON A MISSION.'

'Very subtle,' said Icarus.

'Just keep looking, lad.'

Icarus just kept looking.

They can be big old jobbies, those multi-storey car parks. And it is a fact well known, to those who know it well, that a race of magic gnomes live in multi-storey car parks. And when you're away doing your shopping in the supermarket, they get into your car and move it to another level. They are related to the wallet fairies, who nick the ticket to the multi-storey car park out of your wallet, where you're absolutely certain that you put it, and slip it into one of your carrier bags. So that when you've finally found your car that the magic gnomes have moved, you have to go through every single one of your carrier bags to find your ticket. And you drop your carton of milk and put heavy things back on top of your eggs and mis-place the bag of sweeties you were intending to eat on the drive home and get yourself into a right old fluster.

'Why are there always burst milk cartons in multi-storey car parks?' asked Icarus, as Johnny Boy slipped over on one and fell with a thud to the floor.

'I don't know. Ouch. Help me up.'

They were on the sixth floor now and though they'd seen

an awful lot of red Ford Fiestas, they hadn't seen—

'That's it,' said Johnny Boy. 'If I hadn't slipped over, I never would have noticed it.'

'But it hasn't got an ON A MISSION sticker in the back window.'

'No, it's fallen off. It's here.' Johnny Boy pointed to the inner sill of the offside rear wheel arch. 'It's sticking out through this rust hole, see?'

Icarus saw. And Icarus took out his little roll of tools. Having first assured himself that he wasn't being observed.

Naturally.

Icarus tinkered and Icarus opened the boot.

'Well well well,' said Icarus, peering in.

'Help me up,' said Johnny Boy, struggling up.

'It's here,' said Icarus. 'It's all here. Boxes of tablets. The formula. And what's this electronic doo-dad thing?'

'Oooh,' said Johnny Boy. 'That's the professor's machine. The one that tunes into ghosts. I thought he'd destroyed it.'

'Spectremeter,' Icarus read from the little brass plate on the doo-dad's side. 'And this is a portable version, powered by batteries.' He lifted it out and tinkered with the buttons.

'Don't switch it on in here, for God's sake.'

Icarus returned the spectremeter to the boot.

'He was originally going to call it the Ghostamatic 2000,' said Johnny Boy. 'Spectremeter's probably better. I didn't know he'd called it that.'

Icarus took his roll of tools and applied his talents to the driver's door. Then he returned to the boot, scooped up the contents and flung them into the rear seat of the car.

'Come on,' he said to Johnny Boy. 'We're leaving.'

'You're going to nick the car?'

'I'm going to relocate it.'

'Can you get it started without the key?'

'No, I'll use the spare one that's always kept under the sun-shield visor thing above the windscreen. At least it always is in the movies.'

'You watch too many duff movies, lad. The professor always kept his in the glovie.'

'Come on then, let's go.'

'To where?'

'To anywhere. There's been a big dark car with blacked out windows following us ever since we left the professor's house. I may have pretended not to notice it, but I do watch a *lot* of movies. And I know how all this works.'

'What big dark car?' asked Johnny Boy.

'The one over there, coming up the ramp.'

'Let's go,' said Johnny Boy.

Now, there is a knack to starting a Ford Fiesta. You have to pull out the choke as far as it will go. Give the accelerator pedal a little bit of toe. Turn on the ignition slowly. Keep your foot off the accelerator pedal and let the revs build up. When the revs sound like they are running too high, ease the choke in to about half an inch, and wait until the engine has taken up a regular beat. Then put your foot on the accelerator pedal and pump it a few times, just to sound cool, and then you're away. Then . . .

Johnny Boy fumbled in the glovie and fumbled the key to Icarus. 'Let me explain what you have to do,' he said.

'No time.'

'But you'll flood the engine.'

'No time.'

The long black car drew to a halt, boxing the Ford Fiesta in.

'Well. It hardly matters now,' said Johnny Boy. 'We're trapped.'

'Of course we're not.'

Icarus keyed the engine. And stuck his foot down hard to the floor. The engine roared and the usual glorious cloud of acrid fumes came a-bursting out of the exhaust. Icarus slammed the gearstick into reverse.

'What are you doing? You'll smash into them.'

'Of course I won't.'

Icarus dropped the handbrake and let out the clutch. The Ford swept backwards out of the parking bay.

The long black car did likewise out of its path. Very fast, with its tyres screaming.

'They're letting us out!' cried Johnny Boy. 'Why are they letting us out?'

'Because this is a clapped-out Ford Fiesta, of course. And anyone with a decent car knows far better than to get anywhere near a clapped-out Ford Fiesta. It's a natural instinct with drivers of posh cars. They can't help themselves.'

Johnny Boy glanced out of his window. 'They're getting out of the car,' he said. 'They're wrong'uns and they've got guns.'

'Then let's go.'

Marvellous acceleration, the Ford Fiesta. Simply marvellous.

Icarus swerved out of the parking bay and then took off at the hurry-up.

Johnny Boy was up on his seat, clinging to the headrest. 'They're getting back into the car,' he shouted. 'They're coming after us.'

'Yes, well I thought they probably would.'

'Faster,' cried Johnny Boy. 'Faster.'

Now, it does have to be said, what with Hollywood knowing its own business best, and everything, that the 'car chase in the multi-storey car park' never seems to lose its popularity. Those 'hilly streets with the trams in San Francisco' are always good, of course. And the 'racing under the big overpass jobbies in Brooklyn' and the 'swervy mountain roads in France', which are usually filmed in California, and the 'out on the freeway in the desert' of course. Also in California. But the 'car chase in the multi-storey car park' (or parking structure, as our American cousins like to call it) never ceases to impress. Lazlo Woodbine actually considered adding one more location to his set of four, that of the 'parking structure, where a dodgy drugs deal is being done with racketeers'. But he decided to scrub round it, because it was far too dangerous a location to work. What with all the car chases going on.

And everything.

Icarus did some more swerving and headed down the exit ramp. The long dark car came creeping slowly after him.

'We're losing them,' said Johnny Boy. 'They've slowed down, we're OK.'

'I think not,' said Icarus. 'It has probably occurred to them, as it has occurred to me, that I don't have a ticket. I don't know how we're going to get out of this car park.'

'Oh dear,' said Johnny Boy. 'That would be a problem.'

'Possibly.' Icarus leaned over and whispered words into Johnny Boy's ear.

'Do you think that might work?' asked the small man.

'I'd give it a go,' said Icarus. 'I can't think of anything else.'

'Okey-dokey then.'

The Ford Fiesta moved across the first floor of the multi-storey car park and then rather than going down the exit ramp it went up again. Up to the second floor, all round that, then up to the third floor and all round that. The long dark automobile followed it.

The driver wasn't smiling.

The Ford Fiesta went down to the second floor again and then up two floors to the fourth. The long dark automobile followed the Ford Fiesta. Losing sight, then gaining sight of it again.

The driver had a definite frown on.

The Ford Fiesta went down to the third floor, then up to the fifth, then down to the second again. The long dark automobile followed it.

The driver had a snarl on now.

'What are they doing?' he shouted. He was an evil-looking man, the driver of the long dark automobile. He wore a chauffeur's uniform and looked exactly the way that evil chauffeurs always look. Even down to that business with the chin and the unusual birthmark above the right eyebrow, which resembles the Penang peninsula. 'What are they doing?' he shouted again. 'Driving up and down and round and round until they run out of petrol?'

'Cut them off,' said a man in the back. An unseen man, so description wasn't necessary. 'Park the car across the exit ramp on the third floor.'

'But they're in a Ford Fiesta, sir. It might scratch our bodywork if it bumps into us.'

'Just do it.'

'Yes, sir.'

The Ford Fiesta went up to the fifth floor again and then came down. The long dark car was blocking the third floor exit ramp. The chauffeur was sitting on the bonnet. He had a gun in his hand. The Ford Fiesta came down the fourth floor exit ramp. Which was the ramp leading from the fourth floor to the

118

third, in case you're finding this somewhat hard to follow.

'Here they come,' shouted the chauffeur, raising his pistol. 'Stop or I fire, you sons of . . .'

The Ford Fiesta didn't stop.

'Stop or I fire! Stop or I fire!'

The Ford Fiesta didn't stop.

'Stop or I—' The driver leapt from the bonnet as the Ford Fiesta struck the long dark automobile.

Well, struck it is not exactly the word.

Passed right through it is. But that's four words.

'Aaagh!' went the chauffeur as the Ford Fiesta merged into the long dark automobile, emerged from the other side, drove on round the third floor and then went up to the fifth again.

Down on the *ground floor* the Ford Fiesta had reached the ticket barrier. 'Nice work,' said Icarus to Johnny Boy. 'That old portable spectremeter really gets the job done, doesn't it? I'll bet they'll be chasing the ghost of this car around the car park for the rest of the day.'

Johnny Boy grinned. 'And switching it off on the second floor so the ghost car just goes on in a continuous loop while we slipped down to the exit. Smart idea, Icarus.'

'So let's be off on our way.'

The bloke who worked in the little ticket office next to the barrier grinned at the grinning pair who stood before him.

'Lost ticket?' he said. 'That will be fifty guineas, please.'

9

'Fifty guineas?' said Icarus Smith. '*Fifty guineas?*'

The car park attendant wore a uniform. It didn't fit at all well. They never do.

'Fifty guineas?' said Icarus again. 'What do you take me for?'

'A noble bachelor,' said the bloke in the ill-fitting uniform. 'And who's this? Your little brother is it?'

'I wish it was,' said Icarus. 'I have a brother, but he's barking mad.'

'I'm getting madder by the moment,' said Johnny Boy.

'Come on,' said Icarus. 'Let's go.'

Icarus Smith and Johnny Boy returned to the Ford Fiesta.

'What are we going to do?' asked Johnny Boy. 'Drive through the barrier?'

Icarus gathered up the papers and the boxes of tablets and the spectremeter. 'No,' said he. 'I think we'll just walk from here.'

Down the exit ramp from the first floor came the long dark automobile.

'On second thoughts,' said Icarus, 'I think we'll run.'

★

Johnny Boy couldn't run very fast, because he had very short legs. Icarus managed to flag down a cab.

'Brentford,' said he. 'And fast, please.'

'Ah, you again,' said the cabbie. 'And with your mate out of the box, this time. Hop in then and I'll tell you some more about the knowledge.'

On the journey back to Brentford, which was not achieved in quite the speedy manner Icarus would have hoped for, the cabbie told Icarus some more about the knowledge. And Johnny Boy, who had a passionate interest in the geography of Greater and Inner London, and also the songs of Bruce Springsteen, asked the cabbie how you got to Thunder Road.

'What an interesting man,' said Johnny Boy, when he and Icarus had finally stepped from the taxi.

'Fascinating,' said Icarus Smith.

'But I think he was wrong about turning left in Arnold Layne,' said Johnny Boy, who also had a love for early Pink Floyd. 'So what, exactly, are we doing here?'

'This is a pub,' said Icarus.

'Yes, well, I can see it's a pub.'

'It's called the Three Gables and I'm supposed to be meeting my best friend, Friend Bob, here tonight. I'm going to tell him everything.'

'Do you think that's wise?'

'Absolutely,' said Icarus. 'In movies, people always keep things to themselves until the last minute. It heightens the tension. Personally I don't need any more heightened tension today.'

'You're gonna get it,' said Johnny Boy, 'when you've taken the drug.'

'That's why I want to be with Friend Bob when I take it.'

Johnny Boy made a doubtful face. 'It's a very wise man who

knows who his real friends are,' said he. 'Friend Bob might not be what you think he is. You'd better let me take a look at him first.'

'To see if he's a wrong'un?' Icarus pushed open the door to the saloon bar. Johnny Boy followed him in.

The Three Gables was a proper drinking man's pub. No theme nights or foppish fancies here. It was your honest to goodness, down to Earth, spit and gob, drinking man's pub. And you don't see many of those around any more. It served proper flat ale in proper dirty glasses. Had proper full ashtrays and a proper foul-mouthed barmaid with an enormous bosom and a taste for group sex with Jehovah's witnesses (well, they do keep knocking at your door when you're taking a bath). There was proper unswept lino on the floor and proper unmopped vomit in the gents. There was a proper one man band called Johnny G, who performed there on a Tuesday night. And proper drunken louts who threw proper light ale bottles at him when he did.

The atmosphere was fugged throughout with proper cigarette smoke.

It was all right and proper and the way a pub should be.

'I hate it here,' said Johnny Boy. 'It smells.'

'What can I buy you?' asked Icarus Smith, making his way through the proper crowd of early evening drinkers to the bar.

'Hold on, don't lose me.'

Icarus returned to assist the small man to a quiet corner table.

'Look after all this stuff,' said Icarus, placing the boxes of tablets and the papers and the spectremeter down on the bench seat next to Johnny Boy. 'I'll get us in the drinks.'

'A short for me,' said Johnny Boy. 'But make it a large short, a triple. Vodka, no ice, off you go.'

And so off Icarus went. Presently he returned in the

company of a vodka bottle and two glasses.

'Blimey, I'll bet that cost you a few bob,' said Johnny Boy.

'An understanding exists between myself and the big-bosomed barmaid,' said Icarus.

Presently still, the bottle was uncorked, glasses filled and glasses drained away. Icarus opened one of the boxes of tablets.

He placed a tablet on his palm and rolled it all about. It didn't look all that much. Just a little white pill. There was nothing about it that said BEWARE.

'What *will* I see, when I take it?' he asked Johnny Boy.

'The truth,' said the small man. 'And you won't like it one little bit.'

'And are *you* seeing the truth? *Now*, at *this* moment?'

Johnny Boy glanced all around and about. 'Yeah,' he said. 'And it's all pretty safe in here. There's nothing that should rattle you too much. But out there,' Johnny Boy gestured to out there in general, 'out there is a whole different matter. What you'll see out there will shake you up. You'll never be the same man again once you've taken the drug. The effects don't wear off.'

Icarus lifted the tablet to his mouth.

But then he paused. Did he really truly want to know this truth, whatever it was? Did he really want to take some strange drug, whose unknown effects would be with him for ever? Did he, Icarus Smith, really really truly truly want to change the world? Yes, he'd had the dream. Yes, he *was* the relocator. Yes, he felt that he was on some mission that seemed almost divine.

But he was a lad of eighteen. His whole life stretched before him. He had already got himself into something rather dangerous. Would it not perhaps be better just to cut and run while he still had the chance?

'It's a lot to think about, isn't it?' said Johnny Boy.

'Far too much,' said Icarus Smith. 'And that is not the way that I do business. So let's leave it to fate. It either goes in, or it doesn't.'

'Eh?'

Icarus tilted back his head, closed his eyes and opened his mouth. And then he flipped the tablet high into the air.

The tablet spun into the fug of cigarette smoke, caught a fleeting beam of sunlight when it reached its apogee, became a tiny star hung in a foul-smelling Heaven and then fell back to Earth.

To vanish down the throat of Icarus Smith.

'Fate has it then,' said Johnny Boy.

Icarus gagged and reached for his glass and swallowed down some vodka.

'There's no going back now, lad,' said Johnny Boy. 'Let's just hope that you're up to it. I think you are. In fact, I'm sure you are.'

Icarus wiped at his mouth. Sweat was already coming to his brow. The thought 'Oh God, what have I done?' was crying very loudly in his head.

'Don't panic,' said Johnny Boy, patting the arm of Icarus. 'You won't actually feel anything. You'll experience a bit of double vision at first, but when that clears . . . well, when that clears, we'll talk about things.'

Icarus clutched at his head. There was something going on in there. Something decidedly odd. There was a rushing noise in his ears now. And a queer sensation, as if parts of his brain were being tightened, or bolted up, or realigned in some way.

'Tuned in,' said Johnny Boy. 'Your brain's just being tuned in. It's all to do with frequencies, you see. Like the ghosts. We're all attuned to only a limited range of frequencies, which is why we can only hear and see and smell a limited number of

124

things. We can't see everything that's really going on around us. And that's the way the wrong'uns would like to keep it. That's why they'll stop at nothing to make sure the professor's drug doesn't fall into the right hands. Except it already has. It's fallen into yours.'

The double vision was really kicking in now. Icarus pinched at his eyes. 'I can't see.' He shook his head from side to side. 'I'm going blind.'

'It will clear, lad. It will clear.'

Icarus suddenly jerked bolt upright, his eyes widened and he stared at Johnny Boy. And then his jaw dropped open and then it slowly closed again.

'My God,' said Icarus Smith. 'Johnny Boy, you're beautiful.'

'Well, thank you very much.'

'But you are. You're beautiful. You glow. You've got a golden aura all around you.'

Icarus glanced at the bar. And just as it is when you do some really good acid, it was as if he was now seeing everything the way it really was, for the first time ever.

The only difference was, that Icarus *really was* seeing it.

He gawped at the people standing at the bar. Talking, drinking, smoking, swearing. Just ordinary people. Normal people. But Icarus could really see them. *Really see them.* He could see, not just the people, but what they really were. The very essence of the people. What made the people people.

Some were evidently good people. They veritably shone. Like Johnny Boy, who sparkled. Some, however, were not at all good. These exuded a grimness about them. A dark foreboding.

And it wasn't just the people. The bar itself looked different too. The colours were heightened. Cleaner. Crisper. Everything was more defined. More clarified.

'Wow,' went Icarus Smith. 'And I do mean, Wow.'

'Like it?' said Johnny Boy. 'Like what you see?'

'It's incredible. See that big bloke over in the corner? He's lying to that chap with the moustache. I can't hear what he's saying, but I can actually see that he's lying. I can, I don't know, *perceive* it somehow.'

'Doors of perception,' said Johnny Boy. 'Aldous Huxley wrote about that.'

Icarus took up his glass for a swig. 'Urgh,' he said, gaping at the vodka. 'This stuff's been watered down. You can actually see, my God, you can actually see the water in it.'

'I was too polite to mention that,' said Johnny Boy. 'Seeing as you were buying.'

Icarus looked the midget up and down. 'You're a really good person, man,' he said.

'No, please,' said Johnny Boy. 'Don't start calling everybody man. Break the habit now, while you still can.'

'Yeah, but man oh man oh man.' Icarus whistled. 'This is some trip.'

'It is for now,' said Johnny Boy. 'But sadly it won't be for long.'

'You mean this effect *will* wear off?'

'No, but you've only seen the good side of it so far. And no, hold on, now you're going to see the other side. I don't want you to look just yet, but someone has just come into the bar.'

'Who?' asked Icarus.

'It doesn't matter who, just look at me, please. I'm going to ask you to turn your head in a moment and look. But when you do and when you see what you see, I don't want you to react. Don't scream, or anything.'

'As if I would,' said Icarus.

'Listen, lad. I told you not to look at the ghosts, didn't I? But you didn't listen. Now I'm telling you to keep your wits about you and not to react to what you see. You mustn't give the game away. You mustn't let them know that you can see them.'

'Would this be the wrong'uns?' whispered Icarus.

'Yes it would, lad. He's up at the bar now, so turn your head slowly and keep your mouth tight shut. And don't stare, what-ever you do. Just look and then look away. I really mean it, trust me and do what I tell you.'

'All right,' said Icarus. 'I will.'

And Icarus turned his head slowly and looked towards the man who now stood at the bar. And then Icarus turned his head back slowly towards Johnny Boy.

And Johnny Boy looked into the eyes of Icarus Smith.

And Johnny Boy saw the terror that was in them.

Icarus was finding it hard to form words, but when he could, they came out in a whisper. 'It's not a man,' he whispered. 'It's some kind of monster. What is it?'

'It's a wrong'un, lad. That's what it is. Now take another look and don't react. It doesn't know you can see it for what it really is. You're safe, as long as you don't do anything stupid.'

Icarus turned his head once more and feigned a casual glance towards the figure standing at the bar.

It was hideous. Evil. Loathsome. It was more than the height of a man, with tall quills rising from a scaly elongated head. The eyes were those of a reptile, greeny-red with vertical slits. There was no nose to speak of, but the mouthparts were com-plicated, just as those of some grossly magnified insect. And there was more to it, so very much more. And all this more was fearsome to behold.

Icarus took a gulp of his watered down vodka and slowly turned once more to Johnny Boy. 'It's an alien,' he whispered. 'A creature from outer space. They really *do* walk among us.'

Johnny Boy grinned. 'Alien?' he said. 'You watch far too many duff old movies. That wrong'un isn't an alien.'

'Then what is it?'

'It's a demon from Hell, lad. Although it's not exactly *from* Hell. You see, people have always had the wrong idea about Heaven and Hell. They thought Heaven was up in the clouds and Hell way down in the burning depths. But they're not. They're both right here. Inhabiting the same space we do.

'You see, there is no afterlife. No Heaven or Hell that you go to when you die. When you die, you're finished, gone, kaput. But there are angels and there are demons and they do *walk among us*. This world can be Heaven or Hell, depending how your cards fall. Depending who, or rather *what*, is pulling your strings. I don't know if there's a God or not. But if there is, I'll bet He's down here too.'

'Demons,' whispered Icarus. 'And they've always been among us? And people can't see them for what they are? People just think they're other people?'

'You're catching on, lad.'

'It's all too much. I mean, well, I mean, the demons and the angels both here on Earth. I mean, they don't *get on* with each other, surely, I mean . . .'

'You mean, you mean, you mean. *No*, they *don't* get on with each other. You might have noticed that mankind does indulge in a bit of warfare once in a while. The odd bit of conflict. Well, that's not always the fault of mankind. All those evil despots, those Hitlers and Stalins, people have said that they sold their souls to the devil. But that's not true. They really *were* demons. Waging their wars. Using up people as if they were nothing at all. So that the forces of evil can rule the planet.'

Icarus buried his face in his hands. 'No,' he wept. 'No.'

'Pull yourself together, lad. People will look. The *wrong'un* will look.'

Icarus did some snappy pulling together. 'We have to do something about this,' he said. 'This is big. This is really really big. This is bigger than anything. The knowledge of this could really change the world.'

'So, it's a good thing you won't be telling anybody about it, isn't it?'

Icarus looked up in horror.

The chauffeur of the long dark automobile looked down.

He wasn't a wrong'un. But he was a bad 'un.

He gestured with a bulging jacket pocket.

'Yes,' he said. 'It *is* a gun. You might have seen it earlier. Now pick up all the boxes and the paper and walk quietly before me to the front door.'

'And what if I don't?' said Icarus. Suddenly bold and very very angry. 'Are you really going to shoot me in here, in a crowded bar?'

Icarus heard the pistol cock.

'Without a second's thought,' said the chauffeur.

Icarus could see the man within the man.

And Icarus could see that the man wasn't lying.

Icarus gathered up the boxes and the papers and the spectre-meter, and with Johnny Boy before him and the chauffeur behind, moved across the crowded bar towards the door.

They passed close by the creature standing before the counter. Icarus could feel its pitiless gaze and a chill ran through him. What was he to do? Shout for help, turn suddenly and fight?

The jacket-muffled muzzle of the gun dug into his back. 'Just keep walking,' came the chauffeur's voice at his ear.

Outside and drawn up close to the kerb was the long dark

129

automobile. As Johnny Boy and Icarus approached it, a rear door swung open.

'Get inside,' said the chauffeur.

Johnny Boy peered in, then jerked back in horror.

'Go on,' said the chauffeur, 'both of you get in.'

Icarus climbed into the car. Johnny Boy followed him.

Stretched out on the rear car seat was a single occupant.

The single occupant was not a human being.

The long quills glistened and twitched, moving singly or in pairs, probing, sensing. The cold reptilian eyes swivelled in their scaly sockets. The complicated mouthparts moved and chewed and sucked.

'So,' said the creature in a cold dead voice. 'We meet again.'

'We do?' Icarus Smith whispered the words. His throat was dry and he was shaking terribly.

'Well, briefly,' said the creature. 'In Stravino's barber's shop. You stole my briefcase, I believe.'

10

Now, when I found myself standing in an alleyway, at the back of the Crimson Teacup, looking down at the dead body of God and turning up my collar to the howling hurricane, I stayed as cool as a Conservative councillor caught with a Cockney castrato in a curate's cloakroom.

'Deny everything,' I shouted to Barry, above the wind and weather. 'We'll just have to deny everything. Hide the body. Pretend this didn't happen. Spin some line to God's wife that He's off on a fishing holiday in Norfolk and I'll change my name and grow a beard and become a Muslim.'

'Neat thinking, chief.'

'You think there's a chance I can pull it off?'

'About as much chance as Dr Harold Shipman becoming the Queen Mum's personal physician.'

'Quite a *slim* chance, then?'

'Somewhat thinner than Fangio's waistline, chief.'

'Then that leaves me with only one alternative.'

'And what's that, chief?'

I shoulder-holstered my trusty Smith and Wesleyan chapel,

dropped to my knees in the rain, hail, fog and snow and sleet and sunshine, closed my eyes and clasped my hands in prayer. 'Please forgive me, God's widow,' I wept. 'It wasn't my fault. I tried to save Him. I shot the two hoods who gunned Him down. Have mercy on me, miserable sinner that I am.'

'Turn it in, chief.'

'Sssh please, Barry, I'm praying.'

'She won't be listening, chief. People don't pray to Her, because they don't know She exists. So She doesn't listen to praying. Got me?'

'Gotcha,' I said. 'So it's bury the body, grow the beard and Allah Akbah till the sacred cows come home.'

'Comparative religion not really your strong point, eh, chief?'

A rain of frogs came down upon my head.

'I think we'd better discuss this back at my office,' I said. 'My trenchcoat can't take this sort of punishment.'

Now the last thing I needed at a time like this was another client showing up. So when I walked into my office to find a broad sitting behind my desk, you could have knocked me down with an auctioneer's gavel and bathed my butt in borax.

I've seen some ugly fat dames in my time, but this one took the dog biscuit. She made Mo Mowlam look like Madonna. I didn't figure this dame looked good for anything but using as a roadblock in Belfast. But always being the gent that I am, I gave her the big hello.

'Hi, babe,' I said, as suave as Sinatra. 'Did the circus leave town without you?'

She shot me a glance like she was chewing on a stewed chihuahua and moved more chins than Chairman Mao on his glorious march to the south.

132

'Did you just shake your head?' I said. 'Or was that a Zeppelin docking?'

'Sit down, Mr Woodworm,' she replied, and she didn't smile when she said it.

'The name's Wood*bine*,' I said. 'Lazlo Woodbine.' And added, 'Some call me Laz.'

'Well, I shall call you cadaver, boy, if you don't sit down when you're told.'

This dame had more front than Frinton. But I wasn't in the mood to take a donkey ride.

'Listen, lady,' I told her. 'I've had a rough evening. I've just left three dead men in an alleyway, and the world won't weep for a fat lass. So kindly shift your wide load off my chair and your whole damn trailer-park out of my office.' And I made the kind of shooing motions that you do to a dachshund that's doodling on your dahlias.

Which, as it turned out for me, wasn't the smartest of moves.

The dame lifted a mitt the size of a silicone implant* and zapped me with a lightning bolt that singed my decorum and set my fedora ablaze.

I went up like Crystal Palace and down like a funk soul brother.

'Oooh! Aaagh! Eeek!' I went. 'Oooh! Aaagh! Eeek!' and 'Waaaaah!'

I didn't cotton on at first to just what was happening to me. I figured it was a case of spontaneous human combustion. I get that every once in a while, if I've eaten too much coleslaw. But usually this just makes my socks smoulder. Which is no great shakes.

But what was happening to me now had nothing to do

* A *really* big one!

with coleslaw. This was the full B. K. Flamer.*

I beat at myself like a borderline self-mutilator and hopped and howled like a hedonist.

And then the dame moved her mitt again and my water cooler sort of lifted itself off its stand, swung across the room and emptied its contents all over my head.

Which had a more than sobering effect.

I did a couple more 'Aaah!'s and 'Eeek!'s and then I got down to a bit of serious grovelling. 'Please forgive me, God's widow,' I wept. 'It wasn't my fault. I tried to save Him, I shot the two hoods who gunned Him down. Have mercy on me . . .'

'Shut it!' said Eartha, widow of God, because that's who *She* was.

'Shut it!' She said.

And I shut it.

Eartha raised her bulk from my office chair and leaned across my desk. She glared me glances that jangled my nerves and set my knees a-knocking. 'Mr Woodworm,' She said (I didn't correct Her). 'Mr Woodworm. Am I right in assuming that my husband is dead?'

'Well, ma'am,' I went. 'You see, I, well, in as much as, which is to say . . .'

'*Yes* or *no*, Mr Wormwood?'

'It's yes, ma'am, I'm afraid.'

'*Be* afraid,' said Eartha. 'Be *very* afraid.'

'I am, ma'am,' said I. And believe me, my friends. I was.

'Dead.' She dropped back into my chair to the sounds of splitting floorboards.

* A quarter-pounder of prime char-grilled steakburger, done to perfection and served with a crispy salad topping and a choice of dressings, in a golden toasted sesame seed bun. I've tried others, but these are the best. Yes siree, by golly.

'I'm truly sorry, ma'am,' said I.

'Shut up, you fool, I'm thinking.'

I shut up and I kept my head well down. Outside my office window, the hurricane was gaining further strength. I glimpsed a chewed chihuahua and a pair of Ford Fiestas blowing by.

'Cease that infernal racket.' Eartha raised Her mighty mitt and the storm died all away. 'Get up, Mr Wormwood,' She said. And I got up. 'All right,' She said. 'Now I understand that you were not to blame. Something like this was bound to happen sooner or later. The old fool was asking for trouble. But what I want to know is this: who murdered Him and why?'

'Two guys,' said I. 'I shot them dead. Two slugs, two corpses. That's the way that I do business.'

'And I like the way that you do business. But there were two gunmen. Were they professional assassins, and if so, who ordered the hit?'

I was warming to this dame. She obviously had the hots for me in a big way. 'Ma'am,' I said. 'I shot them dead. And as dead men tell no tales, that ain't my province. Why don't you have a word with their souls? I'm sure you could persuade them to spill all the beans.'

'Because that is not how it works any more. And if you don't put a bit more respect into your voice, I'll burn off your bollocks, got me?'

'Got you, ma'am,' I said.

'Now look at this.' The dame spread out a paper on my desk. It was a pretty big paper. More a broadsheet really, or a double tabloid, which is very much the same as a broadsheet, or possibly just a bit smaller.

'What do you have there, ma'am?' I asked, with a great deal of respect in my voice.

'God's last will and testament.'

'Whoa!' said I. 'And might I take a look?'

'You may.'

I examined the last will and testament of God. Now, I didn't know just what to expect. Well, you wouldn't really, would you? I mean, I might have expected a lot of legal fol-de-rol and perhaps some archangels getting the odd knick-knacks and possibly even me being given all the lands to the south in honour of my services to crime detection. But this was short and sweet. Well, at least it was *short*.

> *To my son Colin, I bequeath my*
> *beloved planet Earth. To my dear wife,*
> *Eartha, the rest of the Universe.*
>   *Signed GOD*

'And that's it?' said I. 'It's, well, it's brief.'

'Very brief,' said Eartha.

'But surely, if I recall my scripture,' I said, 'it clearly states that the meek are supposed to inherit the Earth.'

Eartha made the kind of face that Joseph Merrick made a living out of. 'It's *my* Earth!' She shouted, rattling my ceiling fan and damn near having the remnants of my hat off. 'He gave it to *me* as a birthday present.'

'Ma'am,' said I, as I straightened my flambeaued fedora. 'Ma'am, please, surely now God is dead, you are in complete control of everything. I mean, you just sorted out the weather with a wave of your lily-white hand. You can do whatever you want, can't you? I mean, you could just zap the will and forget all about it?'

'No, Mr Wormwood, I can *not* do that. There are protocols to be observed. Even God had to abide by certain rules. Now I want you to investigate this, Mr Wormwood. I want you to find out who put the hit on my husband and what this will is all about.'

'Ma'am,' I said. 'With all due respect. I do know my business and in cases such as these, it's usually the person who has the most to gain from the death of the subject who's the guilty party. I don't wish to cause any offence here. But I reckon your son Colin is in the frame for this one.'

'If that *is* the case,' She said, 'then so be it and I will deal with Colin myself. But I want proof, Mr Wormwood. Absolute proof. I want to know the truth about what happened to my husband and why. And you are going to find that truth for me, aren't you, Mr Wormwood?'

'Ma'am,' I said, 'you can rely on me.'

'Yes, I know that I can. Because if you fail to deliver, within one week from today, I shall visit upon you such torment that even the devil himself will turn his face away from the horror. Do I make myself absolutely clear?'

'Absolutely, ma'am,' said I. And boy, did I need the toilet.

She didn't leave in a puff of smoke, or anything fancy like that. She just kind of got off my chair and dragged Her big butt out of my door. No thank yous, no fond farewells and no sweet goodbye kisses.

Off She went and that was that and I was left alone.

Alone!

'Er, Barry,' I called. 'Barry, my dear little pea green buddy. Where are you, Barry, my friend?'

In my head was silence. Stillness. Hush.

'Barry,' I called. 'Where are you, Barry?'

In my head was quietude. Tranquillity. Dead calm.

'Barry, dear Barry. Where are you?'

137

'Sorry, chief. I was having a nap. Have I missed anything?'

'Barry! You little . . .' I pummelled at my skull. 'You traitorous cur, you lowdown dirty . . .'

'Leave it out, chief. Stop. Oh ouch! Oh ow!'

'You could have warned me, you lowdown double-dealing . . .'

'Chief, what could I do? I—'

'You let me walk in here and insult God's widow and now I'm in deeper doo than a coprophile in a cow manure Jacuzzi.'

'You've got seven days, chief.'

'Seven days? She *knew*, Barry. She *knew* that God was dead. She turns up in my office less than half an hour after He gets it. And She's even got His will with Her. The will that clearly implicates Her son.'

'Seems like an open and shut case, chief. One that even you could solve.'

'Barry, you little green golly. She *knew*. Do you hear what I'm saying?'

'I think you're saying She knew, chief.'

'That *is* what I'm saying. She was here and She knew and She wasn't even concerned. God is dead and She doesn't give a damn. And why, Barry, why?'

'Well, chief . . .'

'There's no other explanation. I didn't get to be the best in the business by missing the most obvious clues. She was here. She knew. She had the will with Her. The will implicates Her son. *She* did it. Case closed.'

'Well, not exactly, chief.'

'Not exactly, Barry? How much more exactly would you care for?'

'Well, chief, exactly *how* She knew might help.'

'She knew, because *She* ordered the hit.'

'Er, no, chief. She knew because *I* told Her.'

There was silence once again. But it wasn't just in my head this time.

'You told Her?' I fairly roared. I did. I kid you not. '*You* told Her? *You told* Her?'

'Calm yourself down, chief. I had to. I was only doing it to save you from Her terrible wrath, if She'd found out some other way. You'd have never got away with dressing up as a Muslim. I had to come clean with Her. Explain that it wasn't your fault and that you'd find out who'd done it.'

'But *She* did it.'

'No, chief, I've just explained that. She didn't do it.'

'Then it was Colin.'

'Well, chief, I do agree that he looks a likely candidate. And he is a real bad lot. But whether he'd really have the guts to top his own father, I don't know about that.'

I dropped into my chair, dragged open my desk drawer and brought out the Old Bedwetter. At times like these, when the going gets rough, I find that a slug of—

'Don't start that again, chief. And advertising B. K. Flamers. How low will you stoop in the cause of an easy buck?'

'Barry, do you realize the trouble I'm in here?'

'Of course I do, chief. We're in this together, aren't we?'

'Yeah, right!' I took a hefty slug.

'If you go down, I go down, chief. I only get one shot at this Holy Guardian game and if I foul up, I'm on the celestial compost heap. I *do* have your best interests at heart. And I do want you to solve this case. Think of it, chief. This is the Big One. Woodbine brings the murderer of God to justice. How could there ever be a bigger case than that?'

I nodded thoughtfully. And I did it with style. I mean sure, my hat was in sodden tatters and my trenchcoat gone to ruination. My socks were smouldering and I had third degree burns over 60 per cent of my body. I was up to my neck in the deep brown stuff and had just seven days to solve the crime of the eternity, knowing that if I didn't, I would become toast in a million ways more than one. But like I say, I nodded thoughtfully.

And I did it with style.

Now there are some times when you have to sit and think. Mull things over. Cogitate. Employ your mind. Cerebrate. Conceptualize. Contemplate. Commune with your inner self.

And I guess that's all OK if you're one of those tormented-soul detectives with a drink problem and a broken marriage, who's had some big trauma in his childhood and is searching after his feminine side, or however that load of old toot always goes.

But hey, this is Woodbine.

The man. *The* detective.

The guy who makes his own wind and doesn't shoot the breeze.

'OK, Barry,' I said. 'We're gonna make a move.'

'Are you going to change your clothes, chief? You look a right palooka in that charred hat and mash-up trenchcoat.'

'I'll wear my old tweed jacket,' I said. 'It's always good for a bit of disguise.'

'And just why would you want a bit of disguise?'

'Because we're going under cover, Barry. We are going to return to the crime scene in search of clues. I shall adopt one of my many alternative personas and probe this case with a penetrating eye. You just stick with me, little guy, and you'll see why I'm the best.'

'Perhaps I'll grow to like the compost heap.'

'What did you say, Barry?'

'Nothing, chief.'

The alleyway was rather crowded now. There were policemen coming and going and wandering around and stepping on evidence and getting in each other's way and generally carrying on in the manner that all policemen do. They'd set up some lights and stretched a lot of that yellow tape about. And they'd parked their police cars up real close and left the beacons flashing on the tops to give that extra bit of atmosphere.

I shouldered my way tweedily into the blue serge throng. 'Make way,' I said. 'Member of the press.'

A guy turned to face me. And I knew this guy. It was none other than Police Chief Sam Maggot of the L.A.P.D. He and I had run up against each other on more than one occasion and he and I did not see eye to eye.

Possibly due to the difference in height, as he is something of a shorty.

Police Chief Sam Maggot had not been having a good day. He rarely, if ever, had a good day. It was not in his remit to have good days. Police chiefs always have bad days. Every day is another bad day, that's the way they do business.

'Who are you?' asked Police Chief Sam.

'Molloy,' said I. 'Scoop Molloy of the *Brentford Mercury*.'

Police Chief Sam looked me up and up. 'Molloy?' said he. 'Molloy?'

'That's me,' said I. 'What happened here?'

'It's not you,' said Sam. 'It's Woodpecker. Lazlo Woodpecker, private eye.'

'The name's . . .' Well, he nearly had me there. 'The name's Molloy,' I said. 'Scoop Molloy. Some call me Scoop.'

141

'Well, I'll be,' said Sam. 'But you do bear an uncanny resemblance to Woodpecker. Although he wears the snap-brimmed fedora and the trenchcoat and you're wearing—'

'An old tweed jacket,' I said. 'So I must be a news reporter, mustn't I?'

'Well I guess you must. And naturally, as the police always want to help out members of the press, I'll be glad to tell you anything you want to know.'

'That's fine. So what happened here?'

'Murder,' said Sam. 'Murder most foul. Two Greek businessmen. A Mr Georgious Bubble and a Mr Mikanos Squeak. Gunned down in cold blood.'

'And the other guy?'

'*What* other guy?'

'I thought there were three bodies.'

'No,' said Sam. 'Just the two. Just two innocent men viciously murdered. Brutally slain. Cruelly done to death by some pathetic psychopathic scumbag. Some piece of human filth. Some vile loathsome degraded specimen of sub-humanity. Some—'

'Just the *two* bodies?' I said. 'Just the *two*?'

'Are you thinking what I'm thinking, chief?'

'Not now, Barry.'

'What did you say?' said Sam.

'Nothing,' said I. 'But you're absolutely sure that there's only two bodies?'

'Absolutely sure. And I'll tell you more. The murderer barged open that rear door to the Crimson Teacup, then ducked back into shelter. Then he leapt from cover and shot both men dead. Two clean shots. The work of a professional.'

'You're right there,' said I.

'Forty-four calibre ammunition,' said Sam. 'I would say

142

from a trusty Smith and West Indian steel band.'

'Hm,' said I.

'The killer then walked along the alleyway and kicked the corpses. One mean son of a bitch, eh? One heartless evil murdering slimebag. One—'

'I suppose you can tell me next what he was wearing?' I said.

'Absolutely,' said Sam. 'He was wearing a trenchcoat and a fedora. And he was talking to himself. They do that, you know. The real loons. Voices in the head. God tells them to do it. That kind of caper.'

'I'm impressed,' said I. And I was. 'And you worked all this out from scene of crime evidence?'

'No,' said Sam. 'From that.' And he pointed.

I turned my head and I looked in the direction of his pointing. High on the wall above the rear door of the Crimson Teacup was mounted one of those sneaky closed-circuit TV cameras. The type you see, if you look real hard, overlooking nearly every street in the big city nowadays. The type that are linked up to VCRs and record everything they see.

Everything.

'Ah,' I said. 'That was handy.'

I smiled back at Sam.

But Sam wasn't smiling.

Sam held a gun in his hand and that gun was pointing at me.

'You're under arrest, Woodpecker,' said he. 'Loons like you always return to the scene of the crime. They like to have a gloat, don't they? Get off on what they've done.'

'Now just you see here.' I reached for my piece.

'Don't touch that gun,' said Sam. 'That's the murder weapon or my name isn't Sam Maggot and yours ain't Lazlo Woodpecker, private eye.'

'The name's Wood*bine*.' I *had* to say it. 'Lazlo Woodbine', and 'Some call me Laz.'

'Raise your hands and turn around,' said Sam.

'Now listen, please. You're making a big mistake.'

'Just raise your hands and turn around.'

'Aw come on now, Sam.'

'Don't Sam me, you psycho. Raise your hands and turn around.'

'OK. But you're really making a . . .' I raised my hands and turned around '. . . big . . .'

And then he hit me hard on the back of the head.

'. . . mistake. Aaaaaaaaaaaaaaaagh!' I went.

'I'll join you in that one,' said Barry.

And I was falling once more into that deep dark whirling pit of oblivion that all great genre detectives fall into.

But not at this point in the case.

11

When the hurricane hit, Icarus was in a long dark automobile, sitting next to a creature of Hell and being driven to an unknown destination.

'Where are you taking us?' Icarus asked, when he could find his voice to do so.

The creature that was Cormerant flickered its quills and moved its terrible mouthparts. 'To the Ministry,' it said. 'Where you will be interviewed.'

'I have nothing to say.'

'But you will. You will tell us everything we need to know.'

The car took a sudden lurch to the left.

'Drive carefully, damn you!' shouted Cormerant.

'I'm trying.' The chauffeur glanced back across his shoulder. 'The weather's gone mad. A storm's come out of nowhere.'

'Always the weather,' said Cormerant. 'Gets blamed for everything, the weather does. Have you ever thought about that, young man? The way the weather affects everything that people do? The wrong kind of leaves blown onto the track and the trains can't run. The trains can't run, so some man is late for an important meeting. The meeting is cancelled, a business goes bust. Its shares are wiped out on the stock exchange. A shareholder loses everything, goes mad, hangs himself. Leaving a wife who might have given birth to a child who would have one day become the President of the United States and saved the world from terrible war that would wipe out half of mankind. All because of some leaves blown onto the track by weather. Is it fate, or is there a purpose behind it? What do you think, young man?'

'I have no idea what you're talking about.' Icarus hunched himself up and glanced towards the handle of the door.

'Central locking,' said the creature that was Cormerant. 'A new innovation. All the doors and windows are locked. You have nowhere to run.'

Without, the storm raged madly on. Within the car, Icarus Smith sat trembling.

The Ministry of Serendipity is situated beneath Mornington Crescent underground station. Much legend is attached to the station, which for many years was closed to the public and which now does not remain open later than nine thirty at night. The belief amongst conspiracy theorists is that the Ministry of Serendipity is the English Area 51. That a vast tunnel network and massive underground complex exists beneath Mornington Crescent station. And that dirty deeds, involving alien spacecraft and back-engineering and indeed those little grey blighters with the Ray-Ban eyeballs, are done there, whilst Londoners walk blissfully unknowing on the pavements far above.

Icarus knew of such theories, but had paid them scant attention, according them the disbelief he'd always considered they deserved. Such nonsense had always been, in his

146

opinion, more the province of his barking mad brother.

The storm-ravaged automobile turned left at the Station Hotel, crossed the road, and somehow entered the station opposite. Exactly how this happened, Icarus never understood. For at one moment the car was above ground in the wind and the rain and the next it had entered a tunnel and was purring along down a tube of darkness bound for no place pleasant.

The journey time was short, but as to the distance covered, Icarus could only wonder. But he was presently in no mood to wonder. His thoughts centred on a single goal, this being one of escape.

The automobile cruised out of the tunnel and into a great cathedral of a place. It was clearly the work of Victorian artisans, having all those wondrous soaring cast-iron roof-ribs, rising from those marvellous fluted columns, with the rivets and the rusty bits, where pigeons love to roost.

Icarus and Johnny Boy were encouraged to leave the car by the gun-toting chauffeur, who explained to them that hesitation would be rewarded by death. And Icarus found some relief in this, as his nearness to the creature that was Cormerant had troubled him no little bit.

Johnny Boy looked out and up and all around. 'From down here where I am,' he observed, 'this is one bloody big building.'

'And one very deep in the ground,' said Cormerant, climbing from the car. 'Welcome to the Ministry of Serendipity. Take care with all those papers, young man. We wouldn't want any to get lost on the way, now would we?'

Icarus felt that indeed, yes he would. And had been hoping at least to toss the lot out of the window while the car was in motion. As far as he was aware, there were only two men living on the planet who had taken the Red Head drug and knew the

147

truth about what was really going on in the world. And those two men were himself and Johnny Boy and it looked to be a terrifying likelihood that the secret would shortly die with them. 'Go on,' said the chauffeur, 'move.'

Icarus and Johnny Boy were steered across a massive concourse. There were wooden crates and boxes, many bearing enigmatic symbols and letterings, stacked in mighty bulwarks. And thousands and thousands of barber's chairs, all wrapped up in plastic. And on and on, beneath these and between, the two men plodded. Urged at the point of a gun and followed by the loathsome being that was Cormerant.

Icarus did take time to wonder over Cormerant. When first he had encountered him, in his guise as a man in the shop of Stravino, he had seemed a meagre creeping nervous body. Just some put-upon clerk in a city-gent's rig-out, that few would have noticed at all.

And Icarus wondered whether this was what the chauffeur was seeing even now. Whether the chauffeur could hear the cold cruel edge to the creature's voice, or see the arrogant, bombastic manner of its movements.

Evidently not, thought Icarus.

Although, possibly so.

Which didn't really help much at all. So Icarus thought on hard regarding the matter of his escape.

'Down there,' urged the chauffeur. 'Through that door.'

Through that door led them into a hallway. It was a long carpeted hallway. High-ceilinged, papered in richly patterned silk, ornamented with red circles and beryl coronets. Marble busts stared blindly from niches in the walls. Icarus counted six of Napoleon, three of Wellington, one of Churchill and none at all of Noel Edmonds. Icarus didn't count these busts for fun. He was passing many doors and Icarus counted these also. He wanted to remember exactly where the way out was, when he chose to make a run for it.

At length he was brought to a halt before door twenty-three. Just beside the empty niche that awaited Noel Edmonds.

Cormerant knocked and a voice called, 'Enter.'

Cormerant turned the handle and opened the door. 'In,' said he to Icarus.

As Icarus harboured no preconceptions as to what might lie beyond the opening door, he was neither surprised nor disappointed by the sight that met his troubled gaze. But neither was he impressed.

Baffled, yes.

But not impressed.

Beyond the doorway lay a barber's shop.

It was a regular ordinary down to earth, spit and proper barber's shop. It might well have been that of Stravino, but it wasn't. For this one was way deep down in the ground and this one had smarter barber's chairs.

But all the rest was very much the same. The same fag-pocked linoleum on the floor. The same yellow nicotine up on the ceiling. Same pitted mirror with its souvenirs and whatnots. A row of faded cinema seats and even a brown envelope.

Of the smarter barber's chairs, there were three. Stravino had only two in his shop. The second one, he'd told Icarus, was for the son who would one day succeed him. But that particular chair remained for ever empty, as Stravino had fifteen daughters, but no son.

But that is by the by, for we are here. In this subterranean barber's shop, which has *three* chairs. And leaning against the furthest and smoking a cigarette, there stood . . . a barber.

This barber, like Stravino, was obviously a Greek. He had the complicated cookery thing that they always wear above the left eyebrow and the shaded area on the right cheek that looks a bit like a map of Indo-China. And he stood and he grinned and he dished out a welcome.

'Welcome,' he said, 'and come in.'

Johnny Boy edged nervously forward. 'I don't want a haircut,' he muttered to Icarus. 'I do my own. I have a four-in-one home hairdressing set.'

'Shut it, squirt,' said Cormerant.

'Come sit here,' said the barber.

Johnny Boy shook his tiny head.

'No, not you, dolly man. The big boy. The one with all the presents. Someone take his presents, please. And has someone had a look-see in his pockets?'

Cormerant shook his hideous head.

'You no search this boy at all?' The barber raised his unencumbered right eyebrow. 'You no check to see whether he carry big bomb that blow our bottom parts off?'

Cormerant shook his hideous head a second time.

'Then perhaps you'd better do it now, damned clerk with runny nose.'

The chauffeur wrenched the papers and the boxes and the spectremeter from the grip of Icarus. Cormerant reached forward to go through his pockets. Icarus bit hard upon his bottom lip as the creature's terrible scaly hands probed about his person.

'My wallet,' said Cormerant. 'And where is my watch fob and where is my briefcase?'

'All in the time that's good,' said the barber. 'The boy will tell it all to us.'

Icarus eyed the barber. Here indeed lay a mystery. He was not a wrong'un. Not some demon. He was a man, as Icarus. And he was not a bad man. Icarus could see the man within the

150

man and what Icarus could see was loyalty. This man was honest and loyal. He believed in what he was doing. He thought that what he was doing was right. Icarus shuddered. That was how it worked, of course. That was how it all worked. People mostly did believe that what they did was for the best. For the good of others. This man worked here. In this evil Ministry, run by demons in the guise of men. And he believed he was doing the right thing. For queen and country, perhaps? For national security?

'You come sit down here my boy,' said the barber, indicating the middle chair. 'You look like you need a haircut. What shall it be, do you think? Perhaps a Tony Curtis?'

'No thanks,' said Icarus.

'But you sit here all the same.'

Icarus saw the flicker of colour darting round the barber's head. Dark blue for determination. Not a man to be argued with.

Icarus made his way to the chair and sat down hard upon it. The barber flourished a Velocette and swung it over the lad's shoulders.

'We don't have time for this pantomime.' The cold cruel tone of Cormerant's voice jarred in the relocator's ears. 'Call her out, make her get on with it.'

Her? Icarus glanced into the mirror. The barber's expression was grave. The colour of his thoughts was yellow. Fear, that colour was.

'She come soon,' said the barber. 'She out clubbing it up, you know what young ladies are. I just give this boy a Tony Curtis, make him look a regular back street prince.'

'No need for that.' Icarus turned his head at the voice. A woman had entered the barber's shop. She was a most attractive woman. Five feet two and eyes of blue, in a black leather

151

dress and a high-heeled shoe. Golden hair, wide-lipped smile, she moved with elegance and style. Beyond the beauty and the grace, Icarus could see a brooding menace.

'Miss O'Connor,' said the barber.

'Introduce me properly,' said Miss O'Connor.

'Boy in chair, this is Miss Philomena Christina Maria O'Connor. She is an exo-cranial masseuse. She massage your head all nice. Make you feel all dreamy dreamy. Very good for the scalp. Make follicles spring up like little lambs eat ivy.'

'No thank you,' said Icarus.

'Yes thank you,' said Philomena.

'It not hurt a bit,' said the barber. 'You feel grand, I promise.'

Icarus could see the lie and Icarus wanted out. He gripped the arms of the barber's chair, prepared to spring and make a fight of it.

Click and click went the arms of the chair and two steel bands curled to fasten his wrists. Icarus wrenched and twisted, but the steel bands held him captive.

'Just relax,' said Philomena, approaching the chair. 'It really won't hurt *much*. It's just a little massage.'

Icarus fought to keep his head down, but her hands were suddenly in amongst his hair. 'My mother taught me this,' said Philomena. 'Back in the old country. She was a hairdresser, but she'd studied phrenology. She could tell people's fortunes by feeling the shape of their heads. She became very good at it; she had the gift, you see. And she could see a potential in it that few people ever sought to realize. That by applying subtle pressure to precise areas on the skull, you can actually cause changes to occur within the human brain. It's a bit like acupuncture, or acupressure. Once you know exactly where to press and how hard and for how long, you can achieve the most remarkable effects. Here, for instance.'

Philomena pressed a finger down upon the crown of the captive's head. Icarus gasped as a sensation of absolute joy overwhelmed him. A feeling of pure happiness.

'Nice, isn't it?' said Philomena. 'My mother used to get really big tips from her clients when she pressed their heads like that. And yet . . .' Icarus felt a pressure over his right temple.

'Aaaaaagh!' Knives of pain tore through his body. Knives of burning pain.

'That one really hurts, now doesn't it?'

Icarus groaned and tears ran down his cheeks.

'You do have to be very precise, though,' said Philomena, stroking the head of Icarus Smith. 'Just a little bit off and the effects can be devastating. Blindness, paralysis, permanent incontinence, or a total vegetative state. It takes a lot of practice to get it just right. I have a lot of ex-boyfriends who can't do much nowadays but dribble. Shame, but there you go.'

Icarus was shaking now. His eyes rolled and his lips were turning blue.

'So let's see,' said Philomena. 'Let's just see what you have to tell us.'

Icarus awoke in a sweat from a terrible terrible dream. He clutched at his head and blinked his eyes and let out an awful scream.

'Calm down, please, calm down.'

The eyes of Icarus focused on the face of Johnny Boy.

'Can you move?' asked the midget. 'Are all your body parts still working?'

Icarus twitched; his hands were numb. He tried to rise, but his legs offered little support.

'What happened?' he managed to ask. 'Where are we?'

'That evil bitch played havoc with your brain. You told her

153

everything. Where you'd hidden the briefcase. How you mailed the key to yourself. Your address.'

'Oh God, no.'

'I'm sorry,' said Johnny Boy. 'There was nothing I could do to stop her. They flushed all the tablets down the sink and burned the professor's notes. They'd have smashed up the spectremeter too, if you hadn't told them what it did.'

'I don't remember anything.' Icarus rubbed at his knees.

'No, she said that you wouldn't. They made me drag you here and they locked us in. You've been unconscious for hours.'

'Oh God, I'm shaking all over. I think I'm going to be sick.'

'Please don't,' said Johnny Boy. 'This is only a very small cell.'

'A cell.' Icarus looked up and around and about.

'Death cell, I should think,' said Johnny Boy. 'I'm really sorry, Icarus. It's all my fault that you got into this.'

'Don't blame yourself. We're in it now and we have to get out of it and quick.'

Johnny Boy sighed a little sigh. 'We've lost,' said he. 'They've destroyed the tablets and the formula. They win, we lose.'

'Oh no we don't,' said Icarus and he opened his right hand. On his palm lay a dozen tablets, all very sweaty and rather crunched up, but a dozen tablets, none the less. 'I relocated these while we were in the car. We can get some chemist to analyse them. We're not done for yet.'

'Smart lad,' said Johnny Boy. 'But how do we get out of here?'

'Getting out of this cell is no problem,' said Icarus. 'It's what we do when we're out that worries me.'

★

154

Johnny Boy had not counted doors, or busts in little niches. And when Icarus (using certain instruments which he kept in the heels of his shoes) had opened the cell door and glanced up and down a strange corridor, and asked Johnny Boy which way it was to the barber's shop, the small man could only shrug his shoulders and say it was perhaps this way or perhaps the other.

'Best leave it to fate, then,' said Icarus. 'Follow me.'

This corridor had a stone-flagged floor and walls of echoing stone. This was your standard prison corridor, the one along which the cries of tortured souls are wont to echo.

'Your heels really click, don't they?' said Icarus.

'Tap-shoes,' said Johnny Boy. 'I used to do a bit of the old Fred and Ginger.'

'Perhaps you'd like to take them off, or walk on tiptoe or something.'

Johnny Boy stopped and took off his shoes and tucked them into his trouser pockets.

'What happened to your socks?' asked Icarus. 'They look all singed.'

'I suffer from spontaneous human combustion. If I eat too much coleslaw.'

'Well I'll be damned,' said Icarus. 'My mad brother says that he suffers from that. But I never believed him. I thought he was making it up.'

'It's a common complaint,' said Johnny Boy. 'I'd like to meet your brother.'

'No, you wouldn't. He's a nutter. Lives in a world of fantasy.'

'Unlike us,' said Johnny Boy.

'Exactly,' said Icarus Smith. 'But he's one of the reasons that we have to get out of here fast. Cormerant has my address; he'll go there to get the luggage locker key. I don't want any harm to come to my family.'

155

'Shame,' said a voice.

'Oh dear,' said Johnny Boy.

'Just put your hands up,' said the voice. It was the voice of the chauffeur.

Icarus raised his hands and turned around. Johnny Boy did likewise.

'You're very nifty with locks, aren't you?' said the chauffeur. 'I just missed you. Happily I heard your little mate's heels clicking down the corridor.'

'Sorry,' said Johnny Boy.

'Never mind,' said Icarus.

'Yeah well, never mind,' said the chauffeur. 'I wasn't coming to bring you your breakfast, or anything. I was coming to put a bullet through each of your heads. And I can do it as easily here as back in the cell.' The chauffeur raised his gun and pointed it at the head of Icarus Smith.

'No,' said Icarus, 'don't. You don't understand what's going on here. You don't understand who you're working for. *What* you're working for. Cormerant isn't a human, he's a—'

'Forget it,' said the chauffeur. 'You're dead, the two of you.' And he cocked his pistol and squeezed the trigger.

'No, please . . .' Icarus covered his face. 'No, please don't . . .'

But.

There was a flash and a bang.

Icarus gasped and clutched at his head.

And then he heard the screaming.

His eyes, which had been tightly closed, flashed open.

To see before him a terrifying sight.

The chauffeur was squirming, his arms flailing and his head twisting backwards on his neck. From his chest projected a golden crescent. His feet were some twelve inches from the flagstoned floor and kicking violently. The chauffeur contorted

156

in a paroxysm of pain and then went limp and sagged like a broken doll.

The golden crescent swished away. The chauffeur fell to the floor and lay there dead.

And then Icarus saw him. The man who now stood over the chauffeur's body. The man who had driven the blade through his body and lifted him off his feet. The man just stood there, calmly sheathing his golden blade. He was a man, but he was more than a man. A golden aura glowed about him. Bright white light was haloed all around his head.

Icarus stared at the glowing man, then down at the lifeless carcass of the chauffeur and then Icarus did what any reasonable man would do.

He was violently sick.

'How are you feeling now?' asked the saviour of Icarus Smith when the lad had recovered what senses he had.

'Not good,' said Icarus, 'but you. I know you, don't I?'

'You saw me today and I saw you. We were both after the same thing. The briefcase. I've been following you ever since. I hid in the boot of the long dark automobile.'

'In the barber's shop,' said Icarus. 'I saw you in Stravino's barber's shop.'

'Captain Ian Drayton, at your service.' The captain saluted.

'But you're . . .'

'Don't say the word,' said Captain Ian.

'Angel,' said Johnny Boy. 'He's an angel. Only the third one I've ever seen.'

'So both of you know. You've both taken the professor's drug.'

'You know all about that, do you?' said Johnny Boy.

'We've had this place under surveillance for a very long time. We know most of what goes on in here.'

'The professor's dead,' said Johnny Boy. 'They killed him.'

'I feared as much.'

'Hold on,' said Icarus. 'I want to know what is going on here.'

'There's no time now,' said Captain Ian. 'But I'll tell you everything you need to know. There is someone else I have to rescue first. I was hoping that you might assist me in this.'

'I think we owe you one,' said Icarus. 'Who needs rescuing?'

'A detective,' said Captain Ian. 'A very famous detective.'

'Sherlock Holmes?' said Johnny Boy.

'Lazlo Woodbine,' said Captain Ian.

'Lazlo Woodbine?' Johnny Boy scratched at his little dolly head. 'Lazlo Woodbine is *here*?'

'He was brought in unconscious this evening. They're holding him in the medical facility. There's a *doctor* interviewing him now.'

'I don't like the way you said *doctor*,' said Johnny Boy.

'The doctor is, as you might say, a wrong'un.'

'Hold on,' said Icarus. 'This Woodbine character. How was he dressed? Was he wearing his now legendary trenchcoat and a fedora?'

'No, actually he was wearing an old tweed jacket.'

Icarus let out a plaintive sigh.

'That was one hell of a plaintive sigh,' said Johnny Boy. 'Why did you let that out?'

'Because of the old tweed jacket. That's the disguise he likes to wear. He believes that it fools people into believing he's a reporter for the *Brentford Mercury*.'

'I didn't know Lazlo Woodbine ever wore a disguise,' said Johnny Boy.

'He doesn't,' said Icarus. 'Because the man who is here is not

158

the real Lazlo Woodbine. The man who is here is my barking mad brother.'

'What?' went Johnny Boy.

'My brother,' said Icarus. 'The one with the smouldering socks. The one who I told you was a nutter. The one who lives in a world of fantasy. The one who believes that he's Lazlo Woodbine. That's not the real Lazlo Woodbine they've brought in here. That's my lunatic brother.'

12

Now, I'm an only child. They broke the mould before they made me. And being an only child means that you're a loner. You don't have any big brothers to get you out of sticky situations. You have to learn to deal with things yourself. To think on your feet, or even when you're off them.

And, like I've told you before, I work only the four locations. My office, the bar, the alleyway and the rooftop. No great detective ever needs more. So, when I awoke after falling into that deep dark whirling pit of oblivion, to find myself in a fifth and unscheduled location, I had to think on my feet, or in this case, off them.

Yes siree.

By golly.

'Open your eyes, Woodpecker.' I heard the voice of Sam Maggot, but I wasn't opening my eyes.

'Come on, you son of a bitch, we know you're awake.'

'OK,' I said. 'I'm awake already. But I'm not opening my eyes.'

'Oh please do,' said Sam in a voice like syrup. 'There's something I want you to see.'

'What's that?'

'A little piece of video footage.'

'Oh, fine,' I said. 'I'll watch that. Would you mind turning all the lights out, so I can see the screen clearly?'

'You're wacko, Woodpecker. But OK.'

Now Sam had a sidekick. Guys like Sam always have a sidekick. It's a tradition, or an old charter, or something. I've never had a sidekick myself, because, like I say, I'm a loner. Sam's sidekick switched the lights off and I opened my eyes. The room was in darkness, and hey, darkness is darkness, right? I could have been in any darkness. In the darkness of my office, or wherever.

'Just watch the screen,' said Sam and a television screen lit up, as the eyes of a beautiful babe will do when she sees me coming out of the shower.

'Alleyway behind the Crimson Teacup,' said the voice of Sam. 'Closed-circuit surveillance footage. This evening, eight thirty p.m.'

I cast a steely peeper at the footage. There was the alleyway, and there was me, busting the back door. And there were the two guys standing at the end of the alleyway talking. And there was me, ducking back, unholstering the trusty Smith and West End Girls and then leaping out and gunning the two of them down and . . .

'Hold it right there,' I shouted. 'Play that footage again.'

'Oh, you like it, do you, Woodpecker? Want to see yourself committing the murders again and again? Perhaps you'd like me to make you a copy, so you can watch it in the death cell. You murdering piece of—'

'There's something wrong there,' I rightly protested.

161

'Something wrong with that footage. That's not the way it happened.'

'OK, I'll run it again.'

Sam ran the footage again and once again I burst out of the door and once again I gunned down two innocent talkers.

'No,' I said. 'There's a fix in here. This footage has been tampered with.'

'No, Woodpecker. There's no fix. We've got you on video, committing the murders and talking to yourself. You're a wacko, Woodpecker. You're barking mad. It was only a matter of time before you did something like this. Playing the detective and gunning down innocent victims. You're gonna fry in the chair for this one, Woodpecker. You're gonna take that long last walk.'

Captain Ian marched along the corridor. Icarus plodded behind. Johnny Boy ran at full pelt to keep up.

Icarus viewed the captain as he marched. The forceful motions of his shoulders. The confident stride. The sheer sense of purpose. This was certainly not the Captain Ian he had seen in Stravino's. That was a war-scarred veteran, who wore the look of one who had seen too many terrible things.

But now, with his new gift for true vision, Icarus could really see the captain. An angelic being, radiating light. And he'd had a sword, hadn't he? A golden sword, that had driven into the chauffeur's back and dragged him from his feet. But there was no evidence of a sword now. Which had Icarus perplexed.

Was there more that might be seen? More beyond the capabilities of the Red Head drug? More truth? A higher truth?

Icarus didn't have the time for such thinking now.

'He's in here,' said Captain Ian, pointing to a formidable door, all steel and rivet-pimpled.

'That's a very secure-looking door,' said Johnny Boy, catching up and catching his breath. 'And it doesn't seem to have a handle.'

'Or a keyhole, for that matter,' said Icarus.

'We must blow it open,' said the captain.

'This should be good,' said Johnny Boy. 'I like a big loud explosion.'

'I don't,' said Icarus. 'We're in some underground labyrinth here. The noise of an explosion will have those creatures coming running from miles.'

'No problem,' said the captain. 'I'll use a silent explosive.'

'A *silent* explosive?' Icarus made the face of grave doubt.

'Latest thing,' said the captain, drawing out a stick of something dangerous-looking from his pocket. 'The SAS use it all the time. It goes off without a sound. You've heard of gelignite and dynamite? Well, this stuff's called—'

'Don't tell me,' said Johnny Boy. 'Silent nite.'

'No,' said the captain.

Johnny Boy creased double laughing. 'It's a good 'un though, isn't it?' he said, between guffaws. 'Silent nite. Silent night? Get it? Silent night and angels, what a good 'un, eh?'

'It's not *that* funny,' said Icarus.

'No,' said Johnny Boy, straightening up. 'I suppose it's not that funny.'

'It's SHITE,' said the captain.

'Oh come on,' said Johnny Boy. 'It wasn't *that* bad.'

'No, the explosive is called SHITE. S.H.I.T.E. Silent High Intensity Transcalent Explosive. The SAS could probably have called it by a more polite name, but they're – well hard, those lads.'

'What does transcalent mean?' asked Johnny Boy.

163

'It means, permitting the passage of heat. The explosive instantly melts anything within the range of the explosion. So there's no noise, you see. Clever, isn't it?'

'Silent nite was cleverer,' said Johnny Boy.

'No it wasn't,' said Icarus.

'Was.'

'Wasn't.'

'You'd better stand back,' said the captain. 'I'm going to light the fuse.'

'Any chance of a light?' I said, pulling out a pack of Camels.

I don't know about you, but when I'm in a sticky situation that's testing my nerves and calling my mental health into question, I like to light up a Camel. I find that the mellow Virginia tobacco combined with the special filter, with its most distinctive pack and competitive price, gives me everything I need.

Except, perhaps, for a handgun.

'You can't smoke in here,' said Sam. 'This is a—'

'An office,' I said. 'It's an office. Could be any office. Could be my office.'

'I'm going to have my sidekick switch the light on,' said Sam. 'And then we'll see whose office it is.'

'No,' I said. 'Don't do that.'

But I could hear Sam's sidekick moving towards where I knew the door must be and I could almost feel his finger as it pushed down hard on the light switch.

'**!!!**'
••• went the silent explosive.

'My,' said Johnny Boy. 'What a very loud silence.'

Light rushed all about me. But not from some bulb on the

164

ceiling. Or a neon tube. Or several tastefully arranged table lamps of the sort you might buy from Habitat.* Or any number of Art Nouveau style wall lights with tinted Lalique shades. Or one of those ghastly standard lamps with the big fringed shades that your aunty always used to have standing in the sitting room behind the sofa with the antimacassars on it.

No, it wasn't from any of those. The light came suddenly rushing through the doorway from a corridor beyond. And then three men came bursting in. Or it might have been two men and a kiddie.

'It's three,' said Johnny Boy. 'Is this your nutty brother, Icarus?'

I shielded my eyes from the light. But it didn't illuminate the entire room. Just me really, sitting there in a chair. Which could have been anyone's chair. My office chair, for instance.

'That's him,' said Icarus. 'That's my brother.'

'Brother?' said I. 'Buddy, I ain't your brother. The name's Woodbine, Lazlo Woodbine, private eye. Some call me Laz, but none brother.'

'You're my brother,' said Icarus.

'No, kid, I ain't. I know you'd like me to be, love me to be, even. Who wouldn't? It must be every kid's dream to have Lazlo Woodbine as his big brother.'

'It's never been mine,' said the voice of Sam Maggot. 'But you guys better hold it there. And what the bejiggers did you do to my sidekick? Shit and salvation, he's melted all over the floor.'

There was a lot of movement then. And I can never be having with too much movement. I mean, take the suffragette movement for instance. What was *that* all about? A lot of sassy

* Forget it. I have no intention of endorsing Habitat!

165

dames with penis envy, running off at the mouth about equal rights for women. Equal rights? They wish. But hey, I'm only kidding about with you. I'm all for women having equal rights. 'You're equal,' I tell them when I'm on a bus, 'so move your butt and let me sit down, before I move it for you.'

But anyhow, this wasn't movement like that. Or even like the other. This was violent movement. A lot of violent movement. Sam had his pistol drawn, but the guy with the soldier's bearing – not the guy who wished I was his brother, or the tiny dude who looked like Barbie's* boyfriend – the guy with the soldier's bearing comes in swinging.

He knocked the gun out of Sam's hand and gave him an evil beating. Sam slumped down right over my lap. A broken man, with three teeth missing and his left ear half torn off. He looked up at me, and I could tell by the expression on his bloodied face that he was pleading with me to step in and save him further punishment.

My reputation as a great humanitarian can often put me in a situation such as this.

I eased Sam carefully down to the floor. Cradled his head in my hands and smiled him one of my winners.

And then I straightened up and put the boot in. Sending Sam into a deep dark whirling pit of oblivion, from which I trusted he would sometime awaken, an older but wiser man.

'Well,' said I, flicking specks of blood from my old tweed jacket. 'I guess I have to thank you guys for helping me out.

---

* Actually I heard this really good joke about Barbie the other day. So if it's OK I'll share it with you now, before the violence gets under way. This guy takes his daughter to a toyshop to buy a Barbie doll. And there's three of them in the window. There's sporting Barbie, at £9.99. Disco Barbie, at £9.99. And divorced Barbie, at £500. 'Why is divorced Barbie so expensive?' asks the guy. 'Because', says the shop assistant, 'divorced Barbie comes complete with Ken's house, Ken's car, Ken's furniture, Ken's etc.' Well, I thought it was funny.

Sam's sidekick cooked to a puddle and Sam in the land of nod. I'll be taking my leave now. I'll meet you in a bar somewhere.'

'Just a minute,' said the kid called Icarus. 'Mum said I was to give you a message, the next time I saw you.'

'Kid,' said I, 'I'm not your brother. How can I get this through your skull?'

'You certainly look like my brother,' said Icarus. 'In fact you look exactly like my brother. Identical to my brother in fact.'

'Kid, have you ever met Lazlo Woodbine?'

'Of course not,' said Icarus.

'And have you ever seen a photograph of Lazlo Woodbine?' Icarus shook his head.

'Because there are no photographs. No-one knows exactly what Woodbine looks like. All anyone knows for sure about Woodbine is that he wears a trenchcoat and a fedora, but no-one can put a face to the name. And do you know why that is? Don't speak, I'll tell you. It's one of the secrets of my success. My exciting exploits are always told in the first person, so the reader is Woodbine. And the reader projects his own image onto the blank canvas. The reader identifies with Woodbine. Sees himself as Woodbine.'

'You don't look like me,' said Icarus. 'You look like my brother.'

'I haven't finished, kid. If the reader doesn't identify himself with Woodbine, then he does the next best thing. Puts his hero's face on Woodbine's body. You obviously look up to your brother as a hero.'

'Someone hold me back,' said Icarus. 'Someone hold me back, or I'll punch his lights out.'

'Christmas dinner must be a lot of laughs at your house,' said Johnny Boy. 'I'm holding your leg, that's the best I can do.'

'Give it up, kid,' I said. 'I'm not your brother, though I'd be honoured, if I were you, to think I was. If you know what I mean and I'm sure that you do.'

'He's barking,' said Icarus. 'What did I tell you, Johnny Boy?'

'But he thinks he's telling the truth. Look at him, you have the gift, you can see his colours.'

And Icarus could. He could see the intricate webbings of colour that were thoughts and emotions swimming all over the man. And he could see the man inside the man. The man who was his brother?

'We don't have time for this,' said Icarus. 'We have to get out of here and fast.'

'Leave it to me, kid.' I straightened my shoulders with more sang-froid than a San Fernando sandwich salesman at a sanitary-wear symposium. 'I'll have us out of here in less than twenty minutes.' I stepped over the VCR and removed the surveillance tape. I slid this into my inside pocket and then stepped over to the desk. Here I retrieved my trusty Smith and Western Union and slotted this into my shoulder holster. Then I stepped over to the telephone and dialled out a digit or two.

And then I spoke words and received words in return and then I replaced the receiver. 'All done,' said I.

'What is done?' asked Icarus. 'How are you getting us out of here?'

'I dialled out for a pizza, kid.'

'At a time like this!'

'Easy, kid, easy. It's one of those pizza companies where, if they can't deliver the pizza in twenty minutes, you get it for free. And did you ever hear of anybody actually getting their pizza for free?'

'No, I didn't,' said Icarus.

'No, kid, you didn't. Because those guys find you wherever you are. And I've tried hiding. In the spirit of experimentation,

168

you understand, or devilment, when I have imps in me. You know how it is.'

'I know you once hid in the loft,' said Icarus. 'And the pizza man abseiled down the roof and found you.'

'Good example,' said I. 'Not me, of course. But good example.'

'Did you order us all a pizza?' asked Johnny Boy. 'Because I'd like anchovies on mine. I love anchovies, they're small and delicious. A bit like me, really.'

'Gimme a break.'

Icarus sighed. He'd been doing a lot of sighing lately. More than was normally natural for one of his tender years. 'So you really think', said he, 'that if we just wait around here, in this secret underground establishment, a pizza delivery man is going to knock on the door?'

'There isn't a door any more,' said Johnny Boy.

'Knock on the doorpost then. Pizza in hand?'

'And then we just follow him out,' said I. 'You don't get to be the best in the business without having a flair for this kind of thing. I'm telling you, kid, in my business, having a flair can mean the difference between a pair of drainpipe trousers or a pair of bell-bottoms. If you know what I mean, and I'm sure I could have put it somewhat better than that.'

'Barking,' said Icarus. 'He's barking mad.'

'I think we should just run,' said Johnny Boy.

Captain Ian nudged the arm of Icarus. 'Do you want me to punch your brother's lights out?' he asked. 'I could carry him over my shoulder.'

'I heard that,' I said, checking my watch.

'Oh, get real,' said Icarus. 'This rubbish isn't going to work.'

'I'll give you a slice,' I said to Johnny Boy. 'But if there's only one olive, I'm having it.'

169

'Fair enough. I hope you ordered extra cheese.'

'Doesn't everybody?'

'For the love of God!' said Icarus. 'This is insanity. There isn't going to be a pizza man. We're down here in the Ministry of Hell. We have to be serious. We have to escape.'

'Pizza for Mr Woodwork,' said a voice. 'Hot pastrami, double cheese and triple chewing fat.'

I looked at the kid called Icarus.

And he looked back at me.

'Don't say it, kid,' I said. 'Don't go getting all dewy-eyed and all choked up and saying, "Thank you, Mr Woodbine, you're the bestest friend a boy could ever have." Just bow to the inevitable. Forget the rest, when you're dealing with the best. This is Woodbine you're dealing with and Woodbine always gets the job done.'

The kid was speechless and who could blame him? I took his hand in mine and gave it a shake.

A couple of tablets dropped from his hand and into my manly palm. They looked kind of sweaty, but a tablet is a tablet and I had a real old headache from the bopping that Sam had given me.

'Aspirins,' I said.

And I tossed one down my throat.

13

'Sit down,' said Icarus Smith. 'Something is about to happen to you. We don't have much time.'

'Listen, kid,' I told him. 'I'm done with sitting down. I have a case that needs solving.'

'You have to listen, something is about to happen. That wasn't an aspirin that you just swallowed. That was the Red Head drug.'

'Who's paying for this pizza?' asked the pizza guy, doing that thing that they always do with their helmets.

'I'm paying,' said I. 'And I've got fifty big ones for you if you give me a lift out of here on the back of your bike.'

'No,' said Icarus. 'Hold on.'

'Fifty big ones!' said the pizza guy. Now doing that thing they always do with their gloves. 'Hop on, Mr Woodcock, and I'll have you away in a jiffy.'

'No! Hold on!' And Icarus made a pair of fists.

The guy with the military bearing stepped forward to block my passage. And I don't take kindly to that, when I'm not wearing corduroy. I drew out the trusty Smith

171

and 'Go West' by the Village People.

'Out of my way, fella,' said I. 'Or know the joy that a bullet brings, which ain't no joy at all.'

The guy took another step forward and I took a small one back. This guy was brave, I had to give him that.

Now I don't know what might have happened next. Perhaps I might have shot the guy, perhaps I might not. Perhaps the guy would have just backed off and then perhaps he wouldn't. Perhaps I should have noticed the little guy with the singed socks who was creeping up on me and then ducked the pizza, with the double cheese and the triple chewing fat, that he hurled right into my face. But as something else happened at that very moment and none of these things did, I guess I'll never know for sure.

The something else that happened happened suddenly and when it suddenly happened, it was loud. That something was an alarm bell sounding and it brought with it that sense of urgency and panic that alarm bells so often do.

'We're rumbled!' I shouted above the hubbub. 'Follow me and let's go.'

They dithered for a moment, but soon bowed to my natural authority. There was a bit of rushing then and we all got stuck in the doorway.

'Can five fit on your bike?' I shouted at the pizza guy.

'You don't have to shout,' he said. 'I've got my helmet on.'

'Can you get five on your bike?' I reiterated in a moderate tone.

'No problem,' said he. 'As long as three are prepared to run behind.'

'Then let's go for it,' I cried. 'Take us to the nearest bar and don't spare the horsepower.'

★

The nearest bar turned out to be the Lion's Mane, a safari theme pub on the corner of Thor Bridge Road and not two hundred yards from the entrance to Mornington Crescent underground station.

I entered the establishment, hacked my way through the plantain and the jungle vines and beat a path to the bar. The landlord was lean as a leopard and gamin as a gazelle. He wore a solar toupee and one of those khaki safari suits that not even David Attenborough can wear without looking an utter plum.

'Set 'em up, barkeep,' I said. 'Four gin slings and a punka wallah and none of that calling me bwana.'

'Ice and a slice?' asked the lean landlord.

'A squeeze, if you please,' said I.

'Aaagh!' went Johnny Boy. 'There's a big snake trying to eat our pizza.'

'And a machete please, barkeep,' I added.

The landlord did the business and I put paid to the python.

'I'll have to charge you extra for killing the wildlife,' said the lanksome landlord. 'You just missed the happy hunting hour. But for a small surcharge, our in-house tailor can make you up a jacket from the snake's skin.'

'Put me down for a trenchcoat and matching fedora,' said I.

'Hell's mud huts and hinterland!' said the long-legged land-lord. 'It's *you*, Laz. I didn't recognize you in that old tweed jacket. I thought you were that reporter guy from the *Brentford Mercury*.'

I looked the lean and lanksome long-legged landlord up and down. 'Why, Fange,' I said. 'It's you. I didn't recognize you in that solar toupee. I thought it was Ally McBeal with her hair up.'

'Enough of your thinnist remarks, you fat bastard.'

173

'Serve the drinks up, Posh,' said I. 'And put some Karen Carpenter on the jukebox.'

The landlord did as he was bid and I hacked my way to the veranda area. Here we sat ourselves down upon wicker chairs and watched the sun sinking low over the veldt, to the sound of distant tribal drums and the calls of the uzelum bird.

'Damn these mosquitoes,' said Johnny Boy, flicking flies from his forehead. 'And damn those native drums. Beating. Beating. They're driving me mad, I tell you.'

'Turn it in,' said Icarus. 'You're only encouraging him.'

'Listen, kid,' I told the kid. 'I got you out of there, didn't I? A big thank you might be nice. And should you wish to include a large "So sorry to have ever doubted you, Mr Woodbine, sir" you won't find me complaining.'

Icarus threw up his hands. 'Look at him,' he said to Captain Ian. 'The Red Head drug's done absolutely nothing. It hasn't worked.'

'I don't know,' I said. 'My headache's cleared up.'

'But you can't see anything different? Everything looks the same to you?'

'What do you want from me, kid?'

'I give up,' said Icarus. 'He's barking mad. Always has been, always will be.'

I raised my glass to the kid. 'You sure have a funny way of saying thanks,' I said.

'I seem to recall', said Captain Ian, 'that it was *we* who initially rescued *you*.'

'Yeah, well, thanks for that. So now, if we've all finished rescuing each other, I must be off on my way.'

'Perhaps I should punch him,' said Captain Ian. 'Just once, in the face.'

'Help yourself,' said Icarus. 'I don't really care any more.'

174

'Hold up, fella,' I said. 'You raise a hand to me and I'll stick you with this machete where the furtling farmer stuck his toilet duck. But just let me ask you something. Why *did* you rescue me?'

'Because you're the best,' said the captain. 'And we need the best.'

'We don't need *him*!' said Icarus. 'Please, not *him*.'

'We *do* need him,' said the captain. 'And whether he's your brother, or not—'

'I'm not,' said I.

'He *is*,' said Icarus.

'—is neither here nor there,' said the captain. 'We need Mr Woodbine's help. Mr Woodbine is on a case and that case is linked directly to us. If anyone can sort everything out, that anyone is Lazlo Woodbine, private eye.'

'But he's not Lazlo Woodbine. He's my barking mad brother,' said Icarus. 'We'll just get drawn into his madness. Escaping from the Ministry on the back of a pizza man's motorbike. Coming to a pub that's got a jungle with a sun-down in it.'

'And a snake,' said Johnny Boy, munching on the pizza. 'Mr Woodbine hacked its head off.'

I brandished the machete. 'Keep your hands away from that olive,' I told the wee man. 'Or you'll be playing Stumpy, in *Snow White meets the Eighth Dwarf*.'

'We'll end up as mad as he is,' said Icarus.

'I'm afraid I'll have to ask you gentlemen to drink up and leave,' said the landlord. 'The yearly migration of the wilde-beest will be coming through here in a minute and the management can't take responsibility for any patrons who get trampled.'

'See what I mean?' said Icarus. 'Absolutely barking.'

175

'No, they don't migrate through Barking,' said Fangio. 'They go across Streatham Common and down through Tooting usually. Oh, and Laz, I'll have the trenchcoat and the fedora dropped round to your office in the morning. The in-house tailor's just come down with a bad attack of spontaneous human combustion and it will be a couple of hours before the night relief in-house tailor comes on duty.'

'So it's farewell,' said I. 'I'd like to say it's been real nice knowing you guys. But as it hasn't, I won't.'

'Wildebeest!' cried Captain Ian, pointing over my shoulder.

I turned around to take a look and would you believe it, the guy struck me down from behind.

And once more I was falling into that deep dark whirling pit of oblivion. And I for one was frankly getting sick of it.

I awoke to find myself once more in my office, with dawn's crack on the horizon.

'What am I doing back here?' I asked, for it seemed a reasonable question.

'We brought you here.' It was the guy with the military bearing. Captain Ian 'I've-got-a-hiding-coming' Drayton. 'The landlord gave us your office address. We brought you here in a taxi.'

'The driver knew all about the knowledge,' said Johnny Boy. 'We came via Beat Street, Elm Street, Amityville Road, through Little China, past the Breakfast Club and the Cinema Paradiso, turned left at—'

'Forget it, buddy,' I said. 'If that's a running gag, it's lost on me.'

Captain Ian pointed a gun. It was *my* gun. And he pointed it at *me*.

'All right,' he said. 'Enough. We haven't slept and I get very

176

edgy when I haven't slept. I might just lose my temper and beat you about the head with this pistol.'

'So what do you want from me?' I asked, in the manner known as polite.

'I want you to tell us all about the case *you're* on and then we'll tell you all about the case *we're* on.'

'Oh,' said I. 'You're on a case too, are you?'

'The biggest ever,' said Icarus.

'No way, buddy. The case I'm on is far bigger than yours.'

'Isn't,' said Icarus.

'Is,' said I.

'Isn't.'

'Is too.'

'Isn't.'

'Chaps,' said Captain Ian. 'I don't know whether you're brothers or not, but—'

'Not,' said I.

'Are,' said Icarus.

'Not.'

'Are too.'

'I don't know and I don't care,' said the captain. 'But I will beat you most severely with this pistol, Mr Woodbine, if you don't tell me everything you know.'

'I'll tell you, fella,' said I. 'But you won't believe a word of it.'

And so I told them mine and they told me theirs. And when we were all well done with the telling, which took quite a fair old time and required us to send out for several more pizzas, it was slack jaws all round and a lot of heavy silence in the air.

But I for one could hear the sound of distant applause. It was still a week distant, but I felt certain I could hear it, because now I had a handle on the case. Now it made some kind of sense to me.

177

'The surveillance video,' I said. 'The one I have here in my pocket. Play it on my TV and tell me what *you* see.'

'Fair enough,' said Icarus. And he took the cassette and slotted it into my VCR.

Now OK, I know I didn't tell you that I owned a VCR, but hey, come on. Who in this world *doesn't* own a VCR? They're commoner than canker on a tomcat's codpiece.

'Let it roll,' said I and the kid let it roll.

Icarus and Johnny Boy and Captain Ian viewed the television screen. I viewed it too, but I couldn't see what they were seeing.

'Demons,' said Icarus, 'two demons and they're shooting a man. But he's not a man, he's golden, golden. He's . . .'

'God,' said Captain Ian in a croaky choky voice. 'They've murdered God.' And he sank down onto my unspeakable carpet and buried his face in his hands.

Icarus stared at the captain and then he stared right back at me. 'I'm prepared to believe the evidence of the video footage,' said he. 'But I still don't believe that you're Lazlo Woodbine. You are my brother and that is that.'

'Kid, I ain't your brother.'

'And how come you can't see the demons or angels? You've taken the drug, but you can't see them. It doesn't make any sense.'

'I have a theory of my own about that,' I said. 'But if demons murdered God, a whole lot of things make sense and I can have this case wrapped up in a couple of days.'

'Do what you like,' said Icarus. 'I don't care. I have to make the public aware of what is going on around them. That creatures of Hell are here among us, orchestrating everything. I have to tell the world.'

'Just one moment,' said Captain Ian. 'Back at the Ministry of

Serendipity, I said that I would explain everything to you. About what is really going on in the world. Now I think would be the time for me to do it.'

'Do you mind if I take a pinch of snuff before you get started?' I asked, pulling out the silver snuffbox that was given to me by a crowned head of Europe, in reward for certain services rendered, of which I must not speak. 'I always find that a pinch of Crawford's Imperial, the king of snuff, helps me to cogitate at times such as these. As the poem goes, whenever the going's getting rough, take a pinch of Crawford's snuff. I've tried others, but—'

'Shut your face,' said Captain Ian. 'Or I might just shoot you in the head.'

I shrugged. 'God's widow won't take kindly to that,' I said.

'No,' said Captain Ian, 'you're probably right. What I'm going to tell you all concerns Her. You see, God created the Earth as a present for His wife.'

'I knew that,' I said.

'I'll shoot your balls off,' said the captain.

'Pray continue with your most interesting narrative,' I said.

'He created the Earth as a present for His wife. But that was a good many years ago and there have been many many years since, which means many many more birthdays for God's wife. And He had to keep giving Her more and better. Women expect that, you know. God may have infinite wisdom, but even He doesn't have infinite resources. There eventually comes a time when the bills have to be settled and it costs a great deal to construct galaxies and nebulas and black holes and splatagramattons.'

'What's a splatagramatton?' asked Johnny Boy.

'It's a posher version of a carmufti.'

'Oh, I see.'

179

'God kept digging deeper and deeper into His robe pockets until finally they were empty.'

'So who was He paying out to?' asked Icarus.

'The cosmic builders,' said Captain Ian. 'The celestial corps of engineers. Everything is subject to universal laws. God might appear to simply wave His hand and cause the Earth to come into being. But certain forces have to be invoked by that bit of hand-waving. And call those forces whatever you like, they don't work for free. God took a second mortgage out on Heaven and then a third and a fourth. And then He went bust and so the angels got evicted from Heaven. And God had to move His family to Earth. You've heard about people having visions of the Virgin Mary. They couldn't have visions of her if she was up in Heaven, could they? They can only see her if she's down here on Earth.'

'So Jesus is down here too?' said Icarus.

'You'll have seen him on the telly. But I am not at liberty to divulge his earthly identity.'

'This is all too much,' said Icarus. 'Far too much.'

'It gets worse. When God went bust, He had to sell up Hell too. So the demons all got evicted and now they're here as well.'

'And you and they have been battling it out ever since, with mankind in the middle?'

'It was all predicted in the book of Revelation.'

'Isn't everything?' said Johnny Boy. 'But tell me this. Professor Partington reasoned that there was no afterlife. No Heaven or Hell to go to when we die.'

'Not any more,' said the captain.

'But there could be again?'

'I don't know. Perhaps.'

'I know,' I said. And I did. 'I know, because I've solved it.'

180

'What?' they all went. Well, they would, wouldn't they?

'I've solved the case,' I said. 'Now that I've heard everything the captain had to say, I know who did it and why.'

They looked from one to another and then they all looked back at me.

'Well, go on then,' said Icarus. 'Tell us.'

'No way, buddy. Not until the final rooftop showdown. I know, but I need proof. I have to present this proof to my employer. To wit and to woo, God's widow. When I've done that, I'll tell you the lot.'

'He's bullshitting,' said Icarus. 'He doesn't know. He's just making it up.'

'Kid,' said I, 'once I've solved this case, you can forget about angels and demons walking the Earth. Everything will be back the way it should be. Trust me on this, I'm a detective.'

'Well,' said Johnny Boy. 'Where does this leave Icarus and me?'

'Dealing with it ourselves,' said Icarus.

'My advice to you', said Captain Ian, 'would be to lie low until Mr Woodbine has solved the case.'

'Oh yeah, right,' said Icarus. 'As if I'd trust *him*.'

'All I need is a week, kid,' said I. 'And if I don't solve the thing in a week, you can do whatever you want. Tell your tale to the *News of the World*. Whatever you damn well please.'

'A week?' said Icarus. 'One week?'

'That's all I need.'

'No,' said Icarus. 'Out of the question.'

'Listen,' said Captain Ian. 'You trust *me*, don't you?'

Icarus nodded. 'I suppose so, yes.'

'Then if I were to ask you to let Mr Woodbine deal with this, would you do it, for me?'

'Well . . .'

'He did save our lives,' said Johnny Boy.

'All right,' said Icarus. 'I'll do it for you. But when my brother here screws up, as he most certainly will, Johnny Boy and I will sort everything out by ourselves.'

'And how exactly will we do that?' asked Johnny Boy.

'I'll think of something. All right, captain, I agree.'

'Good lad,' said Captain Ian. 'Then I suggest this. I will liaise with Mr Woodbine, you and Johnny Boy take yourselves off to a place of safety and we'll all meet back here in exactly one week's time. How does that sound?'

'All right,' said Icarus. 'But if after a week he hasn't solved the case and everything is *not* put to rights, Johnny Boy and I *will* deal with it.'

'Kid,' said I, 'I *will* solve the case.'

And I would. I knew that I would.

Yes siree.

By golly.

14

Icarus Smith and Johnny Boy sat in the scarlet bar and grill of the Station Hotel.

'So what *are* we going to do?' asked Johnny Boy.

'Lie low,' said Icarus Smith. 'Leave it to Lazlo Woodbine.'

'As if. You lied to them, but you can't lie to me.'

'Lying to them seemed hardly out of place. Everyone in that office was lying about something.'

'I wasn't lying at all.'

'Everybody but you, then.'

'Hold up there,' said Johnny Boy. 'Are you telling me that the captain was lying? Angels don't lie, do they?'

'*He* did. It was nonsense, all of it. Think about it, Johnny Boy. God having to mortgage Heaven. Angels and demons getting evicted. It's all rubbish.'

'It sounded quite convincing when he told it.'

'Well, it might have done in there with my brother. I told you that if you spend time with him, you get drawn into his madness.'

'But surely angels don't lie.'

'And do angels murder people with golden swords?'

'I can't say I've ever heard of such a thing. But do you think your brother was lying too? I could see his colours. It looked as if he thought he was telling the truth.'

'I think you'll find that he gave a somewhat edited account of his side of the story. He neglected to mention Barry, for instance.'

'And who's Barry?'

'Barry the voice in his head. His Holy Guardian Sprout. Barry talks to him and helps him solve his cases. Except he doesn't solve any cases. He's not a real detective. He's my mad brother.'

'I find it all somewhat confusing,' said Johnny Boy. 'And I still don't understand how nothing happened to him when he took the drug.'

'Now that', said Icarus Smith, '*is* a mystery.'

'It's a mystery. It's a mythtery.' I sang it in my finest Toyah Wilcox.

'Ease up on the singing there, chief.'

'Why, Barry, my little green buddy pal. Where have you been all this time?'

'Sleeping, chief. That Sam Maggot bopped us on the head, didn't he? Did I miss anything?'

'Not a lot,' said I. 'But I seem to be missing quite a bit.'

'How so, chief?'

'Well, Barry, I have taken a drug which enables me to see angels and demons, which would otherwise be mistaken for ordinary folk.'

'Good golly Ms Molly, chief.'

'Ms Molly indeed, Barry. Yet, even though I have taken the drug, I can't see any angels *or* devils at all.'

184

'I can't say that I find that altogether surprising, chief. You probably can't see any pink elephants or fairies either.'

'Point taken, yet only a moment ago I was in the company of an angel. And also two men who had also taken the drug. And what they saw on the surveillance video footage, I was quite unable to see. How would you account for that, Barry?'

'Perhaps they were all just pulling your plonker, chief.'

'Or perhaps someone or something was stopping me seeing what they saw. What do you think about that, Barry?'

'Well, chief . . . I—'

'It's *you*, Barry! You little green ball of phlegm! It's you stopping the drug from taking effect on me.'

'Come now, chief, as if I would.'

'You would and you have. Switch it on, Barry. Switch it on now. Or by crimbo, I'll winkle you out of my ear with a pencil and boil you up for my lunch.'

'I was only looking out for your best interests, chief. I didn't want you getting all upset, seeing horrible demons and everything. You wouldn't like them, chief, they're really nasty.'

I took a pencil and began to sharpen its point.

'I'm waiting,' said I.

'Chief, please, you really won't like it.'

'This is a 9H, Barry. Very sharp and pointy. I'll put a saucepan on the stove, shall I?'

'No, chief. Please. All right.'

'All right,' said Johnny Boy. 'So what *do* you intend to do?'

'I am a relocator,' said Icarus Smith. 'That is my vocation.'

'Relocating all the devils and angels might prove a bit of a challenge.'

'Possibly,' said Icarus. 'But there might be a way.'

'You cannot be serious, surely?'

185

'Do I look serious?'

Johnny Boy studied the colours of Icarus. 'Yes you do,' said he. 'Very serious. And very concerned also. Something is troubling you deeply.'

'Yes,' said Icarus. 'It is. With all the nonsense going on with my mad brother and everything, I'd quite forgotten about Cormerant. He'll be coming after the left luggage locker key. The one I mailed to myself.'

'God. You're right. We'd better get round to your house.'

'No,' said Icarus. 'We'd be too late. But I have another idea.'

'I've a really good idea, chief,' said Barry. 'Why don't you just turn off the video and have a slug of Old Bedwetter?'

I rewound the videocassette and played the tape once again.

'But you've watched it thirty-seven times, chief. Surely you've memorized the plot by now.'

'Look at them, Barry. Just look at them.'

'I can see them, chief. They're demons, I know.'

'And they're murdering God and we have it on tape.'

'Yes, chief, so you keep saying.'

'And I couldn't see them for what they really were.'

'No, chief, not until I let the effects of the drug kick into your tiny tiny brain.'

'Look at them. They're horrible. Look at all the quills and the scales.'

'Yes, chief, I quite agree, they're not a pretty sight.'

'But there's no doubt of what's really happening. And so I've solved the case.'

'Yes, chief, you do keep saying that. Would you care to take me through your reasoning and explain to me exactly how you've solved the case?'

'No, Barry, I would not.'

186

'But, chief, we don't have any secrets. Well, you don't from me, anyway.'

'Then read my thoughts, Barry.'

'You won't let me, chief, you're blocking me out.'

'Damn right I am. No-one ever finds out how Woodbine solves the case, or even who the villain is, until the final rooftop showdown. That's the way it's always done and that's the way it always will be done.'

'Well, I'm not bothered, chief. You'll give it away when you go to sleep. You can't keep me out of your dreams.'

'Then I won't go to sleep, Barry. I will stay awake for the entire week, until I bring the criminal to justice.'

'No-one can stay awake for a whole week, chief. They'd go mad if they did.'

'Wanna bet? You just watch me.'

'Watch you go mad? I'd rather not.'

'Watch me solve the case. Just watch.'

Icarus and Johnny Boy watched as the long dark automobile drew into the car park opposite the Station Hotel. They watched as the creature that was Cormerant emerged from the automobile and strode to the left luggage lockers. They then watched as he took a key from an envelope which bore the name and address of Icarus Smith, opened one of the lockers and removed a black briefcase.

They did not, however, watch as he returned to the long dark automobile. Nor did they watch as the new chauffeur drove him away.

They did, however, feel the movement of the car.

Because they were now both in the boot.

'It's really quite comfortable in here,' said Johnny Boy. 'Better than being in the boot of that taxi.'

'I've known better places to be,' said Icarus. 'But this seems the best way to get back inside the Ministry of Serendipity.'

'I'd like to see the look on that Cormerant's face when he opens the briefcase,' said Johnny Boy. 'He'll be well peeved when he finds it empty.'

'It seemed the only solution. I couldn't get to my house in time. And as we were opposite the station, it was only a matter of crossing the road and opening the locker up.'

'You're pretty nifty with your little roll of instruments. What exactly do you plan to do when we get back inside the Ministry?'

'Learn,' said Icarus. 'Learn exactly what is really going on. And then act upon that information.'

'I'm not keen to go back in there. I don't want my little head getting squeezed by that harpy Philomena.'

'I told you, you didn't have to come.'

'I'll stick with you,' said Johnny Boy. 'It may not be safe. But at least it's never dull.'

'Dull,' said I, flicking channels with the old remote control.

'What exactly are you doing, chief?'

'Just watching a bit of TV. Isn't daytime telly really dull?'

'Richard and Judy are never dull, chief. They never cease to inspire me. And there's always *Countdown* of course. That Carol Vorderman's a lovely-looking woman.'

'Oh yeah, right.' I flicked the channel and up came Carol, quills and scales and all.

'Well, who'd have thought that, chief, eh? Our lovely Carol in league with the devil.'

'Who'd have thought it, indeed.'

'But come on, chief, you can't sit here all day watching TV.'

'Just unwinding, Barry. Why don't you take a little nap if you're bored?'

'Well, I wouldn't mind, chief, thanks.'

'You just take a nap then and I'll wake you up later when we go out.'

'Are we going somewhere nice?'

'Oh yeah,' I said, 'real nice. We're going up west to a bar where all the swells get together.'

'Smart, chief. I'll bet you'll cut a real dash in your old tweed jacket.'

A knock came at my office door.

'Enter,' said I with more élan than a Lotus.

A guy entered carrying a large cardboard box. 'Delivery for Mr Woodchip wallpaper,' he said. 'Python skin trenchcoat and fedora.'

'I'll just take a nap then, chief.'

'I'll wake you later,' said I.

Somewhat later, though only a bit, the long dark automobile cruised out of the secret underground tunnel and into the secret underground establishment known as the Ministry of Serendipity. Icarus and Johnny Boy heard the car's doors open and then slam shut. They also heard the voice of the evil Cormerant. And a very grumpy voice it was.

'I think he's opened the briefcase,' said Johnny Boy. 'I wouldn't want to be us, the next time we meet him.'

Icarus shushed the small man into silence. They waited until the sounds of cursing had died away and then Icarus raised the lid of the boot.

'Come on,' he said. 'Let's go.'

They crept through the underground cathedral of a place, marvelling anew at all they saw. Especially all those barber's chairs. Those thousands and thousands of barber's chairs.

'Shouldn't there be workers everywhere?' asked Johnny Boy.

'What, in orange jumpsuits and hard hats, like at the supervillain's HQ in a James Bond movie?'

'Something like that. Have you ever wondered where the supervillains get their workers from? Do you think they advertise in the newspaper? You know, *Supervillain seeking world domination also seeks skilled manual workers to help construct nuclear missile silo in defunct volcano. Apply box 666.*'

'You don't have a lot of truck with movies, do you, Johnny Boy?'

'They'll never replace the music hall. Where exactly are we going?'

'To the barber's shop,' said Icarus. 'We'll find our answers there.'

'Perhaps you should ask the Greek to give you a haircut. You'd look good with a Tony Curtis.'

Tony Curtis had nothing on me when it comes to pulling the womenfolk. I attract women like flies. But then who wants women like flies? The way I figure it, either you have or you haven't got style. And I'm a have, every inch of the way, and quite a few inches that is.

I slipped on the snakeskin fedora and tipped it at the angle that will be for ever rakish. I discarded the old tweed jacket and took up the new trenchcoat. Now this *was* style.

Matching python-skin two-piece. I should have asked Fangio whether there was any chance of getting a pair of shoes made up from the off-cuts. I'd have really mullahed the mustard in a three-piece get up. Or would that be four, as shoes come in a pair? And I could have had a necktie too. And a pair of boxer shorts. I made a mental note to pop back to the Lion's

Mane as soon as I had the time, and butcher a couple more python. And perhaps a white rhino, if they had one. White rhino hide would look pretty good on the seats of the brand new Bentley I intended to buy with my payoff from the case.

Payoff? I hear you ask. Just what payoff might this be, Mr Woodbine? Well, my friends, I'll tell you, it'll be a big payoff.

Because I *had* solved the case. And if you were as smart as I am, then you'd have solved it too. You heard everything I heard when Captain Ian the angel was telling his tale. And if you'd been able to put two and two together the same way that I did, you'd be planning what kind of seat covers you'd be having on your Bentley.

But hey, you're not me. And if you've been asking yourself just how come I've spent most of the day watching TV rather than getting out and about, then that's another good reason why I'll be the one in the Bentley, not you.

But I don't want to give any more clues away here now. So you'll just have to settle for the not inconsiderable joy of watching me ponce up and down my office in my new trench-coat and fedora. Looking like a million bucks.

And I don't mean green and wrinkled.

'Green and wrinkled,' said Johnny Boy. 'That's what I think of sprouts. Horrid green and wrinkly things and your brother, if indeed he *is* your brother, actually thinks he has one that lives in his head?'

'I told you he was mad.'

'Damn right,' said Johnny Boy. 'I can understand an onion. But a sprout? No thank you. Where exactly are we now, by the way?'

'We're here,' said Icarus. 'Outside the door of the barber's shop.'

191

'I don't remember that bust being in that niche yesterday. Surely that's Noel . . .'

Knock knock, went Icarus, knocking at the door.

'Er, just hold on a moment,' called the barber's voice.

Icarus opened the door and walked right in.

The barber sat in the middle chair. He had the now legendary brown envelope open and had clearly been savouring its contents.

'How dare you bustle in here,' the barber complained. 'Me being busy with myself. What game is yours and oh . . .'

'Oh?' said Icarus.

'Oh, it's you, boy, back again. I thought they . . .'

'Murdered me?' said Icarus.

'Not murdered surely. Took you off to have a nice sleep.'

'No,' said Icarus, approaching the barber.

'I not like the look of you, boy. You kindly leave by the door where you came.'

Icarus grasped the chair's back and swung the barber around. The barber gripped the arms of the chair and the steel bands swished and clamped his wrists.

'Now look what you make me do, boy. Press the button on the back and set me free at once.'

'I think not,' said Icarus Smith. 'I have questions to ask and you have answers to supply.'

'I tell you nothing,' said the barber. 'I sign the Official Secrets Act. Say nothing to you about nothing.'

Icarus patted the barber on the head.

'Help!' screamed the barber. '*Help me!*'

Icarus took the Velocette and rammed it into the barber's mouth. 'Now,' said he. 'I am going to give your head a little massage. I think I can remember exactly where Ms O'Connor applied the pressure. Let's hope I don't get it wrong. It would

192

really be a shame if you were to suffer some permanent damage.'

'Mmph!' went the barber, shaking his head violently from side to side. 'Mmph!'

'What was that?' asked Icarus. 'Did I hear you saying that you would answer all my questions, clearly and precisely, without any need for painful measures being taken?'

The barber's head nodded up and down.

Icarus removed the Velocette.

'Please don't think of calling out for help again,' he said. 'Or I will put my thumbs in your eyes and twist them inside out.'

Johnny Boy turned his face away. 'I don't want to watch *that*,' he said.

'You've finished watching TV now, then, have you, chief?'

'That's why I woke you, Barry, yes.'

'And so, are we off on our way?'

'We are, Barry, we are off on our way to Black Peter's Tavern.'

'Black Peter's Tavern, chief? Please don't tell me we're going to Black Peter's Tavern. Oh no no. Not Black Peter's Tavern.'

'You know it, then, Barry?'

'Never heard of it, chief.'

I'd always fancied a night at Black Peter's Tavern. It was the kind of joint where all the big knobs hang out. If you know what I mean, and I'm sure that you do. This joint was swanky. It had class. If you were here, you were someone.

The decor was stylish to a point where it transcended style and entered the realms of perspicuous harmony, shunning grandiloquent ornamentation in favour of a visual concinnity,

193

garnered from aesthetic principles, which combined the austerity of Bauhaus and ebullience of Burges* into an eclectic mix before stripping them down to their fundamental essentials, to create an effect which was almost aphoristic, in that it could be experienced but never completely expressed.

So there is no need to bother with a description.

But trust me, it was sheer poetry.

I breezed in, like a breath of spring
And wafted my way to the bar
The hour was the hour known as happy
Which is happy, wherever you are.

I took in the decor, the dudes and dames
And all found favour with me
They had class written through them, like words in a rock
That you buy in Blackpool on sea.

In the time I've spent as a private dick
I've drunk in all manner of bars
From doss house dives with pools of sick
To the haunts of movie stars.

I've cast my fashionable shadow
In many a wayside inn
And raised my glass to beaus and belles
And sailors and Sanhedrin.

* William Burges, the now legendary nineteenth-century architect, notable for such gothic extravaganzas as Castel Coch. Not to be confused with the other Cardinal Cox.

But you know you are home
When you're in amongst your own
And this was home to me
So I leaned my elbow on the bar
And summoned the maître d'.

'Set 'em up, fat boy,' said I. 'A pint of pig's ear and a packet of pork scratchings.'

The maître d' raised a manicured eyebrow and viewed me down a narrow length of nose. 'Would sir care to rephrase that?' he asked.

'Certainly,' I said, with more savoir-faire than a Sophoclean sophist at a sadhus' seminar. 'A pig's ear scratching packet and a pint of pork, please.'

'Sir has the wit of Oscar Wilde, which combined with the droll delivery of Noel Coward creates a veritable tour de force of rib-tickling ribaldry.'

'I couldn't have put it better myself,' said I.

'Kindly sling your hook,' said the maître d'. 'We don't serve your kind in here.'

'Just make mine a Guinness, then, and forget the pork scratchings.'

'Coming right up, sir.'

The maître d' drew off the pint of black gold, and I waited the now legendary one hundred and nineteen seconds for it to fill to perfection.

'On the house,' said the maître d'. 'And help yourself to the chewing fat.'

'Why thank you very much,' said I. 'And what brings on this generosity?'

'Look at this place,' said the maître d', whose name, if you hadn't guessed, was Fangio. 'This is one classy number. Top-notch clientele, thirty-two brands of whisky, carpet on the floor and even paper in the gents' bog. This is my kind of bar, Laz. Do you think you might keep coming back to this one throughout the rest of your case? I didn't take much to the Lion's Mane, a wildebeest trod on my toe.'

I gave the place a once-over glance about. With my new sense of Super-vision, given to me by the Red Head tablet I'd taken in mistake for an aspirin, I could see the men within the men and the women within the women. They all looked pretty damn fab gear and groovy and not a wrong'un amongst them. This place had everything that a place that had everything had. So to speak.

'It's definitely *us*, isn't it?' I said.

'Too true. And look at this uniform. The waistcoat favours my wasp-waist and the fitted slacks show off my snake hips to perfection. You look pretty dapper in the new trenchcoat and fedora, by the way.'

'We're a regular pair of dandies, ain't we?'

Fangio tipped me the wink. 'So,' said he. 'What brings you here?'

'A cab,' I said. 'But I left it outside.'

Oh how we laughed.

And laughed.

The barber at the Ministry of Serendipity wasn't laughing at all. The hands of Icarus Smith gripped the barber's head.

'Tell me', said Icarus, 'all about this barber's shop. Tell me *exactly* why it's here.'

The barber's lips were all a-quiver. Icarus kneaded his skull.

'It's for training purposes,' whimpered the barber.

'Go on,' said Icarus. 'Tell me.'

'To train up operatives in the art of exo-cranial massage. We've trained thousands. Thousands and thousands.'

'To what purpose?' Icarus asked.

'World peace,' blurted the barber.

Icarus squeezed his head.

'It's true. Everybody goes to a barber's or hairdresser's at some time. By using exo-cranial massage on them, the Ministry's operatives keep them in a passive state.'

'Keep them under control,' said Icarus.

'I wouldn't put it like that,' said the barber, hunching down his head.

'I would,' said Icarus, yanking up the barber's head. 'So the Ministry has infiltrated thousands of these trained operatives into barbers and hairdressers up and down the country, so that they can use their techniques to keep the population pacified and under control.'

'I prefer the term world peace,' said the barber.

'I prefer the term world control,' said Icarus.

'Well, at least we know where all the workers in the orange jumpsuits and hard hats are,' said Johnny Boy. 'They're squeezing heads in barber's shops.'

Icarus released the barber's head. 'There's more to this,' he said.

'What?' said Johnny Boy. 'More than world control?'

Icarus addressed the barber. 'Are there operatives all over the world doing this?' he asked. 'Or only here in England?'

'Only here, as far as I know,' said the barber.

'I thought as much,' said Icarus.

Johnny Boy looked up at the lad. 'There are all kinds of colours whirling around you,' he said. 'Just what's going on in your mind?'

'Only this. What if all this angel and demon carry-on is a localized phenomenon? Centred right here in London. And what if it's natural for people to be able to see

197

demons and angels? Without needing the Red Head drug?'

'Then they'd see them, wouldn't they?'

'And some do. But they're considered mad. But the rest don't. And why? Because they're having their heads subtly massaged every time they go to the barber's or the hairdresser's. From when they're children onwards.'

'And the massages affect the brain so people can't see the truth?'

'That's what I think,' said Icarus.

'Angels and demons?' said the barber. 'You talking the jobbies from the bull's behind parts, that's what I'm thinking in *my* head.'

'Just a couple more questions,' said Icarus, 'and then I'll be done with you.'

'I plead the Fifth Amendment,' said the barber. 'Also the Geneva Convention and the Waldorf salad. I tell you nothing more.'

'How many people work here?' asked Icarus.

'I tell you *that*,' said the barber. 'About half a dozen. Me, Philomena the masseuse, Mr Cormerant the wages clerk, some guards that walk up and down. The chauffeur, no, he got stabbed in the corridor. The *new* chauffeur, the women in the canteen where nobody goes to eat, because the food tastes like pigeon poops. And the guv'nor, of course.'

'The guv'nor runs the Ministry?'

'That's what guv'nors do, ain't it?'

'And what is the guv'nor's name?'

'Mr Godalming,' said the barber.

'*Mr Godalming?*' said Johnny Boy.

And so did Icarus Smith.

'Mr Godalming,' said the barber once again.

Icarus looked at Johnny Boy.

198

And Johnny Boy looked back at him.

'This Mr Godalming,' said Icarus to the barber. 'What does he look like? Does he by any chance look like Richard E. Grant?'

'Ha ha ha,' the barber laughed. 'No, he look nothing like Richard E. Grant. His father look like Richard E. Grant. But he don't. He look more like Peter Stringfellow. He's young Mr Godalming.

'Mr *Colin* Godalming.'

'Still waiting for Mr Godalming, Laz?' said the maître d' with a grin.

'In a manner of speaking,' said I. 'I'm right, I assume, that this is the bar where all the media types come after they've been interviewed by daytime TV.'

'You're right there, my friend.'

'Perfect,' said I. 'Because I saw this guy on TV today and I'd really like to meet him.'

'Yeah?' said Fange. 'Who's that?'

'Celebrity hairdresser,' said I. 'Looks a bit like Peter Stringfellow. The name's Godalming.

'Mr *Colin* Godalming.'

15

'It's a mullet,' said Fangio the malnourished maître d'.
'It's a what?' I asked, in a readiness of response.

'The haircut Peter Stringfellow has. Mullet, the classic 1970s haircut, as favoured by members of the Bay City Rollers and damn near everybody else. Peter Stringfellow is the last man on Earth to favour the mullet, now that Pat Sharp's done away with his.'

'I'm more of a Ramón Navarro man, myself,' said I. 'I can't be having with hair that sticks out under my fedora.'

'Class,' said the string bean Fangio. 'Pure class.'

'So he comes in here, does he, this Colin Godalming?'

'Regular as clockwork,' said the wasted one. 'He should be arriving here', Fangio studied the watch on his twig-like wrist, 'in about ten minutes' flat, or if not flat, then he'll walk in upright, as usual.'

Oh how we laughed at that one.

'Well,' said I, to the half-starved meagre shrimp of a maître d'. 'That leaves us with ten minutes of prime toot-talking time.'

'You won't get a word out of me,' said the scrawny wretch,

'until you drop all those derogatory references to my slender, yet perfectly proportioned, physique.'

'Do you have to run around in the shower to get wet?' I asked.

'I'm warning you, Laz.'

'I heard that you once took off all your clothes, painted your head red and went to a fancy dress party as a thermometer.'

'One more and you're out of here!'

'All right, fair enough. So what do you want to talk toot about?'

'Well, actually, Laz, I'm thinking about buying a sofa. Is there anything you'd particularly recommend?'

'Hm,' said I. 'A sofa. Well, it all depends on getting one that's the right size and shape, at the price you can afford.'

'Go on,' said the maître d' with the slender, yet perfectly proportioned, physique.

'You see, you have your chesterfield, your G Plan three-seater, also available as a two, your classic chaise-longue, your Le Corbusier chaise-longue and your drop-end Bavarian chaise-longue with the tapestried upholstery and silk vanity tassels.'

'You sure know your sofas,' said Fangio.

'Buddy,' I told him, 'in my business, knowing your sofas can mean the difference between buttering scones on a battered settee and licking lard on a love couch. If you know what I mean, and I'm sure that you do.'

'I know where you're coming from,' said the Fange. 'For I've been there myself, on a cheap away-day to Norwich. What else would you suggest?'

'Well, there's your studio couch, your box ottoman, your oak settle, which with the addition of cushions can easily be converted into a sofa.'

'I had an aunt who converted to Islam once,' said Fangio.

'She thought she was converting to North Sea gas, but she ticked the wrong box on the application form.'

'Did she have a sofa, your aunt?'

'No, just an armchair and a pair of pouffes.'

'Ample seating. Did she live on her own?'

'She does now, the pouffes moved out. They've opened a candle shop in Kemptown.'

'The air's very bracing in Kemptown. Someone told me that it was good for rheumatism. So I went there and caught it.'

'You can't *catch* rheumatism, can you?'

'It all depends who's throwing it,' I said. 'Boys will be boys.'

And we paused for a moment to take stock and think of the good times.

'My problem regarding the sofa remains unsolved,' said the slim boy. 'I'd like the best, but I can only afford the very worst.'

'Ah,' said I. 'What you have there is a Couch 22 situation.'

Oh how we laughed once more.

Fangio dried his eyes upon an oversized red gingham handkerchief. 'My, I did enjoy that,' said he. 'That was top class toot. But look, here comes Mr Godalming.'

'Colin Godalming,' said Johnny Boy. 'This would be the third child of God, who inherits the Earth. Mr Woodbine told us all about him.'

'Yes,' said Icarus. 'I'm well aware of that.'

'And it makes sense,' said Johnny Boy, 'if God's family have all been forced to move down here to Earth. Colin has his father murdered and falsifies His will. So he now owns the planet.'

'Yes yes,' said Icarus. 'I get the picture.'

'And he's teamed up with the wrong'uns, which is why he came up with this scheme to massage everyone's heads, so they can't see what's really going on. He's been planning it all for years.'

'Yes,' said Icarus. 'I understand what you're saying.'

'That Mr Woodbine is a genius,' said Johnny Boy. 'He knew it was Colin from the start.'

'No,' said Icarus. 'Just stop that. It all fits too easily together.'

'Well, it would if it's correct. Why go looking for a more complicated solution?'

'Because this is my brother we're talking about. My mad brother. And if we get drawn into his madness we won't be able to escape from it. It's infectious. It's like a disease. I've come down here to try to solve this myself. All I have to do is stay away from him for a week. If that's possible.'

Johnny Boy stared up into the face of Icarus Smith. 'Please don't take offence at this,' he said, 'but surely I detect a bit of sibling rivalry here. If Mr Woodbine really is your brother, then you should be proud of him. And if he's not your brother, then you've projected the face of your brother onto him, because your brother *is* your hero. Which might explain why you are as you are. The lad who seeks to make a name for himself as the relocator who set the world to rights. Either way it means that you really do look up to your brother, but you can't bring yourself to admit it.'

'No,' said Icarus. 'It's not true. I am what I am because I had a dream. My brother lives in a world of dreams, but I inhabit reality.'

'You're just digging a deeper pit for yourself,' said Johnny Boy. 'This is all dead Freudian.'

'Let's go,' said Icarus.

'To where?'

'To find Colin Godalming, of course.'

★

203

'Mr Godalming?' I said, sticking out my hand for a shake. 'Mr Colin Godalming?'

The dude looked me coolly up and down. It was clear that I had the right guy here, I could tell by the way he shone. Streamers of light twinkled prettily about him and a golden glow, which wasn't just the mullet, drenched his shoulders.

'And who might you be?' asked the third child of God, declining my offer of a hearty handclasp.

'I'm a private investigator,' I replied, in a tone which left no doubt exactly where I stood on the matter. 'The name's Woodbine, Lazlo Woodbine.' And added, 'Some call me Laz.'

The guy regarded me as one would a pigeon squit plopped on a pampered pompadour. 'Well, Mr Woodless,' he said, in a tone which left no doubt exactly where *he* stood on the matter. 'I don't need a private investigator.'

'It's Wood*bine*,' I said. 'And believe me, buddy, you do.'

The guy gave me the kind of look I wouldn't waste on a whippet. 'What is this all about?' he asked. 'I don't have time to stand around here talking toot with a chap dressed up as a handbag.'

'*A hand bag?*' said I, in my finest *Charlie's Aunt*. Or was it *The Importance of Being Earnest*? I always get the two confused. Or perhaps it was *HMS Pinafore*. No, I'm sure it was *Charlie's Aunt*.

'It might have been *my* aunt,' said Fangio. 'She used to have a handbag.'

'Keep out of this, Jiffy,' I told the emaciated maître d'. 'This is between me and Dolly Parton here.'

'Handbag!' said Colin and he tossed back his hair and primped at his golden shower.

'Fella,' I said, 'let me ask you one question. What's red and white and lies dead in an alleyway?'

'I have no idea,' said Colin.

'A bullet-ridden corpse,' said I. 'And that corpse is your dad.'

'That was subtle,' said Fangio. 'And who's this Jiffy, anyway?'

'My dad?' said Colin. 'What are you talking about?'

'Your dad bought the big one.'

'My daddy is dead?'

'Deader than a stone gnome in a whore's window box,' said I. 'Colder than an Eskimo's nipple at an Alaskan alfresco piercing party. More bereft of life than a rerun of the *Monty Python* parrot sketch.'

'*That* dead?' said Fangio.

'And then some. Kaput.'

'No,' said Colin, getting a blubber on now. 'It can't be true. Not my poor dear daddy. Tell me that it isn't true.'

'It's true,' I said. 'Truer than the noble love that wins the heart of a maiden fair. More unvarnished than a dunny door in a pine restorer's stripping tank. As factual as a . . .'

'Fat fop in a foolish fedora?' said Fangio. 'Only a suggestion, you don't have to use it.'

'Oh my poor dear daddy.' Colin took to wailing and gnawing his knuckles and carrying on like a silly big girl.

'You've upset him,' said the bone-bag of a maître d'.

'Enough of the thin-boy jibes,' said Fange. 'I'm only human too, you know. Cut me and do I not bleed?'

'We can check that out,' I said. 'Give us a lend of the knife you use to hack up your chewing fat.'

'No, really, Laz. I'm not kidding. You can be very cruel sometimes. And the guy's really upset. Look at him, he's crying.'

'He's faking it,' I said.

'I'm not,' blubbed Colin.

'You are too,' said I.

'Blubb blubb blubb,' went Colin.

'Give him a hug,' said Fangio. 'That sometimes helps.'

'I certainly will not,' I said. 'I'm not getting *Tears on my Trenchcoat*'.*

'What's the trouble?' asked a broad-shouldered dame in a pale pink peplos and Day-Glo dungarees. She had the kind of face that you generally see only on a platter with an apple stuck into its gob.

'Butt out, Miss Piggy,' I told her. 'It's nothing to do with you.'

The porcine dame burst into tears.

'Now look what you've done,' said Fangio.

'And you keep out of it too, skeleton boy.'

'Waaah,' went Fangio, breaking down upon the bar.

'Blubb blubb blubb,' went Colin.

'Boo hoo' and 'snort' went the pig-faced lady.

'Can I be of assistance?' asked a solitary cyclist who'd just popped in for a Perrier water. He wore one of those figure-hugging Lycra suits that only look good on Lynford Christie, and one of those streamlined bikers' helmets that don't look good on anybody.

'Clear off, you Spandexed poseur,' I told him.

'Sob sob sob,' went the cyclist.

Now I don't know what it is about crying. It must be infectious, I guess. A bit like yawning really, I suppose. Somebody yawns and you want to yawn too. Perhaps that's a conditioned reflex. Or something atavistic, dating back to our tribal ancestry. When, if the headman yawned, everybody yawned and the tribe all went to bed. Or, if the headman cried, you joined him too, in a good old howling session. I'm not too hot on the history of man, so I couldn't say for a certainty.

* A Lazlo Woodbine thriller.

What I could say for certain was this, however.

It wasn't *my* fault.

OK, I might have started Colin off, but he was only faking it. And Fangio is a sissy boy and the pig-faced dame had it coming. And as for the solitary cyclist and the three students and the retired colourman and the two young women from Essex and the humpty-backed geezer and the continuity girl from *Blue Peter* and the lady with the preposterous bosom and that oik with the mobile phone, who said he'd call for an ambulance, well sure, OK, I might have pointed out their shortcomings, when they came muscling in to what clearly was none of their business. But for them all to start bawling their eyes out and saying that it was all *my* fault, that was laying it thicker than a concrete coat on a Baghdad bombproof bunker.

I mean, blaming *me*?

I could have wept.

In fact, I nearly did.

'Shut up!' I shouted. 'Shut up the lot of you.'

'Waaaaaah,' they went, in chorus.

'Will you stop all this weeping, you bunch of witless wimps?'

'Waaaaaah!' they reiterated, somewhat louder this time.

'He called me Quasimodo,' whined the humpty-backed geezer.

'He said I had a face like a cow's behind,' squalled a woman with a face like a cow's behind.

'He impugned my manhood,' snivelled a closet shirtlifter.

'He referred to me as a pretentious ninny,' ululated a thespian.

'He murdered my daddy!' howled Colin.

There was a lot of silence then.

'He did *what*?' asked the guy with the sore on his lip, which, I'd mentioned in passing, was probably the pox.

'He murdered my poor dear daddy. Shot him down in an alleyway.'

'I did nothing of the kind,' I rightfully protested.

'Assassin!' cried a crying lady, who, let's face it, *did* look a lot like Jabba the Hutt.

'Murderer!' shrieked the bloke with the birthmark that I'd drawn attention to.

'String him up,' yelled the woman with the questionable hairdo that I'd well and truly questioned.

'I'll get a rope,' hollered Fangio.

'Oi, Fange,' said I. 'Turn it in.'

'Sorry, Laz, I got carried away.'

'Murdered my poor dear daddy,' went Colin again.

And would you believe it?

Or even if you wouldn't.

The whole damn lot of them went for *me*!

'If you ask *me*,' said Johnny Boy, 'we're lost.'

'I'm not asking you,' said Icarus Smith.

'No need to be shirty,' said Johnny Boy. 'Just because I put you straight about the relationship you have with your brother.'

'It isn't *that*,' said Icarus Smith, even though it was. 'But actually, I think you're right. We're lost.'

They had wandered a goodly way amongst the corridors of the Ministry of Serendipity. They had left the barber far behind, strapped into his chair with his Velocette in his mouth. But now, somewhere in the middle of what might have been anywhere, they were well and truly lost, which wasn't a nice thing to be.

'Perhaps we should retrace our steps.'

'No,' said Icarus. 'We'll go on. We'll leave this to fate. Which way would you choose?'

'How about turning left here?'

'Right it is then,' said Icarus.

As they walked and wandered, Johnny Boy tried to lighten things up with tales of the music halls. But Icarus darkened things down again with a tale of a film he'd seen about miners who got trapped underground.

'We might be going in circles,' said Johnny Boy. 'You do that, you know, if you try to walk in a straight line. One of your legs is always a tiny bit shorter than the other, so eventually you walk round in a big circle.'

'Does that work if both of your legs are short?' asked Icarus.

'Don't be horrid,' said Johnny Boy. 'You'll make me want to cry.'

The crying howling mob closed in upon me, but I wasn't going down without a fight. I was prepared to stand my ground and dish out as good as I got. I'd raise my fists and fight a fair fight and devil take the hindparts.

But I was severely outnumbered here.

So I whipped out the trusty Smith and Where's-this-all-gonna-end and let off a couple of shots at the ceiling.

Which started the sprinkler system.

And set off the fire alarm.

Way down deep in the Ministry of Serendipity, other alarms started ringing.

'I think the barber's broken free,' said Johnny Boy. 'What should we do now?'

'I would say, run,' said Icarus. 'But I'm not sure just in which direction we should run.'

'Up might be a good plan,' said Johnny Boy.

'Run *up*?'

'Head up. Up and out of here.'

Sounds of running footsteps could now be heard.

'There,' said Icarus. 'There's a ladder fastened to the wall. It leads up some kind of shaft.'

'That would be the one then. Let's get a move on before the guards get us.'

'Get him!' shouted the bloke with the bulldog jowls which I'd said could be cured by surgery. 'Get the murderer, batter him good.'

And suddenly I found myself in a maelstrom of flailing fists and battering boots.

'I can hear their boots getting nearer,' said Johnny Boy, halfway up the shaft that led to somewhere. 'How are you doing up there, Icarus? Can you see daylight?'

'Er, not exactly,' the lad called back. 'Just a sort of manhole cover. And I can't seem to get it open.'

'They're getting closer, Icarus, I can hear them. They're coming from all directions.'

They came at me from all directions, down as well as up and all about. I pride myself that with my daily workout regime* I am always in peak condition and can take a blow to the solar plexus without even flinching. However, I'd never quite planned on taking quite so many blows and all at the same time.

'I'll have to blow it open,' called Icarus.

'You'll have to *what*?'

* Now available on video. *Workout with Woodbine* is priced at £15.99 at all reputable retail outlets.

'Blow open the manhole cover.'

'How?'

'I took the liberty of relocating a stick or two of SHITE from the captain's pocket while we were in my brother's office. I thought they might come in handy one day. Do you have a box of matches?'

'Sadly no,' called Johnny Boy. 'How about you?'

'Er, no.'

'No!' I tried a 'no' and I also tried a 'have mercy' and also 'you've got the wrong fellow here' and 'I have a heart condition' – but callously aloof to all my pleas, even those regarding the potential damage to my trenchcoat and fedora, the baying mob beat seventeen brass bells of St Trinian's out of me, then hoisted me into the air, marched me over to the bar's rear door and flung me out into the alleyway.

Well, at least it *was* an alleyway.

But boy did it hurt when I hit it.

I was bloody and bruised and chopped up and chaffed, my trenchcoat was in ribbons and my hat had gone missing. And as I lay there in the mud, wondering just how many bones had been broken, I was further saddened to hear the sound of a handgun being cocked.

Especially as I knew the sound of that cocking action all too well. For it was the sound of my trusty Smith and Where's-all-that-help-when-you-need-it-now?

I looked up through the eye that didn't have a big brown plum growing out of it, to view the face of my would-be executioner.

'You're dead meat, Mr Handbag,' he said.

'We're dead meat,' called Johnny Boy.

'No we're not,' called Icarus. 'I'll find a way to light this fuse.'

'But we'll get blown up and melted too.'

'This stuff is directional. It will blow *up* if you aim it upwards.'

'But we don't have a match to light it.'

'I'll think of something.'

A torch lit up Johnny Boy.

'Come down from there,' called the voices, accompanied by the sounds of guns being cocked. 'Come down out of there or you're—'

'Dead meat?' said Icarus Smith.

'Dead meat,' said Colin, third child of God. 'There's just the two of us now, Mr Handbag.'

'Now hold on, fella,' I said. 'Don't do anything foolish that I might regret. I know who you are. *What* you are. I'm working for your mother.'

'My mother?'

'Eartha Godalming, widow of God. Big fat ugly dame with a face like a bag full of car parts.'

'What has my mother got to do with this?'

'I've seen the will,' I said, spitting out a bit of blood, to add a little extra drama. 'God's last will and testament. You're in the frame for the murder.'

'What do you mean?'

'The will's a fake. The Earth gets left to you, instead of the meek, who were supposed to inherit it. I know the truth. I worked it out.'

'You know nothing, Mr Handbag. I didn't fake the will.'

'I know that.' I spat out a wee bit more blood, and what seemed like a couple of teeth. 'I know it wasn't you.'

'I think you know too much, Mr Handbag.'

'I know the truth,' said I. 'And I can help you.'

'I don't need any help. I can take care of everything myself. I've got this world under control. Under my control. Do you have any brothers, Mr Handbag?'

'Me?' I said. 'No, I'm an only child. They broke the mould before they made me.'

'Well, I have a brother. A very famous brother. Jesus Christ, his name is. And all my life I've lived in his shadow. But not any more. Not any more.'

Colin's finger tightened on the trigger. And I stared into the barrel of my gun.

'No,' I said. 'Don't shoot me. I can help you.'

Colin shook his head. 'Just let me ask you one question,' he said.

'Anything,' said I.

'What's red and white and dressed as a handbag and lies dead in an alleyway?'

And then, believe it.

Or believe it not.

He put my gun against my head and went and pulled the trigger.

16

They say that your whole life flashes in front of your eyes at the moment before you die. Or rather, at the moment when you *think* you're going to die. And friends, I have to confess that I was pretty certain at that moment, there in the alleyway, that I *was* going to die.

And I can tell *you*, that my whole life *did* flash right in front of my eyes.

And what a life it was!

I'd truly forgotten many of the great things that I'd done. The noble deeds that I'd performed. The seemingly unsolvable cases that I'd solved. The awards I'd been awarded. The accolades I'd had accoladed all over me. The beautiful women I'd made love to. The fast cars I'd driven. The exotic places I'd seen. The friends I'd known. The laughter. And the joy.

I'd been there. Done that. And bought, not only the T-shirt, but a place in the hearts of millions. I had been Lazlo Woodbine, the greatest detective of them all. And not many people can say that about their lives.

In fact, none can, but me.

So, if this was to be my time, I would face the great unknown with dignity. Accept my fate. Turn a brave face to the ultimate adversity. Go out with a smile on my face and a song on my lips.

'Have mercy!' I screamed. 'Don't kill me.'

But he squeezed the trigger all the same.

And then there was an almighty flash.

And Colin just vanished away.

Huh?

My trusty Smith and Well-I-never-did dropped onto my head, nearly taking my good eye out, and I had the strange sensation that I was now all covered in melted goo.

'Come on,' called a voice that I knew. 'Let's go.'

I raised my battered head and stared dizzily at the spot where Colin had been standing but a moment before.

That spot was now an open manhole and clambering out of this was the lad called Icarus, closely followed by his little dolly chum.

Icarus stared down upon my broken remains and his jaw dropped as slack as a sloe-eyed slapper at a slumlord's slumber party.

'What are you doing here?' he asked.

And I might well have asked him the self-same question. But I chose instead to ask him this: 'Whatever happened to Colin?'

'Colin?' said Icarus.

'Colin, the third child of God. He was standing right there on that manhole cover and now he's just, well, gone.'

'Oh,' said Icarus Smith. And it was the kind of oh that I wouldn't wear as a Homburg.

'Aaagh! They're coming after us,' cried the little man. 'Do something, Icarus, please.'

Icarus glanced around and about the alleyway. 'The

dumpster,' said he. 'Give me a hand to move the dumpster. You too, brother.'

'I'm *not* your goddamn brother,' said I. 'And I can't help, I'm all broken up.'

'Never mind.' The kid grabbed hold of the big dumpster wheelie bin thing and with the help of his small companion dragged it over the manhole. 'That should hold them,' he said.

'Kid,' said I, 'you turn up in the damnedest places. I reckon I'll thank you this time. And I'll . . .'

But I didn't get to say too much more after that. Because with all the beatings I'd taken and with the broken up bits and bobs and frankly with the stress I'd been under, staring death in the face and all, I lapsed from consciousness and found myself falling one more bloody time, down into that deep dark whirling pit of oblivion.

Yes siree.

By golly.

'What's the news?' said Icarus. He was sitting in a doctor's office. The office smelled of feet and fish and fear. A fetid fermentation. The doctor had my case notes on his desk. He leafed through them as he spoke to Icarus.

'Your brother is a very sick man,' said the doctor, adjusting his spectacles and doing that thing with his pencil. 'He was badly beaten up and has not only several broken bones, but some internal injuries also.'

Icarus nodded thoughtfully. 'So when do you think you'll have him up and about?'

'Weeks. Months perhaps.'

'He can't be injured as badly as *that*.'

'It's not so much the physical injuries. It's more his mental health that worries me.'

'Ah,' said Icarus. 'We share in that particular worry.'

'He seems to think he's a detective,' said the doctor, buffing his stethoscope up on his sleeve. 'He is clearly delusional. Claims that he's on the biggest case that ever there was. Something to do with the murder of God. Can you imagine that?'

Icarus shook his head.

'And he talks to himself. When he thinks that he can't be overheard. He seems to suffer from multiple personality disorder. I've heard him arguing with an imaginary character called Barry. He blames this Barry for everything that's happened to him.'

Icarus nodded once again.

'I'm wondering perhaps whether he's tormented by some childhood trauma,' said the doctor. 'I know he's got a drink problem and a broken marriage and I feel that he's trying to reach out to his feminine side.'

Icarus nodded, then shook his head, and then he nodded again.

'So I think it would be for the best,' said the doctor, 'if you signed this form, committing him to a course of psychiatric treatment.'

Icarus nodded and Icarus grinned.

'Lend me your biro,' he said.

'Now that was just plain mean,' said Johnny Boy, looking up from his drink. 'Getting your brother banged up in a loony bin.

They were sitting once more in the Station Hotel and Icarus hadn't stopped grinning since they got there.

'It's not a loony bin,' he told Johnny Boy. 'It's a psychiatric hospital. It will be for the best. He really does need the treatment.'

'You realize', said Johnny Boy, 'that you might just have signed his death warrant.'

'It wasn't a death warrant. Just a form to commit him to care.'

'And he's been in that hospital for five days already, which means that his week is nearly up. And if he doesn't solve his case, by tomorrow, God's wife is going to punish him big time.'

'But the case *is* solved. Colin was the culprit and Colin died in an accident.'

'Nothing is solved,' said Johnny Boy. 'Take a look over at the barman.'

Icarus glanced over at the barman. The barman wasn't Fangio, but Icarus hadn't expected him to be. The barman was the usual barman, the one who wore Mr Cormerant's relocated watch fob.

But the barman's true form could now be seen by Icarus. The barman had quills that rose high above his green reptilian head.

'Nothing is solved,' said Johnny Boy once again.

'I'm working on it,' said Icarus. 'I haven't been idle. The men at the Ministry don't know that Colin is dead. I've forged memos using letter headings from Cormerant's briefcase. I've sent them to all departments at the Ministry, closing down the exo-cranial programme. And dismissing all the operatives in hairdresser's and barber's shops. *And* desisting from any further harassment of our good selves. I don't see what more I can do than that.'

'Nor me,' said Johnny Boy. 'But the demons and angels are still among us and only we know that they're here.'

'Perhaps there's nothing we can do but wait.'

'Wait for *what*?'

'Wait for a new generation to grow up. A generation that doesn't have its head massaged. That generation will see the truth.'

'That's a cop-out ending, if ever there was one,' said Johnny Boy. 'Have you given up on being a relocator now? Perhaps now your brother is in the loony bin, you don't have to try any more. You don't have anything to prove. Is that it?'

'No, that's *not* it.' Icarus sighed. Perhaps that *was* it. Perhaps now, with his brother safely locked up, perhaps he no longer did have to prove anything.

'And something I haven't asked you,' said Johnny Boy. 'Whatever happened to your mum? Did Cormerant do something horrible to her when he went to your house to get the left luggage locker key you'd mailed to yourself?'

'No, she was out at the time. Apparently he smashed open the front door and simply snatched the envelope from the floor.'

'Well isn't that hunky-dory? So you don't even have any revenge to take. Let's just have another drink and wait for the next generation.'

'Give it a rest,' said Icarus. 'I've done all I can. I don't know what else I can do.'

'No,' said Johnny Boy, finishing his drink. 'You don't. But I bet your brother does. I'll bet if he was out of that loony bin and back on the case, he'd sort everything out.'

'He's too sick,' said Icarus. 'He's a regular dying detective. He's got broken bones and everything.'

'Has he hell,' said Johnny Boy. 'I've visited him. He's just got a couple of teeth missing and a few bruises. He could have been out of there and back on the case, if you hadn't signed his death warrant.'

Icarus went up to the bar to get in another round of drinks.

The barman with the watch fob leered at him. Icarus stared into the evil face. The long reptilian head, the eyes with their vertical pupils, the quivering quills, the hideous insect mouthparts.

'You haven't put any little treats in my direction lately,' said the barman, fingering the watch fob with a terrible talon. 'You'll just have to pay for this round of drinks. Nothing comes for free in this world, you know.'

Icarus paid and returned with the drinks to his table.

'We're going to the hospital,' he said. 'We're going to get my brother.'

'I'm an only child,' I said. 'I don't know why you keep going on about me having a brother.'

'I do have your case notes here,' said the doctor. 'I do know who you really are.'

'I'm Woodbine,' I said. 'Lazlo Woodbine,' adding, just for the hell of it, 'Some call me Laz.'

'Woodbine,' and the doctor nodded. At least he'd got my name right. 'The world famous private eye. Everybody knows his name, but no-one can put a face to it.'

'That's the way that I do business.'

'Are you sleeping well?' the doctor asked.

'I haven't slept for five days. I daren't sleep, I'll give away the ending if I sleep.'

'Barry will give the ending away, will he?'

'I don't want to talk about Barry,' I said. 'Forget about Barry.'

'All right, let's forget about Barry. Let's talk about you. Mr Lazlo Woodbine, private eye.'

'Good choice of topic,' I said. 'Could I have another wide-awake pill?'

'Now according to my notes . . .' The doctor was at those goddamn case notes once again. 'According to my notes, Lazlo Woodbine works in only four locations.'

'You got it,' I said. 'The office, the bar, the alleyway and the rooftop. No good detective ever needs more.'

'Not even a bedroom, for all that gratuitous sex you genre detectives are so noted for?'

'There are some promises that even a detective can't keep.'

'So you stick to the four locations.'

'I do,' said I. And I did.

The doctor stretched out his arms and put his hands behind his head. 'So how do you explain your present location?' he asked.

'Name any location,' said the taxi driver. 'Anywhere in Inner or Greater London and I'll tell you how to get to it from here.'

It wasn't the same taxi driver. But you'd have been hard pressed to tell the difference. He had that same curious thing with hair on the left hand side and that same odd business with the tongue when he used the word 'plinth'.*

'I'm not really in the mood,' said Johnny Boy.

'Oh go on,' said the cabbie. 'It will make me go faster.'

'All right,' said Johnny Boy. 'How do you get to the Flying Swan?'

'That's easy,' said the cabbie. 'You go up Abbadon Street, along Moby Dick Terrace, turn left into Sprite Street, right into . . .'

'He's making it up,' said Johnny Boy.

'I think they always do,' said Icarus Smith.

*

* Have you tried that with a woman yet? Yes? Well, I told you it was sexy, didn't I?

'You make all this up,' said the doctor. 'It's all a fantasy. If you were the real Lazlo Woodbine, you couldn't be sitting here now.'

'Hm,' said I. 'Well.'

'Over the last five days you have told me a story that is a complete fantasy. About a voice in your head that put in a word with the widow of God. About a drug which enables people to see angels and demons. And if I'm not mistaken, you've been under the impression that I'm one of these demons. One of these "wrong'uns", am I correct?'

'Well,' said I. 'Hm.'

'And there are these bars that you go to, where the barman is always your friend Fangio. Who was a fat boy and now is a thin boy, because he bopped you on the head, so that you could stay within the rules of your genre. The nineteen-fifties American detective genre. One that only truly existed in fiction. You live your life in fiction, my friend. You have no hold on reality.'

'No,' I said. 'I do, I really do.'

'You don't,' said the doctor. 'Just think about this. Every time you are in what you call a "tricky situation", you are rescued.'

I shrugged.

'And who rescues you?'

I shrugged again.

'Your brother rescues you,' said the doctor. 'And the evil men who have you in the sticky situation, the doctor and the third child of God, another brother, you note, who was telling you about living in the shadow of *his* brother, these evil men vanish away to melted goo the moment *your* brother arrives to save you.'

'Coincidence,' I said.

222

'Tell me about your brother,' said the doctor.

'I like to think of myself as a relocator,' said the cabbie. 'I re-locate people. Take them from one location to another. In my small way I help to put the world to rights. If people weren't in the wrong places at the wrong times, there'd be no need for cabbies. We put people where they want to be. Where they should be. You could learn a lot from cabbies.'

Icarus looked at Johnny Boy.

And Johnny Boy looked back at him.

'If I asked you how to get to Shangri La, do you think you might drive a little faster?' said Johnny Boy.

'Perhaps *quite* fast,' said Icarus, glancing into the driver's mirror. 'There's a long dark automobile following us.'

'Are you following me?' asked the doctor. 'Do you see where my reasoning is taking us?'

'We're here,' said Icarus, paying off the cabbie. 'Please wait, we'll be back in just a minute, we have to pick up my brother.'

'Sibling rivalry,' said the doctor. 'You admire your brother, but you can't bring yourself to admit it. He is your hero. He always arrives in the nick of time to get you out of your sticky situation.'

'No,' I said. 'It's not like that at all.'

'I don't like this at all,' puffed Johnny Boy, as he and Icarus ran towards the entrance of the hospital. 'That horrid dark automobile again. Why is it following us?'

'Perhaps my forged memos didn't convince them. Come on, try to keep up.'

'The pretence you're keeping up is nothing more than that,' said the doctor. 'If you could come to terms with your relationship with your brother, you would be well on the way to recovery.'

'Which way to Mr Woodbine's room?' asked Icarus.

The male nurse looked up from the reception desk. He had on a little badge that said, 'Hi, my name is Cecil.'

'Mr Who?' asked male nurse Cecil.

'Mr Woodbine,' said the breathless Icarus. 'He's being held in the psychiatric wing. I've come here to sign his release form.'

Nurse Cecil made little lip-smacking sounds. 'There's a lot of paperwork involved in that kind of thing,' he said. 'Perhaps you should make an appointment. Next week some time.'

'Next week will be too late. I have to see him now and take him out of here.'

'Are you a relative?'

'I'm his brother. I'm Icarus Smith. I signed the form to commit him.'

'How come your name's Smith and his is Woodstock?'

'It's Wood*bine*,' said Icarus. 'Lazlo Woodbine. Some call him Laz. Not that I ever have.'

'Shit!' said Johnny Boy. 'They're coming in the door, Icarus. Two of them and they're wrong'uns.'

Icarus made fists at male nurse Cecil. 'Which room is my brother in?' he demanded to be told.

'I shall have to ask you to leave,' said Cecil. 'Leave of your own free will, or I'll get out the big stick that I punish the naughty loons with and ram it right up your . . .'

★

224

'Tunnel of love,' said the doctor. 'We call it our tunnel of love therapy. We will bring together you and your brother. Take you slowly through the darkness of despair and out into the light of love. At the other end of the tunnel.'

'I don't belong here in the psychiatric wing,' I told the doctor. 'You've got it all wrong. I'm not a loon.'

'We never use the word loon here,' said the doctor. 'All our staff are highly trained psychiatric carers. You'll be treated well here. Here where it's quiet and peaceful.'

'That's SHITE!' said Johnny Boy, as he and Icarus ran along. 'Another stick of SHITE. What are you going to do with that?'

'What do you think I'm going to do with it?'

'Blow the door off your brother's room?'

'Or wherever he's being held.'

'I never did ask how you managed to light the fuse last time without any matches.'

'Then don't ask this time either.'

'Time,' said the doctor, rising from his desk and taking himself over to the door. 'Time is all you really need, Mr Woodbine. Time to put all the pieces back into the right places. Time to understand the true relationship that you have with your brother. That you do admire him, which is why you have created this fantasy life for yourself. Why you always believe that he can ultimately get you out of any sticky situation, although you remain in denial of this.'

The doctor took down his jacket from the back of the door.

'This door,' said Icarus.

'Why?' asked Johnny Boy.

'Fate,' said Icarus. 'Let's leave it to fate.'

And Icarus lit up the SHITE.

I looked dumbly at the doctor. I'm rarely lost for words, especially wise ones. But I was lost for words now.

I mean, hey. This was Woodbine he was dealing with. Lazlo Woodbine, private eye. The greatest dick that ever there was. I wasn't some wimp with a brother fixation. I could handle *myself*. I'm the best in the business and I didn't need this creep trying to make out that I was some kind of a loon.

'**!!!**'

... went the silent explosive.

'That silence doesn't get any less loud,' said Johnny Boy.

The doctor was there, putting on his coat.

And then the doctor was gone.

Gone.

Just gone!

Melted to a steamy pool of goo upon the floor.

Icarus burst into the office.

'Come on, Laz,' he said. 'I need your help. I'm busting you out of here.'

I stared at the guy as he stood in the doorway.

And friends, I got all choked up with tears.

'Brother,' I said, breaking down in a blubber. 'Brother Icarus, it's you. I'm not Lazlo Woodbine any more. I'm cured. I'm your brother Edwin. Come and give me a hug.'

17

'Come on, Laz, we have to go,' said Icarus breathing hard.
'There's wrong'uns after us. Come on.' The resident
patient had his arms out for a hug. Icarus shook him by the
shoulders. 'There's no time. Hurry.'

'Come on, Mr Woodbine,' Johnny Boy tugged at the
patient's leg. 'We need you, we do. Come on.'

'I want to give my brother a hug,' blubbed the man who
once was Woodbine.

Johnny Boy's mouth became a perfect O and then an
inverted U. 'He's lost it,' he gasped. 'He's not working in the
first person any more.'

Icarus grasped the weeper's hand. 'They've done something
to him. They've drugged him up.' He gave the hand a squeeze.
'Come with me and hurry now,' he said.

Johnny Boy scampered over to the doctor's desk.

'What are you doing?' Icarus glanced to the door. Marching
footstep noises were coming from the corridor.

'We can't go out without his trusty Smith and Wassaname.'
Johnny Boy rooted around in the desk drawers. 'Got it,'

he said. 'Oh, and *this*.'

'What's that?'

'The spectremeter.'

'Bring *that*!' said Icarus. 'And come on.'

They didn't leave through the melted door hole, they left via the window. Windows are always good in movies, good for busting through. All that splintering glass in slow motion. It never fails to excite.

'You could have leapt right through that window,' puffed Johnny Boy, as he and Icarus dragged the bewildered brotherly type across the hospital lawn.

'It was easier just to open it.' Icarus yanked and pulled. 'Come on, Laz, you can go faster than that.'

'I need my bed,' blubbered the stumbler. 'I haven't slept for a week. I can't keep my eyes open. Take me home to Mum, Icarus. Tuck me into my cosy bed and send me off to the land of sleepy-byes.'

'What a wimpy little voice.' Johnny Boy pushed as Icarus pulled. 'Do you think he's trying to reach out to his feminine side?'

SMASH and CRASH went the window behind them as two demons burst through. Splintering glass in slow motion, in a manner which failed to excite Icarus.

'To the taxi,' cried the lad. 'Keep up, Mr Woodbine, please.'

The cabbie was chatting with a passer-by. 'You go along the Road to Morocco,' he said, 'turn left at the Road to Rio, right at the Road to Mandalay, straight along the Road to . . .'

Icarus came puffing up.

'Ah,' said the cabbie. 'You're back. I was just telling this gentleman how you—'

Icarus gave the cabbie a head-butt.

The cabbie fell down in a flustering heap.

Icarus dragged open the rear door of the taxi and thrust the blubbering stumbler inside. 'I'm relocating your taxi,' he told the groaning moaning cabbie, who was lying on the ground. 'I won't do any harm to it. You can have it back a little later.'

Icarus swung open the driver's door and keyed the cab's ignition.

Johnny Boy hastened into the taxi, slamming the door behind him.

The cabbie staggered to his feet. 'Stop, you bastard!' he managed to shout, as the tyres of his cab burned rubber and Icarus swerved away.

'You bloody bastard,' roared the cabbie. 'I'll . . .'

But then two demons knocked him once more from his feet.

'Bloody, bleeding . . .'

Doors slammed shut on the long dark automobile.

'My taxi, my taxi.' The cabbie dragged himself once more into the vertical plane.

And was promptly run down by the long dark automobile.

The passer-by looked on, as the two cars roared away into the distance.

'I suppose I'll never know how you get to Xanadu now,' said he.

'Put your foot down, Icarus,' shouted Johnny Boy. 'They're coming after us fast.'

Icarus put his foot down. 'Keep Laz awake!' he shouted back. 'Don't let him fall asleep.'

'Zzzzzz,' went the sleeper.

SMACK! went the hand of Johnny Boy. 'Wake up call for Mr Woodbine.'

The new evil chauffeur looked much like the old one, as may well have been mentioned before. But if not it will be now. He had the same evil-looking face, with that same business with the chin and the unusual birthmark above the right eyebrow which resembles the Penang peninsula. He even wore the same cuff links.

So no further description is necessary.

'Faster,' cried a voice behind him. It was the voice of Cormerant, and it was an angry voice. Cormerant sat in the car's rear seat, flanked by a deuce of demons. Hideous monsters the pair of them were, but not quite so hideous as Cormerant. There was something even worse about him now. A fearsome energy. Sparkling oil-beads of colour ran up and down his quills. His cruel reptilian eyes appeared lit from within. His scaly features glistened and the horrible insect mouthparts chewed and sucked.

Icarus chewed upon his bottom lip. 'Where to, Johnny Boy? Where should we go?'

'You're the relocator, relocate us.'

'Somehow I thought you might say that. Do you fancy a left at the top of the road here, or a right?'

'Definitely a left.'

'Right it is, then,' said Icarus.

They'd done the Chiswick High Road and the Chiswick Roundabout and now they were hurtling along the Kew Road at the bottom end of Brentford.

'Surprisingly little traffic for this time of day,' said Johnny Boy. 'Keep awake now, Mr Woodbine.' SMACK!

Icarus spun the taxi right, through red lights and up into the Ealing Road. The long dark automobile was definitely gaining.

It swerved right after them, mounting the safety island, shattering one of those little jobbie lights that drunks so love to sit upon and scattering several pedestrians into the bargain.

'What is all *that* about?' asked a scattered pedestrian called Pooley.

'Nothing to do with us, my friend,' his friend called Omally replied.

SMACK SMACK SMACK went the hand of Johnny Boy. 'I can't keep Mr Woodbine awake,' he shouted to Icarus.

Icarus leaned over and opened the glove compartment. It was full of gloves (they always are) but nothing else. Strapped to the floor was the medical kit that cabbies always carry. It's a tradition, or an old charter or a City of London Commercial Vehicle Regulation number 432, or something. Icarus ripped the kit from its mount and the box fell open, showering him with hundreds of small plastic sachets filled with glistening white powder.

'I always wondered how cabbies managed to work such long hours under such stressful conditions and still remain so unfailingly cheerful,' said Icarus. 'Here, give him some of this.' And he flung several handfuls of plastic sachets over his shoulder.

'But surely this is . . .'

'Just pour a bag or two up his nose. That should keep him awake.'

BASH went the bumper of the long dark automobile into the taxi's rear end.

'Oh!' went Johnny Boy, lost in a sudden snowstorm.

Icarus swerved the taxi off the road and up onto the pavement.

Shoppers and strollers and dog-walking debutantes screamed and dived for cover.

The long dark automobile mounted the pavement, bringing down a lamppost.

Johnny Boy knelt on the slumberer's chest and emptied sachets of white stuff into his nose.

'I'm going to try to lose them in the back streets,' Icarus shouted. 'Do your thing with the spectremeter again when we're out of sight.'

'He's still not waking up,' Johnny Boy shouted back. 'And I've poured at least a quarter-pound of this stuff up his hooter.'

'Then give him the missing three-quarters. In for a penny, in for a pound.' Icarus signalled right and then turned left at the football ground.

Brentford football ground is rightly famous. Not only because Brentford normally contributes at least four of its players to every England World Cup squad, but because it is the only football ground in the country which has a pub at each of its four corners.

The four pubs in question are the Copper Beeches, the Golden Prince-nez, the Sussex Vampire and the Mazarin Stone.

Out of these, the Mazarin Stone is undoubtedly the best for a pub lunch. Run by one Reginald Musgrave, inheritor of certain West Sussex estates and a manor house at Hurlstone, it serves many an illustrious client and it was here that the famous Brentford naval treaty was signed, which officially ended Britain's war against Spain. Built on the site of the original Priory School, it boasts two ghosts, a veiled lodger and a creeping man, and its upper rooms are available for parties and wedding receptions. There's karaoke every Tuesday night and a raffle on Sunday lunchtimes.

'Get ready to use the spectremeter,' shouted Icarus.

'Aye aye, captain. Oooh, I feel really odd. It's good odd though, not bad.'

Johnny Boy tugged the spectremeter from his pocket and smiled stupidly at it. 'This is a really nice spectremeter,' he said. 'This is the nicest spectremeter in all the world.'

'Turn it on then, please.' Icarus glanced into his mirror. Johnny Boy now resembled a miniature snowman, but at least the sleeper was starting to stir.

'Whoa!' he went, jerking upright. 'Oh yeah! Wow! God do I feel great. Wow! I mean, hey!'

'I love you, man,' said Johnny Boy.

'I love you too,' the other replied.

'We've lost them, boss. Which way did they go?' The evil chauffeur peered through his tinted windscreen.

'I hate them!' Cormerant rocked in his seat. 'Find them! Kill them!'

One of the demons peered through a tinted rear window.

'There.' He pointed. 'There they go, down there.'

The chauffeur tried to reverse the car, but there was a dust-cart coming up from behind and the back roads of Brentford are narrow.

'Get to the top end of the road!' bawled Cormerant. 'Cut them off. Get to it.'

'You got it, sir.' The evil chauffeur put his foot down.

'*Drive!*' roared Cormerant. '*Drive!*'

'That's my brother driving,' said a foolishly grinning individual with a lot of white stuff round his hooter. 'He's my hero, my brother, I love that man.'

'I love him too,' said Johnny Boy.

'When we were kids,' said the foolish grinner, 'he used to

lock me in a suitcase and push it under our mum's bed.'

'I never did,' shouted Icarus.

The taxi scraped along a row of parked cars, sending up a glorious shower of sparks.

'You did too. And you used to hide my teddy and leave clues around the house that I'd have to follow so I could find him again.'

'Lies, every bit of it.' Icarus knocked an old boy off his bike. 'Sorry,' he called through the window.

'There, he's said sorry,' said Johnny Boy. 'He wants you to forgive him.'

'Oh, it's all right,' said the foolish grinner, putting his arm around Johnny Boy's shoulder. 'I love him. I forgive him. It really got to me though, that suitcase. Gave me a real terror of cases. Suitcases, briefcases, handbags, shoulder bags, duffel bags, pormanteaus, dressing cases, pigskin valises, steamer trunks, sea chests, Gladstone bags, overnight bags . . .'

'You sure know your luggage,' said Johnny Boy.

'Buddy, in my business, knowing your luggage can mean the difference between . . .'

'Go on.'

'I don't know. Could we stop off for some lunch, do you think? I'm getting really hungry. We could have a walk in Kew Gardens afterwards. It's really beautiful there. Watch out for that lady with the pram.'

'Sorry,' called Icarus, out of the window.

'And there's a long dark automobile blocking the street ahead.'

Icarus put his foot on the brake and swerved the taxi around.

The woman, who was picking up her baby from the road, fled screaming as Icarus performed a remarkable U-turn.

234

You can do that, you know, in a taxi. They have virtually the smallest turning circle of any wheeled vehicle; cabbies are always proud of telling people that. But then cabbies have so many things to be proud of. They're wonderful people, are cabbies.

And of course, they *never* use drugs. Especially whatever weirded-out mixture it was that Icarus had found.

Icarus put his foot once more to the floor and the taxi took off at the hurry-up, through the maze of roads that was back street Brentford.

It rushed up Abbadon Street, along Moby Dick terrace, turned left into Sprite Street and right into the Ealing Road once more and passed the Flying Swan again.

'That cabbie you head-butted was quite right about his directions to the Flying Swan,' said Johnny Boy. 'They *do* have the knowledge, those boys.'

'I love taxi drivers,' said the grinner, giving Johnny Boy a hug. 'And I love you and I love my brother Icarus.'

'Nice,' said Johnny Boy, licking his snow-covered fingers.

Icarus turned left at the Mazarin Stone and they passed the football ground once more.

'After them! Faster, Faster!' Cormerant made taloned fists.

'I'm doing my best, sir,' the chauffeur said. 'But it's a bloody labyrinth round here and those taxis have virtually the smallest turning circle of any wheeled vehicle. And they are, of course, driven by highly skilled professionals who have the knowledge and never use drugs.'

Cormerant smote the chauffeur on the back of his smartly capped head. 'Drive after them. Faster, you buffoon.'

'They're going down *there*!' A demon pointed as the taxi came momentarily into view.

'No,' said the other demon. '*There*. They're going down there.'

'No, they're coming *up* there,' said the chauffeur. 'No, hang about, you might be right.' The long dark automobile raked along a row of cars on the other side of Mafeking Avenue.

'I think we've lost them,' said Icarus. 'Switch off the spectremeter.'

'*Off?*' said Johnny Boy.

'Yes, switch it *off*.'

'Oh,' said Johnny Boy. 'I hadn't got around to switching it *on* yet. Mind out for that wheelchair.'

'Sorry,' called Icarus, out of the window.

'I don't think he's ever *really* sorry,' said the grinner. 'Our dad was in the removal business, you know.'

'I didn't,' said Johnny Boy. 'Go on.'

'Icarus used to shuffle up his delivery schedules.'

'I never did. Will you switch on the spectremeter? *Please?*'

'And our dad couldn't read very well, so he used to deliver all the furniture and stuff to the wrong locations.'

'That's not true.'

'It is.'

'Perhaps I *did* have this switched on all the time,' said Johnny Boy. 'Is this *off* or *on?*'

'I don't know,' said the grinner, suddenly ceasing to grin. 'But I seem to have double vision. I can see two of you now.'

'And I can see two of you.'

'There!' shouted one of the demons. 'They're coming straight at us. Smash into them.'

'It's two cabs,' said the chauffeur. 'Driving side by side.'

'Well smash into both of them.'

'Get out of the way!' shouted Icarus. There was a taxi in front of him now.

'Is that *us*?' asked Johnny Boy, climbing up. 'That looks like the back of Mr Woodbine's head.'

'What, *the* Mr Woodbine?' asked the erstwhile grinner. 'Lazlo Woodbine, private eye? The world famous detective? Is that *really* him, do you think?'

'I'm backing up,' said Icarus. 'I'm going to go another way.'

'There's a taxi coming behind us now, really fast.'

Smash went something into something.

No it didn't.

'They went right through us,' said the chauffeur. 'Like ghosts.'

Cormerant made tighter fists. 'They're using the bloody spectremeter. Just smash into every taxi you see, we'll get the right one sooner or later.'

'Whoa!' went Johnny Boy. 'We just went right through ourselves. Or rather, ourselves just went right through us. Or was it . . .'

'Far out,' said the grinner, grinning again. 'I'm tripping out here, man. So, like I was saying. Our dad got into real trouble with the company he worked for, because he kept delivering stuff to the wrong locations. And eventually they sacked him. And then he was on the dole and we couldn't keep up the mortgage payments on the house and we had a nice house and he had to sell it and get a tiny one instead. And it was all the fault of Icarus and I was going to tell Mum, but Icarus said he'd lock me in the suitcase if I did and never let me out.'

'He's making this up,' said Icarus, desperately swerving to

237

avoid an oncoming taxi which turned out to be driven by himself.

'I never told Mum, but Icarus used to have nightmares. He'd wake up screaming that he could put everything back in the right places.'

'Shut up!' shouted Icarus. 'Shut up, or I'll throw you out of the taxi. You're no good to us like this. Pull yourself together. Be Lazlo Woodbine again.'

'You want *me* to be Lazlo Woodbine? How could I be Lazlo Woodbine? That was him in the other taxi, wasn't it?'

'That was *you* in the other taxi.'

'Johnny Boy said it was Lazlo Woodbine. When are we going to have lunch?'

Icarus Smith glared over his shoulder. 'You've *got* to help us,' he growled. 'You *are* Woodbine. The greatest detective of them all. You tell him, Johnny Boy.'

'Stop being horrid to your brother,' said Johnny Boy.

'Oh no!' shouted Icarus. 'Look out.'

Something smashed into something else.

No it didn't.

Yes it did.

The long dark automobile ploughed head on into the taxi, mashing up its bonnet to oblivion and bringing the 'Oh no'ing driver through the windscreen in slow motion amidst the shattering glass.

The driver crashed down onto the bonnet of the long dark automobile.

'That's him,' shouted Cormerant. 'Get out and shoot him dead.'

The demons hastened to oblige.

One took hold of the crash victim's bloody head and twisted it around.

238

'Kill him!' shouted Cormerant. 'I've suffered enough of this young man.'

The demon did as he was told.

And shot the young man dead.

18

It really was true.

About your whole life flashing right in front of your eyes at that terrible final moment. As the taxi struck the long dark automobile and Icarus Smith shouted 'Oh no!' his whole life flashed before him, right in front of his eyes.

And it really hadn't been the best of lives.

Icarus could see himself as a child, locking his brother in the suitcase and pushing it under his mother's bed. Tormenting his brother, hiding his teddy, making him play the manic detective in order to find it again. Shuffling up his father's delivery sheets and dreaming the guilt-ridden nightmares, where only he, Icarus Smith, could put the world to rights.

Icarus saw all this as the taxi's brakes failed and the cab ran into the long dark automobile.

Into the *rear* of the long dark automobile.

It was a considerable smash-up, but as the long dark automobile was already ground into the front of another taxi, the long dark automobile didn't move very much at all.

The demon who had despatched the driver of the other cab looked up from his murderous business and wiped away at the spatterings of blood that sprinkled his terrible visage.

'I think I just shot the wrong bloke, sir,' he said.

And of course it was true.

An innocent man lay dead on the long dark bonnet of the long dark automobile. An innocent man who did bear an uncanny resemblance to Icarus Smith. Could almost, in fact, have been taken for his twin. What are the chances of that happening?

Eh?

'Kill the right one then,' shouted Cormerant. 'Hurry up. Do it now.'

'Right one, yes sir.' The demon hastened once more to oblige.

'Out of the taxi.' Icarus was out and dragging the rear door open.

'I'm all shook up,' said Johnny Boy.

'I'm hungry,' said the other. 'Are we going to have lunch now?'

Icarus bundled them out of the taxi. 'Run,' said he. 'It's the only hope we have.'

'Brother,' said the other, 'I'm really not in the mood to run.'

A gun went bang and a bullet parted a Ramón Navarro hairstyle.

'I'll race you, brother Icarus, come on.'

Icarus ran, and Johnny Boy ran and the man with the parted hairstyle ran as well.

The demons marched behind, quills high and quivering, evil reptiloid faces thrusting forward, nasty nasty mouthparts sucking in the air.

241

Oh, and guns held high and firing all the way.

The three men ran across the Ealing Road, towards the tower blocks on the other side. They ran across a forecourt area which seemed strangely deserted, considering the time of day, and then they ran between the first two mighty buildings.

Why do they call buildings buildings? Have you ever wondered about that? I mean a building is only a building when you're actually building it. When it's built, it's built. So they really shouldn't call them buildings, should they? They should be called builts.

'These builts are really high, aren't they?' said Johnny Boy, as he ran.

'These whats?' Icarus answered him.

'Oh nothing, just a thought.'

'In here,' said Icarus, 'quickly.' And he pushed upon a door.

The door was locked.

Icarus fumbled out his little roll of tools.

A bullet ricocheted off the doorpost.

'We're gonna die,' cried Johnny Boy. 'Hurry, Icarus, hurry.'

Icarus hurried.

The lock clicked and the door came open.

Icarus pushed the two men through the doorway. The little one with the terrified expression. The big one with the stupid look on his face.

Icarus slammed shut the door and locked it.

'There,' he said. 'We're safe.'

'There *what*?' said Johnny Boy. 'We're not safe. Those buggers will shoot the lock off.'

Icarus turned. They were in a corridor, *another corridor*! It seemed to be all corridors these days. And underground or overground, a corridor looks like a corridor. Except, of course, when it's a passage, or a hall. But then they're all pretty much the same when you get right down to it, except for the carpets. And perhaps the lighting; you can do a lot with a corridor if you light it tastefully. Not that you could have done much with this particular corridor. It looked really ill kept. Uncared for. This was an unloved corridor. It did have some stairs leading up from it, which was something, although not really something worth cheering about.

'Up the stairs,' shouted Icarus.

'Up?' said Johnny Boy. 'Since when did escape ever lie *up*?'

'It did the last time.'

'We were *underground* the last time.'

The sounds of gunfire echoed from without.

'*Up* it is,' said Johnny Boy, taking a very big breath.

'Brother,' said the other, 'you won't let those beastly things get me, will you? You will protect me?'

'Where's the gun?' said Icarus.

'Here,' said Johnny Boy.

'Then I'll hold them off. You run upstairs with my useless brother here and knock on someone's door. Call the police, or something.'

'And which police would that be? The good police, or the wrong'un police? Should I ask them to send cops without quills? Do you think they'll understand what I mean?'

'Are you trying to be difficult?'

'No, it's just . . .'

The sounds of close-quarters gunfire and the lock exploding from the door put paid to further conversation.

'*Up!*' said Johnny Boy. '*Up* it certainly is.'

And so they ran up. First up one staircase. Then another. And they ran along further corridors, knocking on doors and shouting for help. But do you know what? Not a single door opened to them. Not one. And why was that? Was it because the good people of Brentford turn deaf ears to callings for help? No, it wasn't that. Was it, then, that they were afraid to answer their doors, what with all the shooting going on, and everything? No, it wasn't even that. If it was anything at all, and it was, it was because, but for the three men running and the demons firing shots, the entire flat block was deserted.

There wasn't another living soul in that flat block.

And why was that?

Had all the occupants gone out shopping? No. Had they gone on holiday then, a coach outing, or something?

No, not even that.

They had all, in fact, moved. Every last one of them.

Because the tower block had been declared an unsafe structure. It was scheduled for demolition.

Today, actually.

In about fifteen minutes.

Now normally, when a local council decides to blow up one of its flat blocks, this gets on to the news and thousands of people turn up to watch the detonation and cheer as the block comes tumbling down. And the streets get sealed off for half a mile around and policemen stand in their shirt sleeves and smile at everybody and some cherub-faced kiddie who's won the 'Why I'd like to blow up the flat block' competition gets to light the blue touch-paper or press down a plunger of whatever and it's all a right old carry-on and how-do-you-do.

But not *here*.

Not in Brentford.

Brentford doesn't go in for all that hullabaloo.

Brentford does things in a quiet and sedate manner.

In Brentford, the council simply rehouses the flat block's occupants, in new and finer homes, then calls in the SAS to demolish the tower block with SHITE. So the flat block simply ceases to exist. In silence. In the twinkling of an eye.

Down on the ground level, the SAS were even now setting up the charges and unrolling metres of fuse.

Up on level twenty-three Icarus banged on more doors.

'Perhaps they've all gone to the shops,' puffed Johnny Boy.

'Or on holiday, on a coach outing. What do you think, brother Icarus?'

'I think we're in trouble here.'

'Oh, you'll get us out of it. You always get me out of every sticky situation.'

Sounds of marching feet came up the stairwell. Sounds of handguns being reloaded. Ugly sounds of sucking breath and grunting.

'Onward, ever upward,' said Icarus.

'I'm all done,' said Johnny Boy. 'Leave me here to die.'

'Icarus will save us, Johnny Boy, don't fear.'

Icarus gestured with the trusty Smith and Where's-the-sense-in-going-up-any-higher-why-not-simply-make-a-fight-of-it-here?

'Up,' urged Icarus. 'Up.'

But of course, going up has to stop eventually. Eventually you *are* up and you can't go up any more. Eventually, you hit the top and when you've hit it, you know, just know, exactly where your going up has got you.

They crashed out through a door and onto the tower block roof.

An acre of blank tarmac, relieved only by four of those whirly-whirly-air-conditioning-sucky-out-extractor-fan jobbies

245

that you always find on tower block roofs, along with all the pigeon poo.

Johnny Boy crawled onto the rooftop. 'Seventy-two floors,' he wheezed. 'But at least we got here at last.'

Icarus staggered onto the rooftop. He whirled around like one of the whirly-whirly things, the gun in his hand and a rather horrified look on his face. 'Where is it?' he managed to say. 'Where is it?'

'Where's *what*, brother? Ooh, the view's lovely from here. You can see Kew Gardens; look at the sunlight on the glasshouses.'

'Where's the cradle? The window-cleaning cradle. I thought we could abseil down on the ropes.'

'Now that would have been exciting,' said Johnny Boy, clutching at his heart. 'I'd have been right up for a bit of abseiling.'

'We're trapped.' And Icarus whirled around again.

And got himself dizzy. And fell right over.

Johnny Boy sat on his little bum and laughed. Laughed, that's what he did. 'There's no way down,' he laughed. It was what they call *hysterical laughter*. 'You've got us up here and there's no way down.'

'Shut up!' shouted Icarus. 'I'm thinking.'

'Better think fast, then.' Johnny Boy laughed some more.

'I could soar down,' said the other, making wings with his arms. 'I could soar down, like a swan, or a mighty condor, spread my wings and . . .'

Icarus dragged him back. 'Sober up,' he shouted. 'Pull yourself together. Be Woodbine. You *are* Woodbine. He'd get us out of this. He would.'

'You'll get us out of this, brother. I trust you. You're my hero.'

'No. I'm nobody. *You're* the hero. You're *my* hero. Really.'

'You're not *my* hero.' A gun-toting demon stepped out onto the rooftop.

'Nor mine,' said his hideous companion. 'I only like Carol Vorderman.'

'I don't like anybody,' said Cormerant, pushing the demons aside.

Icarus raised the gun to fire. But guns have safety catches. Click went the gun. And click again. Icarus fumbled to drop the safety catch, but there is a knack to these things.

Cormerant strode over the rooftop and tore the gun from the hand of Icarus Smith. 'Here,' said he. 'Why don't you let your companion here have a go at it?' And he thrust the gun into the limp-looking hand of the man who had once been Woodbine.

'Oh no,' said that man. 'I can't be having with guns. Nasty things, guns. They go off and shoot people.'

Cormerant laughed. 'He's sort of lost his edge, hasn't he?' he said, and he offered the gun to Johnny Boy.

'I'll have a go,' said the midget. 'But I might need a hand pulling the trigger.'

'I'll give you a hand,' said Cormerant. 'But not for that.'

And he reached down to Johnny Boy, took hold of his head and snapped the little man's neck.

'No!' Icarus screamed and sank to his knees beside the body. 'No, Johnny Boy, no.'

Cormerant turned to his two evil henchmen. 'Go back to the car,' he said. 'I can handle everything here. Take the car back to the Ministry. I'll join you later for a nice cup of tea.'

The demons departed, laughing all the way.

'You killed him.' Tears flowed down the face of Icarus Smith. 'You callous monstrous bastard. There was no need to kill him.'

247

'I'm cleaning up,' said Cormerant. 'Cleaning up all the mess you've made with your interfering. He's dead because of you. Because you stole my briefcase. You're the one who has to live with his death on your conscience. But don't worry yourself, you won't have to live with it for long.'

'I've posted the cassette tape.' Icarus looked up through his tears. 'I've posted the cassette tape of you torturing Professor Partington. To a newspaper. Along with a signed testimony and one of the Red Head tablets. And I've had a chemist analyse the drug and produce gallons of it in liquid form. A friend of mine has it and if I don't phone him at a specified time today, he'll pour it into the local water supply. People will see you and your kind for what you really are.'

'I don't think so,' said Cormerant. 'Your friend. Would that be your best friend? Friend Bob?'

'How—'

'I've been keeping a careful eye on you. Your best Friend Bob is now sadly deceased.'

'No,' wept Icarus. 'No.'

'You should never have messed with me,' said Cormerant. 'You don't know who I really am.'

'You're a piece of shit,' said Icarus.

'Language,' said Cormerant. 'You shouldn't talk like that to me. You should call me by my official title. You should call me Your Satanic Majesty.'

Icarus stared up at Cormerant. And the face of evil stared back down at him.

'You have seriously fucked with me,' declared the Evil One. 'You've fucked with my plans. I had that moron Colin right in the palm of my hand. He was mine. And with his father dead and the Earth passed on to him, I would have had it. He would have sold the Earth to me, just to spite his mother. But then you come along. Stupid petty criminal and you fuck everything up. There's no Hell for you to go to now. But I will make your final moments more hellish than your puny little mind could ever comprehend.'

And the spawn of the pit took hold of Icarus and lifted him from his feet.

'Eyes first,' said His Satanic Majesty. 'Eyes plucked out and pushed down your throat, then other bits too, one slowly after another.'

Icarus shook and fought to break free, but you really don't have too much chance against the devil.

Icarus tried to close his eyes and turn his face away, but the taloned claws pressed in upon his eyeballs.

And once again Icarus found the whole of his life flashing right there in front of his eyes.

And once again he felt it hadn't been the best of lives.

'Time to suffer, you thieving little gobshite.' And the claws of Hell went pressing in.

'Hey, scumbag,' I said. 'Leave the kid alone.'

The creature turned to face me and I could see by the look on his big ugly puss that he didn't like what he saw.

'And what's this?' he asked in a tone that I didn't take to.

'This is where you get it,' I said, cooler than a Carmelite in a coprophiliac's karsy. 'This is where you get what's coming to you.'

The Beast of the Revelation looked me up and down then up and down some more.

I raised the trusty Smith and Wes Craven's *Nightmare* and thumbed back the hammer. 'The safety catch is off this time,' I said.

Cormerant let Icarus fall to the rooftop. 'You have got to be kidding,' said he.

'Me, buddy, I never kid. This is the final rooftop showdown. This is where you get yours.'

'You dare to point that gun at me, you cringing gutless piece of shit!'

I cocked an eyebrow and smiled him one of my Woodbine winners. 'I might not have slept for a week,' said I. 'And I may be drugged up to the windows of my stainless soul. And I may have had to adopt a different persona, that of this kid's brother, in order to cover the scenes where I left the hospital and travelled in the taxi and through the streets and up the stairs and everything. But this is *my* territory here, buddy. This is my fourth location. The rooftop where the villain gets his and I get all the glory.'

'Ha,' the devil-made-filthy-flesh laughed and evilly he did it too. 'You dare to mess about with me?' he asked. 'When you know who I really am?'

'You must be the devil, pal, because you sure as hell smell just like shit. But you ain't no immortal any more. Not with there being no afterlife. You can catch a bullet like the rest of them.'

Mr Evil lunged towards me, but I took a duck to the side. Taking a duck to the side can often save your life when you're a private eye. Mind you, you have to know which side to duck to. Knowing which side to duck to can mean the difference between bathing the babe in béchamel sauce and burning your butt on a Bessemer converter. Or chewing the fat with the fattest of friends and biting the bullet in Brixton. Or any one of a number of similar permutations, most of which are obscene.

If you know what I mean. And I'm sure that you do.

The creature lunged and I took a duck.

And damn me if I didn't duck the wrong way.

But hey, gimme a break, I hadn't slept for a week and I had more nose candy up my proboscis than Noah had knobbing on his ark.

And all of a sudden, and a very bad sudden it was, I had talons around my throat and more bad breath in my face than a necrophage's dental hygienist.

'So you burn, Mr Woodsmoke.'

'Can't you do better than that, buddy?' I asked, trying to lighten up the situation. 'Surely Wood . . . er . . . Wood . . .' But damn me if I could think of another one myself.

But hey, gimme another break, I . . .

'Time to die,' said Cormerant.

'You first, shitface,' I said. And I stuck my gun right into his plug-ugly gob and let him have six of the best.

Which lightened the situation right up for me.

But darkened it somewhat for him.

The top came off his horrible head and it was raining quills.

He staggered about, and I'll tell you, friends, he didn't look like he was making whoopee.

'You shot me,' he said.

And I could see clear through his mouth to the sky.

'Yeah,' said I. 'And if you think that's rough. I'm now gonna kick you in the balls.'

And, my friends, that's what I did.

And he took the rooftop plunge.

And down at ground level, and all but forgotten in all the excitement, an SAS demolition man went 'three, two, one' and pushed down on the plunger, in that way they always do.

'!'

went the SHITE. Which was one very loud bit of silence.

Yeah, well, it might have been. But it wasn't.

I'm sure he would have pushed upon that plunger. That's what they always do, when they're blowing things up.

But a hand fell on the soldier's shoulder and the voice of Captain Ian Drayton said, 'Hold fire.'

Back on the rooftop, I helped Icarus up. 'Are you OK, kid?' I asked. 'You look a little shaky on your pins.'

'Thanks, Mr Woodbine,' he said. 'You came through for us. Well, you came through for *me*.'

He dropped to his knees beside the little broken dolly man.

'The bastard killed him,' Icarus wept. 'Merciless bastard.'

'He's one dead bastard now,' said I. 'I'm sorry about your little buddy.'

Icarus lifted the tiny man up in his arms and kissed him on the forehead.

'Oi!' went Johnny Boy. 'None of that. I know we're friends. But not *that* friendly.'

'It's a miracle,' said Icarus Smith.

'You never can tell,' said I.

252

19

We headed back to my office, Icarus, Johnny Boy, Captain Ian and I. We took a taxi, I recall, and the cabbie told us all about the knowledge. I don't remember too much about what he said, but I'm damn sure he was wrong about the route to Heartbreak Hotel.

Once we were safely back in my office, I leaned my butt on my desk.

'OK,' said I, with more suavity than a Swiss sword-swallower in a Swedish swivel chair. 'I guess you'd like me to explain it all to you.'

Heads nodded all round, as they generally do when I ask a question like that.

'The first thing you have to understand is that Colin did *not* put the hit out on his old man.'

'He *didn't*?' said Johnny Boy. 'But he was the prime suspect.'

'Little guy,' said I, 'this isn't some episode of *Columbo*. In the world of Lazlo Woodbine, it is *never* the prime suspect.'

'I knew that,' said Icarus.

'Well you never told *me*,' said Johnny Boy.

'Might I continue?' I enquired, with more retort than a Reigate squire on a cardboard box in Carfax.

Heads nodded all round again and I was set into telling of my tale. 'It wasn't Colin and it wasn't Eartha.'

'*Eartha?*' said Icarus.

'Put a sock in it, kid. Eartha was number one on my list. She called me in to search for Her missing husband. I figured that She wouldn't have done that unless She cared about him. Unless, on the other hand that rocks the cradle, She wanted evidence for a divorce. Which She didn't, because God had got up to His capers with the Jewish girls before and She's taken him back every time. So, at the start off, I figured She cared. *But.* She shows up at my office, less than an hour after He's copped it, with the will in Her hand and She's hardly the grieving widow. She doesn't show a flicker of emotion on that plug-ugly puss of Hers. And that made me suspicious. She's got the will and the will fingers Colin. I tell Her that. But She doesn't care about that either. It seems that She's happy to have Colin put in the frame. And as investigations prove that Colin is running the Ministry of Serendipity, an organization dedicated to dumbing down the public – *thumbing* down the public in fact – to keep them unaware that demons and angels are walking on the face of the Earth, it looks like Colin all the way. And it seems that Colin's mum doesn't give a flea's fart about *him* either. To me it all smells worse than a Baskerville do-do in a devil's footbath. But, like I say, it wasn't Her.'

'So who *was* it?' said Icarus.

'Well, it wasn't Colin and it wasn't Eartha and it wasn't even Captain Ian here.'

'Me?' said Captain Ian. 'You thought it might have been *me?*'

'Sure, guy, I had you right up there on my list. Icarus goes

to the movies a lot, he'll tell you how it works. There's only
ever a limited number of suspects. And you get to meet them
all early on in the plot. Like Cormerant, right? *You* tipped me
off when you told me that Jesus could be seen on TV, but you
weren't at liberty to divulge his identity. You knew I'd take a
hint and watch TV and you knew I'd see your brother being
interviewed. You led me right to him.'

'His *brother*?' said Icarus.

'Sure, his brother,' said I. 'Don't you realize who this guy
really is?'

'He's an angel,' said Johnny Boy.

'He's Jesus Christ,' said I.

There was a bit of a silence then, but I could live with that.

'Jesus Christ!' said Johnny Boy. 'I mean . . . well . . . *Jesus
Christ!*'

'Please don't,' said Captain Ian. 'No matter how people say
my name, it always sounds like swearing.'

'But I mean . . . well . . . you are . . .' Johnny Boy dropped
down to his knees, though the change in height was negligible.

'How did you know, Mr Woodentop?'

I let that one pass, because after all, he was the Lord. 'I
wouldn't have guessed,' said I, 'if it hadn't been for Barry. He
was stopping the effects of the Red Head drug working on me
and he had to be doing that for a good reason. He knew that
with the help of the drug I could solve the case and he wanted
me to solve the case, but I figured that you'd tipped Barry the
wink to stop me from seeing who *you* really were.'

'But *we* couldn't see him for who he really is,' said Icarus.
'And we still can't. I mean, well, sir, you just look like an angel
to me. No offence meant, of course.'

'None taken, I assure you,' said the Lord.

'He does look like an angel,' said I. 'But an angel with a

golden sword. Check out a copy of the *Bibliomystikon*,* "And the Lord of Hosts shall come amongst them and slay them with a sword of gold." It ain't your regular practice for angels.'

'You certainly know your occult scripture,' said Jesus.

'Lord,' I told him, 'in my business, knowing your occult scripture can mean the difference between singing a psalm at a Sunday school clam-bake and spearing a clam with a jaded jackeroo. If you know what I mean and if you don't, who does?'

'You have me on that one,' said Jesus. 'But it wasn't me who murdered my father. So just who was it?'

'Well, it wasn't your sister Christene, either.'

'Actually I thought it might have been,' said Jesus.

'His *sister*?' said Icarus. 'Where does his sister come into this?'

'Philomena *Christina* Maria O'Connor,' said I. 'The dame with the dangerous digits. She was in cahoots with Colin. More of that sibling rivalry, you see. Mr Christ here, the elder son, got all the glory. Barry told me how he had his sister edited out of the New Testament. Because he had full editorial control. And they'd stopped writing Bibles by the time that Colin came along, so he never got a mention anywhere. The Godalmings are a very dysfunctional family. There's a lot of jealousy going on there. The same as in any other family, I guess.'

'I tried to be nice,' said Jesus. 'I always try to be nice. I'm noted for it.'

'It's not your fault, Lord. Well, some of it is. But let's just have a suspect head-count here. It wasn't Colin and it wasn't Eartha and it wasn't Jesus and it wasn't Christene.'

---

* The secret Bible for the initiated. Not that you'll get it in W. H. Smith's.

'So it was Cormerant,' said Icarus. 'He was, after all, the devil incarnate.'

'Right up there in my listings,' said I, cooler than a catechumen at a canon's coffee morning. 'Along with Fangio for a while; you can never trust a skinny guy. But no, my friend, it wasn't even Cormerant.'

There was a lot of sighing then and a fair bit of scratching at heads.

'So who *was* it?' Icarus shouted.

'It wasn't anybody,' I said. 'Because God *wasn't* murdered. God *isn't* dead.'

'*WHAT?*' they all went, and very loudly too.

'He isn't dead,' I said. 'The whole thing was a scam. A set-up from the beginning. Jesus here gave it away when he told us all about how God had to take out mortgage after mortgage on Heaven and Hell until He ran out of money. I figured, how had He done that? He'd have had to have taken out life insurance, right? A whole lot of life insurance, to cover all those extra mortgages. And who wouldn't insure God's life? The guy's eternal, right? A pretty safe bet. But what if God was to die and His wife cashed in His life insurance policies to pay off all the debts and reclaim Heaven and Hell? If He faked His own death, everything would get sorted.'

'It makes some kind of sense,' said Icarus.

'Pray continue with your most interesting narrative, Mr Woodbine,' said Johnny Boy.

'I was set up,' said I. 'From the very beginning. I was diverted away from the briefcase case, because I would have found things out in the wrong order. Barry told me all about how God had this thing about Jewish virgins, so I head off to the Crimson Teacup, where God conveniently shows up and then conveniently gets shot in an alleyway, right in front of my eyes.

257

'Making me the star witness. And what an unimpeachable witness, the greatest private eye of them all, in the pay of a most illustrious client, to wit, the wife of God. She was in on it with Him, as if you hadn't guessed.'

'I hadn't,' said Johnny Boy.

'I'm losing the plot here,' said Icarus. 'I'm becoming confused.'

'Try to keep up, kid. It's all pretty simple. Well, at least it is for me. So I'm right there, right? At the right place at the right time to witness the murder of God. And it might have worked too, if I hadn't gone back disguised as a reporter and been recognized by Sam Maggot and bopped on the head. I'd have fingered Colin for sure, which was what his mum intended. But I wouldn't have been able to prove it, so he would have walked free. So God's wife would have got the money. Colin would have got the Earth and I'd have probably ended up in the fiery place without a sweet thank you for being such a sucker.'

'But there is no Hell any more,' said Icarus.

'Yeah, but there will be again, kid. As soon as Eartha gets the money and pays off all God's debts, Heaven and Hell will be back on the go and all will be right with the world once more.'

'Explain about the video footage,' said Icarus. 'We all saw that. We all saw God getting murdered.'

'We saw what God wanted us to see. Or rather what He wanted the insurance company to see. It would look pretty kosher through angelic eyes. They'd see two demons shooting God dead then me dealing death out to the demons. What with that, and my testimony and the weather going mad, what more proof would they need?'

'A body?' said Icarus.

'Yeah,' said I. 'You'd think so, wouldn't you? But would

they really expect God's widow to let them view the body of God? Especially as He died in such shady circumstances. His reputation would have to be kept intact. He was God, for God's sake. When I was in that alleyway, I saw what God wanted me to see. And on the tape the angelic insurance assessors would see what God wanted *them* to see. Ordinary folk would see what I saw when I saw the tape for the first time. Me shooting two innocent guys. But after I'd taken the drug and Barry let the effect kick in, I played that tape again and again and I saw something more. I fast-forwarded the tape and after the bit where I fall to my knees and sully my trenchcoat and then I get up and walk from the alley with all the wild weather and everything, there's a bit more. You have to look real close, with a true professional's eye. But you can just make out through all the wind and rain and storm, *God getting to His feet and sneaking away.*'

'*What?*' went Icarus and Johnny Boy and Captain Ian Christ as well. 'You saw *that*?'

I guess Eartha would have wiped that bit off the tape before She showed it to the insurance company.'

'So that's it,' said Icarus, shaking his head. 'You actually solved it. You solved the greatest case that ever there was.'

'Who else but me, kid? But the sadness of it is that nobody is ever going to know.'

'Why not?' asked Icarus. 'I don't understand.'

'Kid,' I said, 'what did you want more than anything else in this world?'

'For everything to be put right,' said Icarus. 'That was my dream, my vocation. To put the world to rights.'

'And the only way that the world can be put to rights is if all the angels and demons who fight it out down here and get mankind into a lot of sticky situations go back to where they belong. To wit, Heaven and Hell. And the only way that is going to happen is for us to keep our big mouths shut, pretend that God is dead and let Eartha pick up on the insurance. She pays off God's debts and the world is put to rights. Am I right, or am I right?'

'You're right,' said Icarus.

'And as no-one else on Earth but us knows anything about this, they won't know that God's insurance company thinks God is dead. They'll still go on worshipping Him and God, wherever He happens to be, will be happy to let them do it. Things will be a lot better on Earth. There'll be an afterlife once more, the good people will go to the good place when they die and the bad ones will go to the bad place. And that's why I can never take the credit for solving the greatest case that there ever was.'

'He's right,' said Jesus. 'That's how it has to be.'

'But it's . . .' Icarus threw up his hands. 'It's dishonest. I thought that God was all good.'

'I think we've all had enough theology for one day,' said Johnny Boy. 'Let's just settle for this as a happy ending.'

'Yeah,' said I. 'Well you would say that, wouldn't you?'

'I just did say it,' said Johnny Boy.

'You know,' said I, with more gravitas than a gut-shot gunman at a herring-gutters' ball. 'You got me thinking back there, on the rooftop. I really couldn't understand just how it was that you didn't die up there.'

'A happy happenstance,' said Johnny Boy. 'All's well that ends well. Isn't it?'

'Oh, please,' said I. 'I've come this far, I've worked the lot of it out. You wouldn't deny me a little bit of glory, seeing as how I can never ever talk about this case.'

'Eh?' said Icarus. 'What's all this?'

'Ask Johnny Boy,' said I.

Johnny Boy grinned. 'Go on then,' he said to me. 'Do it.'

I reached down to him and with more panache than a pool-shark on the poop deck of a Pooh-Bah's paddleboat, I took hold of his hair and ripped off his wig and his mask.

To reveal the face of . . .

Yes, you've guessed it.

No you haven't? Then let me tell you.

The face of Richard E. Grant himself.

Otherwise known as God.

'Dad!' said Jesus. 'It's *you*! You've shrunk.'

'I've always been a master of disguise, my boy.'

'No,' said Icarus. 'This can't be happening. It can't.'

The face of Richard E. Grant smiled handsomely up at Icarus Smith. 'It can be,' said He. 'And it is.'

'No,' said Icarus, and tears were in his eyes once more. 'No, it's not fair. It can't be.'

'I know,' said God. 'You feel cheated, don't you? Cheated and deceived. You feel now that you really didn't do anything. That I helped you out every step of the way. But I didn't, you know. You did it all yourself.'

'No,' said Icarus. 'I didn't. *You* did. From the very first time I met you. It was you all along. You helped me at Professor Partington's. When you opened the shed door and the breeze blew the map pieces conveniently into place. And in the pub, when I threw the tablet into the air and said "Let's leave it to fate" and the tablet fell straight down my throat. You did it. And you've done it again and again. I trusted you. I thought you were my friend. But I was nothing to you. Just another pawn in your game.'

'Hey, kid,' I said. 'I'd ease up if I were you. This is God you're talking to, you know.'

261

'Hm,' said Icarus, biting his lip.

'Best show a little respect, eh?'

'It's all right,' said God. 'I understand. After all, I understand everything. That's what being God is all about. It's just that I've never been too good with money. And I did marry a wife who made a *lot* of demands. She never really understood me, you see. But listen, Icarus, I might have helped you out a little. But I did it because I was acting as your Holy Guardian Angel. Lazlo had Barry and you had me.'

'You made a fool of me,' said Icarus.

'No, my boy. I just helped you to achieve your ambitions. Getting all the angels and demons back where they belong, that is the ultimate piece of relocation work. And you played a major role in doing that. Why, if you hadn't released Lazlo from the psychiatric hospital . . .'

'*You* talked me into that!'

'Details, details,' said God. 'Always details. You played your part and you did your bit and it has brought you and your brother back together again.'

'That kid is no brother of mine,' I told God.

God raised an eyebrow.

'Whatever you say, sir,' said I. 'But he ain't.'

God smiled and tipped me the wink. 'Right,' said He. 'Well, everything seems to be tied up, with no loose ends. There will be a knock coming on your door in just a few minutes. It will be my, er, widow. And by the by, Mr Woodbine, you did get one thing wrong. She *doesn't* know. She really thinks I'm dead. Ours wasn't exactly what you'd call a happy marriage. She's not a very caring woman, my wife. I gave her the world, literally, but it wasn't enough. She didn't care about me and she didn't care about Colin. Mind you, he was an evil little wretch and he was going to sell the world off to the devil, which really

262

wasn't playing the game. I wrote my will to implicate him in my murder, but I knew he'd walk free. I thought it would be a good laugh to see him and my wife arguing over who really owned the world. I'm sorry he's dead, of course, but then accidents will happen.'

Icarus opened his mouth to speak, but then thought better of it.

'So, I'll be leaving you now,' said God. 'I know I can trust you to do the right thing and sell the story of my murder to my wife. We all want the same thing, don't we? The angels back in Heaven and the demons back in Hell.'

I nodded and Icarus nodded. And Jesus nodded too.

'I'll be glad to get back to Heaven,' said Jesus. 'You can't get a decent haircut down here.'

'And I did like you, Icarus,' said God. 'I do like you. It was great to be your friend.'

'It was great to be yours,' said Icarus. 'You were like a brother to me.'

'And it was never dull. I really enjoyed that bit when you used the spectremeter to make it appear that the professor's Ford Fiesta was still going round and round the multi-storey car park. That was really clever of you. I liked that.'

'Thanks,' said Icarus.

'So, good luck to you, my boy. You'll do all right for yourself. Although I'd advise you to find yourself a new vocation. Relocation can be a dangerous profession. But you'll succeed, I know you will. You have my word on that.'

'Thanks again,' said Icarus.

'Well, I must be leaving you now,' said God. 'I have a hot date at the Crimson Teacup, and it would be rude to keep a lady waiting. So I'll say goodbye for now. Goodbye and God bless.'

And with a wink and a wave and a nod and a grin, He vanished.

Just like that.

'I think I'd better be leaving too,' said Jesus. 'I've never been too good at lying to my step-mum. She doesn't care too much for me, you know.'

And he gave a nod and a wink and a wave.

And then he vanished too.

I looked at Icarus.

And Icarus looked at me.

'That just leaves the two of us, kid,' said I.

And then there came a knock knock knocking at my office door and I could see a big fat shadow on the frosted glass.

'I think you'd better leave all the talking to me, kid,' I said. 'This will be my last bow. I've solved my final problem. After I've talked to the dame, Lazlo Woodbine Investigations is shutting up shop for good and all. I've had enough of this business.'

Icarus smiled and stuck out his hand for a shake.

'You're a hero, *brother*,' he said. 'Put it there.'

I smiled back at the kid in the way that only Woodbine can do.

And then I shook my brother by the hand.

THE END